USA TODAY BEST SELLING AUTHOR

KRISTEN PAINTER

BOOK
THREE

THE FORGETTABLE MISS FRENCH

The Forgettable Miss French
Shadowvale, Book Three

Copyright © 2019 Kristen Painter

This book is a work of fiction. The characters, events, and places portrayed in this book are products of the author's imagination and are either fictitious or are used fictitiously. Any similarity to real person, living or dead, is purely coincidental and not intended by the author.

Published in the United States of America.

Shadowvale isn't your typical small town America. The sun never shines, the gates decide who enters, magic abounds, and every resident bears some kind of curse.

Werewolf Virginia "Ginny" French's curse means no one can remember her. Not even for as long as it takes to ring up her groceries or make her favorite iced coffee. And being that forgettable has turned her life into an incredibly lonely existence. So much so, she's thinking about doing something really wild just to entertain herself.

Werewolf Ezekiel "Easy" Grayle loved his life until he got struck by lightning and lost control of his shifting abilities. It's led to some uncomfortable situations – and the decision to move to a town where the unpredictable is acceptable.

He didn't realize just how acceptable until he catches his hot but maybe-crazy neighbor sneaking out of his pool in a barely-there bikini. He's too busy unpacking to pursue her, but when she comes knocking, all bets are off.

Can a forgettable woman ever find love or is her curse too much for even the most determined man to overcome?

CHAPTER ONE

Ginny French sipped her iced coffee and stared out the window of Deja Brew, watching people, almost all of whom she recognized, and thinking about her life. She'd been doing that a lot lately, and she knew it was a sign that she was sinking into a dark place.

It happened periodically, but this time...it felt darker than usual.

During times like this, the idea of turning to a life of crime held a certain appeal. Not really bad crimes. A little bank robbing, maybe. Or an art heist. That might be fun. Although those kinds of shenanigans probably needed a whole crew of people to pull off, and that was where she got stuck.

Becoming a criminal wasn't what interested her. It was the thrill of such acts and everything that she guessed went into pulling off such a stunt. But not just the preparation, the execution, and the exhilaration of a job like that, but the successful getaway.

All of that would go a long way toward taking her mind off how very alone she was.

The whole life-of-crime thing was definitely one of the crazier thoughts she'd had, but lately, her wild ideas were getting, well, wilder.

Being forgettable could do that to you.

It could also wear you down.

A life of crime would at least be exciting. At least, it *seemed* like it might be exciting. Real jail, on the other hand, would be a nightmare. And considering that she never so much as jaywalked intentionally, she couldn't really be sure a big crime would thrill her as much as she imagined.

Still, it had to be more exciting than the life she was leading now.

Jaywalking was probably where she should start, though. But in this town, there wasn't much in the way of law. Sure, there was Deacon Evermore, peacekeeper, but she wasn't positive he'd ever actually arrested anyone.

Not in the ten years she'd lived in Shadowvale anyway. Unless events like that were kept secret. That could be, too.

The town had a way of protecting itself from all sorts of things, which was what made it such a haven for the odd, unusual, and downright cursed. That's why she lived here. She was the latter. And had been since she'd had the sad misfortune of touching a haunted mirror on the wall of the Myrtles Plantation during a vacation to Louisiana.

She picked up her drink, the heavy, silver ID bracelet on her wrist clanking against the table when she moved.

To the best of her deduction abilities, that was the incident that had caused her to become an invisible woman.

Not really invisible, because invisibility didn't truly define her problem. It was close, a symptom perhaps, but it didn't capture the true depth of what had become of her. Ever since touching that mirror, no one could remember her. Not even for as long as it took to make her coffee order, or ring up her items at the drugstore, or do her hair, or bring her food order.

Nothing she'd done so far had changed that fact either. Not even a return trip to Louisiana to touch the mirror a second time. Wasted time and money were the only results of that trip.

She gave her cup a little swirl, rattling the ice. It was something, really, to live in a place for ten years and have everyone treat you like a stranger.

Everyone. The mailman. The dentist. The butcher at the Green Grocer market where she bought her meat every week, something a werewolf like her needed to satisfy her protein requirements.

She'd learned to deal with being a perpetual stranger. Mostly. But one of the parts she still struggled with was the reaction from her fellow wolves, the shifters who made up the pack in this town. The pack she couldn't join because she was a permanent outsider.

Without the approval of the pack's alpha, Rico Martinez, there was no joining the pack. She'd tried talking to Rico in person and, finally, approaching him in her wolf form.

Getting his approval was the easy part. Getting him to remember her...that's where things went sideways. She hadn't expected that seeing him in person would secure her in his memory, but as a wolf? She'd had hope for that. Until that had failed, too, and she'd figured that even her scent was forgettable.

That's how she knew the curse she was under was serious.

Never a quitter, she'd tried to join the pack on a group run on two occasions, hoping to slip into the crowd unnoticed. The first time, they'd snarled at her, but the second and last time, she'd gotten nipped on the flank, an injury that had hurt not only physically but mentally and emotionally.

After that, she'd stopped trying.

Being a lone wolf wasn't the daring existence books and movies made it out to be. In truth, it was depressing. She had no real support system. No wolves to run with. No core group who understood what being a shifter meant. Having a pack was like having a family.

And she'd involuntarily become an orphan.

For a second time.

Her gaze fell to the ID bracelet again. The first time had happened when she was three, too young to remember the car accident that had claimed her parents' lives. The ID bracelet, a gift from her mother to her father, was the only personal item that survived the wreck. Even now, as she stared at her father's name engraved into the silver, she found comfort in the connection.

Thankfully, her aunt Gwen had stepped in all those years ago, becoming Ginny's guardian and a phenomenal parent. She was the only one who sometimes remembered Ginny, an ability Ginny attributed to their blood connection. And when Aunt Gwen didn't remember Ginny, that wasn't because of Ginny's curse.

Aunt Gwen's memory troubles came on after her stroke, but thankfully, the retirement community in Shadowvale, Emerald Manor, had an assisted-living wing where they knew how to care for supernatural patients with such issues. Unlike the assisted-living home Aunt Gwen had been in the first time.

They'd called animal control upon finding a wolf in Aunt Gwen's room. What a mess that had been.

At least here in Shadowvale, inappropriate shifting wasn't a deal breaker. Not in the care home anyway. The move to this town had benefitted both of them. Well. Mostly Aunt Gwen. Ginny wasn't getting a whole lot out of it. No matter where she was, she'd be forgotten.

But this way, Aunt Gwen was safe.

Ginny just wished her aunt could remember her *all* the time. On the days when Aunt Gwen looked at her with that blank stare...that's when Ginny's world really went dark. Aunt Gwen was her safe place. Always had been, but these last ten years, more than ever.

So when she couldn't remember Ginny, the loneliness was almost suffocating.

Ginny swallowed against the lump forming in her

throat and took a few deep cleansing breaths. This line of thinking was going to turn her into a weepy mess, and that wasn't something she wanted, not in the middle of her favorite coffee shop.

Not that making a scene was such a big deal when it would be forgotten in minutes. All she'd have to do was slip into the bathroom for a couple moments, and when she came back out, she'd be brand new to everyone who saw her.

How crazy was it, that despite coming here almost every morning, she couldn't even order her usual, because no one who worked here had any idea what her usual was. Nor would they ever. Not unless she could find the legendary curse-lifting book in the town's enchanted forest.

But there was as much chance of her finding that book as there was of being remembered. She'd been looking for ten years and hadn't even come close. Not that Aunt Gwen could ever know that.

Ginny had told her all about the book and the forest when she'd first found out about them, and Aunt Gwen had almost had a second stroke. She was sure that their family was cursed as a whole and was convinced that Ginny would only come to further misfortune if she dared enter the enchanted forest.

From that day on, Ginny kept her searches for the book to herself.

She finished her iced coffee and thought about going home. Her job as a graphic designer was her only real solace, because online seemed to be the one place she wasn't forgotten. At least in emails.

But she wasn't ready to disappear into her work just yet.

There was one other...*creature* who was always happy to see her, one other being who *seemed* to remember her.

First, she had to get pie. More like *pies*, actually. Seymour was a big eater.

She left Deja Brew behind and walked a couple blocks up to the Black Horse Bakery, another place she'd probably be considered a regular if anyone remembered her. She got into the short line at the counter and checked her phone while she waited, mostly to see if there were any business emails that needed dealing with.

Someone was looking for a logo. That was good. Usually easy work. Another client wanted some new graphics for a product launch. Awfully short notice, but Ginny still wasn't rushing home. It could wait.

"Next."

Ginny approached the counter. "Hi, I'd like six of the blackberry pies."

Blackberry had been the Pie of the Day for as long as she could remember, which was since she'd lived here. Touching the mirror hadn't affected her memory, only the memories of those around her.

Nasha, the woman who owned the place, nodded. "You must have a houseful of blackberry pie lovers."

Since it didn't really matter what Ginny said, she sometimes told the truth instead of falling back on comfortable small talk. This was one of those

11

moments. "Nope. I live alone. Except for my three goldfish, but they're not much on pie."

Nasha's brows lifted a little, but to the woman's credit, she didn't comment further. Being the daughter of one of the Four Horsemen of the Apocalypse had probably given her the ability to stay cool in any situation, no matter how odd. "Coming right up."

Of course, Ginny wasn't going to eat any of the pies. They were all for Seymour.

Nasha presented her with two shopping bags, each holding three boxed pies. "Here you go. Hope you enjoy them."

"Thank you. What do I owe you?" Ginny knew they were free. All the baked goods were. But Nasha thought she was new here, and Ginny was so used to the routine, she played along without thinking about it.

"Nothing." Nasha nodded knowingly. "I thought you were new to town. Everything at Black Horse is free, except the coffee. Come back and see us."

"I will for sure." Ginny headed out, smiling, but the smile faded as she hit the sidewalk. Why had she gone along with all that? She hated the fakery, the pretending, the—she sighed. She didn't really hate it, but it did wear thin. And she didn't do it for herself. She did it for the people she interacted with. To make their lives easier.

What good would it do to explain her problem to everyone who asked her if she was new in town? None, that's what. And it wouldn't make a lick of difference.

She got to her car, a navy blue Jeep that was currently topless and would be until the weather turned cool again, put the pies on the floor behind the driver's seat, and climbed in. She took the ponytail holder off the shifter stick and knotted up her hair on top of her head. Then she dug her sunglasses out of her purse and popped them on.

Lastly, she started up the Jeep and cranked on the tunes. Today she was going to play her music louder than was polite. She liked it that way, and since no one could remember that she was the one doing it, why not?

She pulled out of her parking space and onto Main Street. If she'd been in any other town in the Carolinas, she was pretty sure the sun would have been shining down on her. She tipped her head toward the sky while still keeping her eyes on the road. She swore she could feel the warmth on her skin, but in Shadowvale, there wasn't ever any sun. Sometimes, like today, there was a hint of a golden glow.

But never any visible sun.

It was the town's big curse. Or blessing, depending on what kind of supernatural you were. For some, like the vampires, it was a major draw. But no matter what kind of overcast skies the day had, the evenings were almost always clear.

Which meant the moon was almost always visible. Something the shifters in town enjoyed.

She turned off Main Street, drove through one of the residential sections, past Emerald Manor where

Aunt Gwen was. She'd been to see Aunt Gwen the day before and taken her a box of cupcakes from the bakery. Aunt Gwen loved sweets—who didn't? But especially the cupcakes.

Beyond Emerald Manor, she entered a more rural area, then turned again onto the road that led to Miller's Lake. Once she got there, she took a mostly dirt road that led around the lake to the old fishing pier and boardwalk that wrapped around the shore.

Since they'd built a new public park area on the other side of the lake, the old boardwalk wasn't used nearly as much anymore.

Ginny's Jeep bumped over the uneven road. She dodged some of the bigger ruts for the sake of the pies, slowing as she neared the water.

No one was out here today, which was perfect. On a warm weekend, the lake was a popular place, but during the week, people had other things to do. Not everyone, but today no one had shown up at the old pier. That definitely increased the chances of Seymour making an appearance. He often didn't when a lot of people were around.

She took a deep inhale of the air and smiled. The lake was beautiful. The water was crystal clear until it got deep, and then it turned the loveliest shade of blue-green. She imagined with sun on it, the color would be spectacular. That would never happen, of course, but she could picture it all the same.

Most times, she came to the lake with her swimsuit on under her clothes, but not today. Not for the past few visits, really. Not since her next-door neighbors had moved, leaving their house empty and their pool rather *available*.

Sometimes, when the wolf inside her needed the release, she'd come out to the lake at night to run one of the many trails that followed the shoreline. It was a safe place for the most part, as the local pack preferred the enchanted forest or the mountainsides. Nightingale Park, above the twilight line, was another of her favorite places to run, especially when she was in the mood for sun, although the pack liked the park, too. But that was easy to avoid. If the parking lot was full, she went elsewhere.

As often as she could, she took Aunt Gwen out with her. Sometimes here to swim as well.

Ginny parked, got the pies out, and walked toward the pier. The little boardwalk followed the shoreline for a good bit, bending around behind the trees where it jutted into the lake for fishing. She went out to the end, sat down with the shopping bags next to her and her legs crisscrossed, then got one of the pies out. It did smell good. And that smell was usually enough to bring Seymour out.

She opened the box and held it up, letting the breeze travel over the golden crust and pick up the scent of the juicy berries inside. Smiling, she called out for him in a singsong voice, "Seymour...I have pie..."

A second passed, then two.

The water near the deep center of the lake rippled. Her smile widened. "Pie," she repeated. "Blackberry. Your favorite."

The ripples moved toward her, picking up speed as they approached.

He surfaced a few feet away, his gorgeous head breaking the water's tension like a submarine rising. The thin spines that ran in v-shaped ridges from his brow all the way down his back to the tip of his tail glistened with beads of water, but lay flat to his skin. His dark, luminous eyes blinked at her, then focused on the pie. A little trilling sound left his throat, and he smiled eagerly.

"Nice to see you, too, Seymour." She felt like he remembered her, but there was a chance it was just the pie. She rarely came to the lake without bringing him some, unless she'd come for an evening run, and then she didn't always see him. Hmm. She hoped it wasn't just the pies.

He lifted his front right flipper, barking at her and pawing the water.

"I didn't come to swim today. I should have, though." The neighbor's pool was just a lot more convenient than driving to the lake every time she wanted to swim. She liked swimming with Seymour, though. He was like a giant dog, eager for attention.

Although, she'd learned that he could give off little electrical shocks, like an eel, when there was contact. Since the first time that had happened, he hadn't done it again, though. "I just came to see you and bring you pie. You still like pie, don't you?"

He nodded, sending droplets flying.

She laughed. "Just a second."

She worked her fingers gently between the crust and the tin on either side, her thumbs braced on the bottom of the plate. "Ready?"

His tongue lolled out, a sure sign of his affection for all things pie.

"Here goes." With a much-practiced forward motion, she flipped the pie out of the tin and into the air.

Seymour craned his neck, mouth open in a display of teeth that were more accustomed to shredding fish, and caught the pie. He swallowed it down in one gulp, then looked at her expectantly.

She shook her head in amusement. "You really need to learn to chew."

CHAPTER TWO

Ezekiel "Easy" Grayle stared up at his new home and sighed. Not because of the house, though.

The house was the nicest home he'd ever owned. It was pale gray with white trim and a dark blue door, and it had more than enough room for a single guy. Way more. But instead of using one of the two upstairs rooms for an office, he was converting the main floor dining room instead. Doing that would allow him to live on one floor, saving the upstairs space for the rare guest.

Besides that, the dining room was a large space and near the kitchen.

He was a writer who liked to eat while he worked. He was also a werewolf, and most werewolves needed to eat a lot to keep up with their fast metabolism.

The house also had a pool, something he'd only shared in his condo building. Now he didn't have to. Water was great for the creative process, and he was looking forward to seeing what effect it had on his.

No, the house wasn't the problem. It was everything else in his life.

Like how this was not where he'd imagined himself at this stage in his life or career. But he hadn't expected anything that had happened to him in the last three months either.

Sure, the movie deal was a dream come true. A dream he'd let himself have only a couple years ago when his books really started taking off. Tomahawk Jones, supersoldier, was going to be on the big screen.

Easy grinned at the idea as he found the key under the mat, just like the realtor had promised. His book, his characters, coming to life as a movie. That really hadn't set in yet. It was crazy.

Much like this town. Key in hand, he looked around at the cul-de-sac from his new front porch. At the mature oaks dripping with Spanish moss, the white picket fences, the beautifully manicured lawns with colorful flower beds and carefully cultivated topiaries. The whole street was like that. Picture-perfect.

Except the house next to his, which was a little less pristine, but he was okay with that. Nice to know someone else had a life that kept them from spending every waking moment on whatever neighborhood beautification project had to be underway.

He felt a kinship with whoever lived there. Like they might already be friends. Him and them against the neighborhood. He shook his head. That was his writer's brain, getting away from him and creating a story from nothing.

Whatever the situation was with all this perfect landscaping, he was going to have to hire a yard guy. He had a furry thumb, not a green one. He didn't have any intention of puttering around in the yard either. Not when he had a book in desperate need of writing and a looming deadline that was a constant reminder of that.

He walked back to the moving truck he'd rented. He'd towed his motorcycle behind it, but his car was arriving by transport tomorrow. He got to work getting the bike off the trailer and into the garage, then he unlocked the truck's rear door and slid it up as he made a mental note about finding a yard guy.

At least being a werewolf was okay in this town. Especially a werewolf with problems. That had really helped solidify his decision to move here.

He'd had to go somewhere, though. Since he'd been struck by lightning three months ago, his shifting abilities had become less than predictable. Living among humans was getting dicey.

He frowned. Truth was, even living among his own kind might cause problems, but he'd been assured that in this town, weird wasn't just okay, it was normal.

He prayed that was true. Because if the moon was full, there was no controlling his urge to shift. It was going to happen, no matter how hard he tried not to, no matter where he was, or who he was with. Now that he understood that, it wasn't such a big deal. He could prepare.

Sort of.

Problem was he never knew if he was going to end up a wolf or not. Crazy. He'd never realized he was such a mutt until the lightning strike.

Now it was anybody's guess what he was going to turn into because, apparently, he was cycling through every random bloodline ever introduced into his gene pool. So far, he'd seen himself become a pack's worth of different wolves, a fox, a coyote, a Siberian husky, and, most curious of all, a beagle.

Whichever one of his relatives was responsible for that indiscretion, they had a *lot* of explaining to do.

A lot.

It was embarrassing. He'd stopped joining his pack for group runs because of it, but he'd been able to handle that. Running alone wasn't as fun, but it still worked the kinks out.

Then, two weeks ago, everything had changed. He'd been about to do a book signing at a big-box store, and the visual of a full moon on another book's cover had caused him to shift. A freaking picture.

He'd managed to get off the retail floor, but then, right there, in the middle of the Saver's Club employee breakroom, he'd turned into a red wolf.

That incident had sent him on a downward spiral. He couldn't write. He didn't want to leave his house. He no longer knew what the day would bring. Or how to handle what was happening to him.

Him. Easy Grayle. Decorated former Army Ranger. Onetime candidate for pack alpha. *New York Times* bestseller. Semifamous author.

Current hot mess.

He'd started to question his mental stability.

Then he'd gotten an anonymous note telling him to visit Shadowvale, that it was a safe place for his kind. Attached to the note had been a full-color pamphlet that included GPS coordinates. It had felt like a lifeline.

So he'd gone. The place had been a little hard to find, and the gates had looked like they were new a hundred years ago, but they'd opened for him.

He'd spent a long weekend in town exploring and quickly realized Shadowvale might be the only safe place left for him to live until whatever was going on with him got cured. If it could be cured, which he desperately hoped was the case.

For one thing, he really, really wanted to attend the premiere of *Operation Lone Wolf*. For another, he didn't want to spend the rest of his life as a voluntary outcast. Wolves weren't meant to be alone. They needed packs.

And mates. But bringing a woman into his life was a nonstarter until his issues were behind him. No one needed to shoulder that burden but him. And no female wolf was going to want a mate in his condition anyway.

Jobwise, moving was no big deal. He could write from anywhere, and often had, although most of his remote locations were in places like Bali and Berlin, exotic settings that were more research than vacation. Tomahawk Jones traveled a lot on his missions.

And when he was whole again, he'd move back to the city and resume his life there.

But in the meantime, Shadowvale would be home. As peculiar as it was. In theory and in practice, this place didn't even exist. Although he'd been assured by Pam, his realtor, that deliveries to town, like the transport bringing his car, would have no problem getting in or finding his new house.

They'd just conveniently forget all about the town when they left. Apparently, the town's magic was a strange and powerful thing.

In a way, it was ironic that he'd end up in a town like Shadowvale. He was on the cusp of becoming a household name. And yet, here he was, moving into a town that prided itself on being invisible.

He stuck the key into the lock, and a zap of static electricity snapped at him as his fingers touched the metal. Since the lightning strike, these little electrical glitches happened a lot. So much so that he'd become almost immune to the little zings when he came into contact with metal, or the way the lights sometimes flickered in response to his emotions. All part of his new, cursed existence.

He unlocked the front door and pushed it open.

This was home now. And while he might still become a household name, the high life in the city wasn't going to happen. It was a gut check to realize how much he'd been looking forward to some of that fame and fortune.

Maybe this was fate's way of keeping him in check.

Well, job done.

With a sigh, he tossed the key onto the kitchen counter, walked back to the moving truck, and started unloading his stuff into the house. Nothing, from the leather sofa to the king-size bed, was too heavy. His shifting might be on the fritz, but his strength was still there. All of his senses were, thankfully.

That was something good. He tried to focus on that and on all of the good things in his life, which were many.

Despite that, he couldn't shake the feeling that moving to Shadowvale was like admitting defeat. Or accepting what had happened to him. He didn't want to do that. He was a fighter. And he wanted to keep fighting.

He would, too. He'd gently reach out to the alpha here and see if he was receptive to having a new member who might not actually show up as a wolf.

And if he wasn't, which Easy expected, he'd go back to solo runs.

Another thing he was going to do was get to work on his book. Immediately. With the movie being made, he couldn't afford to miss out on the momentum the release would create. He had to make his deadline, which was still six months off, but if he didn't get going, the time would fly by. Getting settled in this house would eat up a chunk of that.

His editor would probably give him an extension—this movie deal had earned him a lot of leeway—but he didn't want to push the book back either.

He was afraid doing it once would mean doing it again. And again. And that wasn't a road he wanted to go down.

No, it was time to get everything back on track. His life, his career, and somehow, his wolfiness.

He hoisted his leather recliner, balancing it on his shoulder, and started for the house.

There had to be a way.

CHAPTER THREE

"This is the last one, Seymour." Ginny readied the pie like she had all the others, and when Seymour gave an eager nod, she flipped it to him.

He snatched it midair and gulped it down. A couple seconds later, he burped, sending out a pungent waft of blackberry pie and fish.

Ginny rocked back and waved a hand in front of her face. "Oh, Seymour, that's gross. It's a good thing you're cute."

He panted, tongue out, like a happy dog. A giant seaweed-green dog with spines and flippers and a bewhiskered face that was more seal than sheepdog. He trilled at her, a questioning little sound.

"Nope, pies are all gone." She held her hands out to show him, then tipped both shopping bags so he could see into them.

He exhaled soft clicking noises.

"I know. Always sad when they're gone." She extended a hand. "Want some chin scratches?"

He nodded.

"Okay, but no shocking me. Right?"

He made a little woof and came closer, lifting his head and stretching his neck, an indicator that, yes, he did want chin scratches.

She obliged him, raking her nails down his slick skin. More trilling, this time slower and more like a purr. Electricity crackled over his skin, a mild buzz against her fingers. She knew he could really throw sparks when he wanted to, but since that first time, which she'd chalked up to him being overly excited, he'd never done more than what he was doing now. They were friends, after all.

The word brought a knot to her throat. "You know, Seymour, you're basically my only friend. And I don't think you have a clue about that, but that's okay. You don't need to. I just hope the day doesn't come when you forget me, too."

He bent his head and bumped it against hers, an affectionate gesture he sometimes greeted her with. She preferred it later in the visit, like now, when he wasn't dripping wet from just surfacing.

Just because no one would remember didn't mean she wanted to go home looking like she'd been caught in a rainstorm.

"All right, you sweet beasty, I'd better go home. I have clients waiting and work to do." She stood up, brushed herself off, and gathered the shopping bags, stuffing one inside the other with the pie boxes and tins. "I'll see you again, soon. I promise."

Seymour honked at her and bobbed his head from side to side.

"I don't want to go either, but I have to." She waved. "See you later, okay?"

He reared out of the water to shake one of his front flippers at her, honking again.

Knowing what came next, she backed away from the splash zone. "Bye."

He dived forward, sending a shower of water into the air, and disappeared below the surface.

She stood there a bit longer, watching the wake from his movements turn into ripples, then those ripples travel away into nothing.

This moment always filled her with sadness. And a wish that things were different. For her, but for Seymour, too. As far as she knew, he was as alone as she was. There was always the possibility that lake monsters were solitary creatures.

But no one really wanted to be alone all the time, did they?

She walked back to her car, glad she had work to dive into when she got home.

She smiled. *Dive into.* She threw the bakery bags into the back seat, climbed behind the wheel, and put her seat belt on. She glanced at the lake one more time. "Until next time, Seymour."

Then she headed home, happy about the visit, but unable to shake the melancholy that was becoming her constant companion these days.

It wasn't a feeling she liked or wanted. Happiness was far preferable. Happiness didn't send her down dark, introspective thoughts about robbing banks just for the fun of it.

Sometimes, seeing Aunt Gwen helped, but those days were becoming fewer as her memory issues seemed to give her more bad days than good ones.

Ginny needed to get a hobby. Besides feeding the Pie of the Day to her favorite lake monster. But something like that. Something that got her out of the house. Maybe she'd start watching the rugby matches on Sunday afternoon again. Ogling hot, sweaty men was always fun. Although she wasn't sure if that qualified as a hobby, exactly. Aunt Gwen might like it.

Stuff like that was always more fun to do with someone like an aunt or a girlfriend or two while sipping on wine slushes and pretending to take selfies while actually taking snaps of their favorite players.

At least that's how she imagined it could be. But that whole idea might be built around something she'd seen in a chick flick once. There had been a time in her life when that kind of group activity was possible. She'd had lots of friends in college.

Now…not so much.

Still, the rugby match might be fun. Or it might just make her more miserable, seeing as how none of those guys was ever going to be hers. Not because they wouldn't ask her out. She was cute enough to get that far.

It was just they never remembered that they'd asked her when she showed up for the date. *If* the guy had somehow remembered even making the date. And there was no attempting to go through with the evening at that point. Trying to explain over and over that you were sitting at a guy's table because he'd asked you to was no way to spend an evening.

She could go to more movies. But again, not the most fun thing to do alone. And Aunt Gwen didn't always have the concentration necessary for something that long. As a result, most of their movie watching was done at Emerald Manor.

Truth was, nothing was that fun to do alone. Except reading, which she already did constantly. She sighed. The library was another place she'd be considered a regular if the librarians could remember her.

She turned onto Beech Lane, which would take her home to Crab Apple Court. At least she had a library card. That was about as close as she'd come to belonging to anything in the last ten years.

The library had all kinds of classes in the community room, too. Painting, art appreciation, writing workshops, history talks, even a self-defense class. But attending any of those would mean having to introduce herself over and over and over again.

It got old. Ginny only had so much patience for it anymore. And most of that was reserved for visits to Aunt Gwen and the staff at the Emerald Manor who never remembered her either.

That lack of patience worried her. Especially when she thought about her life in another year. Or five. Or ten.

How was she going to get through more of this same existence? Maybe it was time to step up her efforts to find the book in the enchanted forest.

Which meant more running through the woods alone. And more lying to Aunt Gwen about it.

She shook her head as she turned onto Crab Apple Court. Something had to change and soon or—there was a rental truck in front of the McKinleys' old place.

Had someone bought it? They must have.

Well, that was a bummer. That meant the McKinleys' pool was now closed to her. Getting her own pool wasn't in the budget. Maybe someday, but being able to use theirs for the last couple of months had made her want one even more. Mostly, she swam in her human form, but sometimes she went in as her wolfy self, something she felt odd about doing at the lake. And would never dare do at the community pool.

She sighed. She'd really gotten used to using the pool whenever she wanted. Except for Tuesdays. That's when their pool service came.

The McKinleys were nice people, but she wasn't sure they'd have granted her such access. Wolf hair in the filter had to be a drag, but hey, that's what they were paying a cleaning service for, right?

They were wolves, too, so it wasn't like hairballs in the skimmer were a new thing.

They'd moved out after their son, Ryan, had outgrown his curse on his sixteenth birthday, the lucky dog. Poor Ryan had been unable to shift into his true form. He'd managed a tail a few times, and ears and a snout once or twice, but it wasn't until the full moon a week after his sixteenth birthday that he'd gone complete wolf.

His parents had been overjoyed and had promptly moved back to Iowa and their home pack.

She got it. She would have done the same. She didn't have a home pack, not since moving to Shadowvale. Growing up, she'd run with Aunt Gwen's pack, becoming a member as soon as she was old enough. But there'd been college and Aunt Gwen's stroke, and a lot of old ties had been severed due to distance and the constraints of life.

Now she and Aunt Gwen just went for runs together whenever they could, which meant on Aunt Gwen's good days. So not as much as Ginny would have liked.

It was okay, though. Any sacrifices she had to make for Aunt Gwen were no big deal.

Despite losing her parents so young, Ginny had still had a happy childhood. All thanks to Aunt Gwen, who'd put her own life on hold to make sure Ginny had everything she needed.

Which was why Ginny would take care of that woman until her dying day, something that hopefully was a long ways off.

But all this time without a pack had a way of leaving a person isolated, no matter what the reasons.

She parked in her driveway and got out of the car, still looking at the moving truck. Maybe this new family would have kids, too. Good kids, though. Not the kind that turned into wolves and ran through the neighborhood, peeing on people's fences. She glanced down the street at the house that sat on the corner of Beech and Crab Apple and narrowed her eyes.

Those Freeman kids needed a good swat with a newspaper.

Her attention returned to the rental truck. The back was open. Looked like it had been about half-emptied. Most of what remained was in boxes. Lots and lots of boxes. There was an empty flatbed trailer, too. Maybe it had had bikes on it. Or a golf cart.

Those were becoming more popular in Shadowvale these days.

She rolled her eyes. Aunt Gwen would laugh at that. But she'd probably get a kick out of riding in one, too. Maybe Ginny could rent one for a day out. That might be a fun thing to do.

Enough looking. She went inside, her stomach grumbling. She should have gotten herself something at the bakery. Instead, she dug around in her fridge for leftovers that could be turned into lunch.

Penne Alfredo with chicken and broccoli from last night's dinner went into the microwave to heat up. While that was happening, she went back into the living room to check on her goldfish. She was pretty sure they didn't remember anyone or anything.

Except for feeding time.

She waved at them. "Hi, guys." Bob, Comet, and Sparky swam to the surface in hopes of flakes. "Sorry, you got fed this morning. I guess you don't remember that."

Everyone had their burden.

When her food was ready, she'd take her bowl into her office and answer emails while she ate, then get started on that logo or the new product graphics.

That was the exciting life she lived.

Maybe later, she'd go see what the new neighbors were up to.

The microwave dinged, and almost simultaneously a soft, metallic *thunk* came from outside. The rental truck's door maybe? She went to get her food, grabbing a can of pop on her way out of the kitchen.

A low, throaty rumble vibrated through the house. She frowned. What was that?

An engine. But what kind of car made a sound like that? It was coming from the McKinleys' former home. She put her meal down and ran to the front of the house to look out the window. A man in a T-shirt, jeans, and full helmet was pulling out of the McKinleys' garage. Well, his garage now.

The bike was a swirly, metallic, sparkly black where it wasn't leather or chrome. The motor snarled like a wild animal, and as he adjusted something on his helmet, she became well aware that, even from the back, this wasn't just any man.

This was hotness. In the most tantalizing male form she'd ever seen.

Her mouth went dry, and she swallowed in an effort to unstick her tongue from the roof of her mouth. His jeans were…very tight. Molded to him, really. Which made it hard not to look at his backside. His T-shirt was just as tight, frankly, showing off a trim waist and broad shoulders. She rubbed her lips together. Maybe he'd recently grown all those muscles, and nothing fit him anymore.

Actually, his clothes fit him just fine.

Just. Fine.

A few tattoos peeked out from his sleeves. Nothing she could make out. An insignia of some kind, maybe.

She hoped he wasn't a Hells Angel or something like that. This wasn't that kind of neighborhood. Or that kind of town.

Of course, if he was, maybe he could talk to those Freeman boys for her. She grinned. "Hello, Mr. Neighbor."

Helmet secured, he put his feet on the bike, revved the engine, and went off down the road.

Ginny watched him until there was nothing left to see. Then, still smiling, she went back to her lunch.

Until she knew more about him, she wouldn't really be able to say, but this new neighbor might be worth giving up her pool time for. Although now that he was out of the house, this might be her last chance for one final swim.

He'd probably gone to eat lunch. Made sense. He wouldn't have food in the house yet. That should buy her at least forty minutes. Maybe an hour.

The impulse to do something crazy struck her. At least this was safer than robbing a bank.

With great haste, she stuck her plate of food and her can of pop back into the fridge and ran to her bedroom to change into swimming attire.

She had exactly three bathing suits. The first was for visits to the lake or occasionally the Shadowvale community center's public pool, which she tended to avoid because of her curse and all that entailed, despite having a membership card. The suit was a rather sedate one-piece navy blue number with three bands of gold braid at the waist. Classy, nautical, and not the least bit naughty.

The second was a tiny hot-pink string bikini bought on a whim and used once on a trip to Nightingale Park, where she'd lain out for twenty minutes, then gotten cold feet, put her cover-up back on, and gone home. Now she just used it to lay out on her own back deck. It was naughty and then some.

The third was a cute, retro-styled two-piece in red and white polka dots.

Her comfort suit. A little sexy, but still covering her up. Sadly, one of the straps was hanging on by a thread and needed to be sewn back on before it could be worn. She really needed to do that tonight.

The navy suit would have been her second choice, but she'd gotten spaghetti sauce on it two nights ago, and it was still sitting in the laundry basket. She'd known better than to eat dinner while wearing it, but she'd come back starving from an evening swim at the McKinleys'.

Which left the hot-pink suit.

She bit her bottom lip. Crumpled up, the entire suit fit in the palm of her hand. What had she been thinking when she'd bought it? It wasn't her at all.

What she'd been thinking was *why not*? No one was going to remember her anyway. It was the same principle behind the days she sometimes wore a gown from her vast collection of bridesmaid dresses to the Green Grocer or the library. (Her curse had struck her at the age of twenty-six, the previous two years being when every single one of her college friends had decided to get married and include her in the wedding party.)

So what was she worried about? Even if anyone saw her, they weren't going to remember.

She shucked her clothes, tied the suit on, grabbed a towel, and snuck through the tree line that separated her backyard from the McKinleys'. Or what's-his-name's.

With a smile, she tossed her towel aside, then stood at the edge of the pool, put her hands together, and dived in. The water was gloriously refreshing. She surfaced, blissful, but bummed that these stolen moments were coming to an end.

She swam laps. Butterfly, backstroke, front crawl. They all made her happy. She really should get her own pool, but that would be so expensive. Too bad the community pool was always so busy.

Thankfully, she could still swim with Seymour.

At last, she slowed. Treading water, she studied the back of the house. Too bad her curse meant she couldn't make friends with the new guy and talk him into letting her swim.

A thought hit her so hard she started to sink. What if he was married? Or had a girlfriend? And his significant other was home right now? Ginny was shocked she'd been so dumb as to not consider that sooner. Getting caught in the new neighbor's pool in this swimsuit by his female companion wasn't going to make a great first impression.

For once, her curse might not be so bad.

Then the low, throaty rumble she'd heard earlier resonated through the neighborhood.

It no longer mattered if he had a wife or a girlfriend in the house, because the motorcycle man himself was home.

Crap.

Ginny swam for the side, heart thumping, and grabbed hold of the edge. As she pulled herself up, one of the bathing suit's strings on the top caught under her hand.

The movement of pushing up untied the top of her suit. Somehow, she made it to her feet in time to clamp her hands down over her chest to keep the suit in place.

With a firm grip on the girls, she ran for the tree line, hoping against all hope that she'd avoided detection. If that was possible for a half-naked, dripping-wet woman wearing a few tiny triangles of Day-Glo pink.

In what was probably mere seconds later (but seemed like an eternity), she finally stood in her own kitchen, breathing hard and dripping contraband pool water onto the tile.

"Dumb, Ginny. Really dumb." She exhaled. "Well, even if he did see me, he won't remember."

Except…she'd left her towel.

CHAPTER FOUR

Easy found his way to the grocery store via GPS. Looked like a nice one, too, judging by the produce and the meat department. As a carnivore, he measured a supermarket by its butcher, with the produce section coming in second. Mostly because of his love for potatoes. Because what went better with steak? Fried, baked, au gratin, mashed, boiled... however they were served, he'd eat them.

The Green Grocer was no slouch in either the meat or produce areas. Maybe because of the wide variety of shifters who lived in town, but the glass butcher cases were stocked full of all varieties and cuts of meat. The seafood department was the same way, and for him, a big salmon or trout fillet was right up there with a ribeye any day.

He couldn't carry much on his motorcycle, so stocking his place would have to wait until his car arrived, but he got enough steaks and fish for a few meals.

He picked up a few other things, including a bag of baking potatoes and some butter. And, because it was one of his favorite things, a gallon of ice cream. He chose caramel cookie crunch this time, but he wasn't stuck on any one flavor. However the mood moved him, he went. Ice cream was his one real vice, but thankfully, his metabolism could handle it.

The last thing he grabbed was a large Italian hoagie from the deli. It would make for an easy lunch on a day he really didn't feel like cooking.

He paid, bought two reusable bags for his stuff, then managed to fit it all in the storage well on his bike.

The first time he'd been to Shadowvale, he'd mostly house-shopped. There was still a lot more of the town to discover. But as much as he would have loved to tool through town to check things out, the ice cream didn't really allow for that. Nor did the fact that he still had a lot of unpacking to do.

That had to come first. Nothing else was going to get done until he was settled.

Home it was. Home. Huh. He put his helmet on. Funny to think of this new place as home. It didn't really feel that way. Not yet. Probably wouldn't take too long, though. He'd never been overly attached to any one spot.

Maybe after a few more hours of unpacking, he'd see what that pool was all about. He'd already contracted the same company as the previous owners to keep up with the cleaning. That was another task he had no interest in taking on.

The backyard had a small summer kitchen, too. The grill that was part of it was going to get a lot of use, starting tonight. He was definitely throwing some steaks on there for dinner.

He smiled. Maybe living in the country wasn't going to be such a bad thing. His condo in the city was pretty low on amenities compared to his new house.

As he drove home, he saw a few interesting characters, but also noticed that quite a few pedestrians turned to look as he went by. It was the bike, not him, he knew that. Shadowvale either didn't have a lot of motorcyclists, or those it did have weren't on bikes this loud.

Maybe time to put new baffling in the muffler. He liked the rumble, but in a small town, it might not be as appreciated. And he didn't want to be known as the noisy biker. That was no way to make a first impression.

As he pulled into his driveway, his peripheral vision caught the strangest thing. A streak of bright pink and a whole lot of tantalizing female flesh.

He parked, put the kickstand down, and took his helmet off. He knew what he thought he'd seen. The curves of a gorgeous brunette in a barely there bikini running away from his house. While...holding on to her chest?

But there was no logical explanation for that. Was there? He ran a hand through his hair to comb it into place after the helmet, then frowned. Maybe the lightning strike was starting to affect his brain. First, he'd seen a guy in town with horns, then this woman. He supposed anything was possible after the Saver's Club incident.

He sighed, feeling less than optimistic about his future. He had to find a cure for this stupid thing before it was too late.

He popped open the storage well, got his grocery bags out, and went inside to put everything away. The house was a chaotic mess of boxes and random furniture, and he didn't feel like being in the midst of all that, so he took his hoagie and went outside to sit on the front steps and eat.

The day was warm despite the softly overcast sky, and everything had a golden glow to it, like the sun might come through at any moment, but he knew from what his realtor had told him that that wasn't going to happen.

She had assured him there was never any sun below the twilight line. Pam said that was just how the town functioned. She'd offered to show him houses above that line, but he liked being closer to the action of downtown. Such as it was.

She'd also told him about a place called Nightingale Park, which was apparently where a lot of people went to soak up the sun. Maybe he'd check that out in a day or two. Getting used to no sun was going to be a change.

He kind of thought she'd been angling for him to take her there, and she was cute enough, but he wasn't interested in dating. Not with all of his baggage.

The hoagie was good. Not like those from the place he usually got sandwiches in the city, but it held its own.

He'd be happy here. He hoped. But the way his mind was changing gave him concern. At what point did he need help? Would there come a time when he couldn't manage things on his own? He was a young guy. Still two years from forty. And in good health.

Other than the problems from the lightning strike.

He finished the hoagie, wadded up the wrapper to throw away when he had a trash can, and went back to work unloading the rest of the truck, happy for the distraction from his thoughts.

He was carrying two barstools to the kitchen counter when he stopped and looked longingly at the pool. He tucked the stools under the counter. He'd sweated through his T-shirt half an hour ago. But if he stopped now to swim, he wasn't going to feel like finishing the rest of the unpacking.

The blue water called to him.

He shook his head, staring at the pool through the sliders that led onto the rear porch. "Not yet."

Something caught his eye. He went closer to the glass doors. Was that the remains of a wet spot at the pool's edge? In this warmth, there wasn't much left to it, but he was pretty sure that's what he was looking at.

Then he saw something else. A blue-and-white-striped towel a few feet away. And there was no chance that was a hallucination.

He glanced toward the house next door and laughed softly as three new thoughts came into his head. One, he wasn't completely crazy after all, which went a long way toward restoring his good mood. Two, anyone willing to wear a bikini that small—and look that fine in it—while sneaking a dip in his pool was going to keep life interesting.

And three, Miss Hot-Pink Bikini was a total smokeshow.

He wanted to meet this woman. Not in his current sweaty state, but after he'd had a shower and cleaned up a little. Maybe he'd invite her over for steak. If she didn't have a husband.

If she was single and had a boyfriend, well...he might still invite her over. So long as the guy didn't live there, too. That wasn't a line Easy was going to cross. But no ring and no live-in? Fair game.

Not because he wanted to date her. Just to be neighborly.

He went back to the truck, smiling. It was nice to have something new to think about. And while he reminded himself again that he wasn't looking to get involved, a diversion wouldn't be such a bad thing. So long as she didn't think he was being anything more than neighborly.

He had a book to write, after all.

He stacked three boxes marked Kitchen and carried them in, unable to keep himself from looking at the house next door.

Was she watching him? Probably not. Why would she? She was most likely bummed someone had moved in and curtailed her chances of using the pool, because there was no way she'd taken advantage of its availability just this once.

He snorted. Well, if she was going to wear a bikini like that, she was welcome anytime. Anytime he wasn't writing. Because there was no way he could concentrate on Tomahawk Jones with a woman like that all wet in his backyard.

It took him until nearly eleven p.m. to get the rest of the truck unloaded and his bedroom set up enough to function. He'd tackle his office tomorrow, after he returned the truck. Which reminded him, he needed to call his realtor. She'd promised to meet him at the rental place and drive him back.

He rolled his head and shoulders, working out some of the wear and tear he'd put on himself today. Not a big deal for a shifter, but it had still been more effort than he was used to. Sitting at a desk all day was making him soft. Something else he needed to change.

But what he wanted right now was a steak and a swim. Even at this hour.

He went back to check out the grill and was happy to see the previous owners had left the propane tank, and from the gauge on the side, it looked about half full. Plenty for him to cook dinner. He turned it on and left it to heat up, then grabbed the striped towel and went back inside, but not before noticing there were no lights on at Miss Hot-Pink Bikini's house.

Sure, it was a little late to invite her over this evening, but that didn't mean he hadn't been thinking about it. But it was probably for the best that she'd already gone to bed. He was pretty beat, too. And in no shape to meet someone for the first time.

He put the towel on the kitchen counter, then went to get the pack of steaks from the top shelf in the fridge. He unwrapped them, got them seasoned up, and let them sit while he went to change.

Which was when he realized he had no idea where his bathing suit was. He knew he had one. Although he couldn't quite recall when he'd worn it last. That time he'd gone boating with the pack? Maybe.

But what box was it in? He had no idea. And no real desire to dig through a score of boxes to find it.

Well, it was his house, his pool, and screw it, he didn't need to wear a bathing suit if he didn't want to.

Besides, Miss Hot-Pink Bikini was already in bed, probably asleep, too. So it wasn't like his naked self in the pool was going to harm her delicate sensibilities.

Although he wasn't really sold on her being all that delicate when it came to skinny-dipping. That suit of hers almost qualified. He grinned. He had to find out her name and her relationship status and soon.

For purely platonic reasons. Mostly.

With a little laugh, he stripped down to nothing, put on his robe, and went to get the steaks started.

CHAPTER FIVE

Ginny considered herself a pretty good sleeper, but she doubted any werewolf around could have slept through the delicious aroma of steaks grilling.

For a werewolf, that was like clanging a giant dinner bell.

She blinked a few times, shaking off the sleepiness and inhaling, nose twitching at the smell. She sat on the edge of the bed, rubbed a hand over her face, and looked at the time. Eleven twenty-seven.

She'd only been asleep for about half an hour. But why was she smelling steak? She'd had pork chops for dinner. Even so, she had to wonder if she'd left the stove on.

Might as well check, she was up now.

She went to the kitchen, but everything was off. Yeah, that smell wasn't coming from her house. She followed her nose onto her back deck, opening the door carefully so as not to make any noise. The air was warm and balmy and steak-scented.

Quite appealing to the werewolf kind.

She stayed close to the house. Fireflies danced in the line of trees on the boundary between her house and the McKinleys'. Because the lots were pie-shaped, the backyards didn't really look directly into one another.

Even so, she didn't want to be caught spying. Which was exactly what she was about to do.

Because not only was the steak-grilling happening next door, but the motorcycle-riding hotness who'd bought the place was in the pool. The same pool she'd snuck out of hours earlier. She could hear the water splashing as he swam.

She groaned internally. He'd have seen her forgotten towel by now, which meant getting it back would require a confession from her. Then he'd know she'd been in his pool.

She could just leave it, but that would break up a set. And she'd have to make sure he never saw the matching one, or he'd know. So many complications from a towel!

She frowned. Why did he have to go for a swim tonight? She knew why. He'd had a long day of unpacking. And that was hot, sweaty, tiring work. Of course he'd want to swim. She couldn't blame him. That pool was amazing.

She was a little jealous. Without any actual right, she felt like he was swimming in her pool. Which was nonsense, because that wasn't even remotely true. He owned it now, well and clear. And she never had.

But for three glorious months, she'd had the use of it. That felt like it had to be worth something. Even if it wasn't.

She sighed. Well, at least she had him to look at now. A reasonable trade-off if ever there was one.

She glanced toward his house. Speaking of looking...she snuck down off the deck to the thickest section of the tree line and tried to find a gap in the branches. She had no idea what he looked like from the front or without a helmet. She probably should have paid more attention today while he was unpacking the truck, but she'd gotten lost in her work.

The foliage was thick, but she found a spot where a good section of the pool was visible. He had only the pool light and the summer kitchen lights on, but those were more than enough for her shifter vision.

He swam past.

Her eyes widened. The movement of the water made it hard to say for sure, but what she'd just seen could only be described as a naked butt.

Blowing out a breath, she turned away and put her back to the tree. He was skinny-dipping. Of course he was. What else would a man do on his first night in a new house with a pool? She wanted to look again, but that felt awfully intrusive. And a teensy bit wrong.

Even if he spotted her and then forgot about it, she'd still know she'd pulled a Peeping Tom on him. *Not cool, Ginny.*

She rolled her eyes at herself, the same woman

who'd been contemplating a life of crime only this morning.

Maybe one more quick look. Thirty seconds, no more. Just enough to see if a woman was with him. A second look that was purely based in fact finding. That was all.

She found the spot between the branches again. *Oh my.* He was getting out. Climbing up the ladder and about to leave the water—she turned away.

Maybe ten seconds went by before she looked again. He had a robe on now and was facing her. Had he heard her? Seen her?

She spun away from the trees and went very still, a little mortified that she'd possibly been discovered. He couldn't see her through all these branches, could he? At least he'd forget in a little bit.

Even so, as bad neighbors went, she was getting close to the top of the list. Not as bad as those pee-happy Freeman boys, but still. She needed to get inside and go back to sleep, which was not going to be easy with the current image of his bare backside in her brain.

Wow. The dude was fit. Hot and fit. And he drove a motorcycle. Also, his tattoos weren't just on his arms. There was another one on his right shoulder blade, but nothing from the waist down. Which was something she really shouldn't know.

What kind of game was fate playing here? Teasing her with a man like that, knowing he was never going to remember her. That was just cruel. Terrific eye candy, but totally unfair all the same.

Frowning, she crept back inside and returned to bed. To sleep, of course, but also to think about what she'd done.

And what she'd seen.

She was still smiling when she drifted off.

When she woke again, at a much more reasonable hour, the previous night's activities came flooding back. So did her smile as she tucked a hand behind her head. Today was going to be a good day.

Today she was going to meet her new neighbor for the first time. Well, the *first* first time. Every meeting from here on out would be his first, but not for her. Her smile slipped away as the bitter reality of that set in.

It was what it was. She couldn't change it, so she focused on the bright side. Because of her curse, she felt no pressure about how meeting him would go.

Hard not to feel *some* pressure, regardless. She wanted him to like her right away. Not after two weeks of trying.

Because she'd done that before with a guy at the post office. Every time she'd gone in, she'd learned something new about him. What baseball team he liked, what his favorite color was, and so on. Then she'd put it all into play on the same day, and he'd asked her out.

Which had been great, but pointless. Other than she'd amused herself for a couple of weeks. But that amusement had turned sour fast, making her feel more alone than ever.

There was no dating a forgettable woman.

That hard truth wasn't going to rain on her parade today, however. She was too fired up about this new guy. Why, she wasn't sure.

Maybe hope never really died?

She hopped out of bed and went to the kitchen to make some coffee and figure out a game plan. No doubt he'd be working on stuff inside today, unless he hadn't emptied the truck yet. Hmm. Either way, she'd go over and introduce herself right away. As in, right away after she showered, did her hair and makeup, and put on a fabulous outfit.

She dropped a K-Cup into the coffeemaker and pushed the brew button. Hazelnut mocha this morning. One of her favorites. Did he drink coffee? Probably. Most people did.

That made her think. Maybe she'd run into town and get him some. He might not be able to make his own yet if his kitchen wasn't set up, so that would be a nice thing to do. On second thought, she'd get him coffee *and* something from Black Horse Bakery. Bringing something she'd baked herself would be better, but that would take too long and it just wasn't going to happen.

When she made cookies, they came from a slice-and-bake roll. Oh, who was she kidding—she ate the dough directly from the tube. Martha Stewart she was not.

That was the plan, then. Some kind of crazy-good thing from the bakery (something perfect for sharing, like cake), plus coffee, plus her looking super cute. He'd invite her in for sure, then.

And if he did have a wife or girlfriend, which Ginny was leaning heavily toward him not having, then he'd introduce Ginny to her. Or at least bring her up in conversation if his significant other wasn't home. But none would be preferable. *Please let none be the case.* That was the least fate could do.

The coffee finished streaming into her cup. She added sugar and half-and-half and gave it a stir. The creamer was almost gone. She added it to the grocery list she kept on the fridge.

It was selfish to want him to be single, she knew that. Especially when she couldn't have him. But she didn't need him to be single permanently. Just today. Or for a week. That would be plenty of time for her to dream about what never could be.

Then he could meet someone he could actually remember, fall hopelessly in love, fill that house with kids, and she could weep for the life she'd never have. An upbeat, healthy kind of weeping, of course.

"Gin, you're a mixed-up ball of crazy." She lifted her cup, saluting her reflection in the microwave. "But at least I don't feel like robbing a bank anymore."

She took her coffee back to the bedroom, put the morning news on the television, and picked out an outfit while half-listening and drinking her hazelnut mocha. That's when she saw the package on the dresser that needed to go to the post office.

"Ugh." Well, she was going out anyway. Might as well get that done, too.

Based on what she'd seen of her new neighbor and what she thought he might like, she decided on cutoff jean shorts, a mint-green gingham top that tied at the waist, and her hair in a ponytail. Or was that trying too hard to be cute?

Actually, it was super cute, and she didn't care if it was over the top. Plus, she could wear her white wedges with the cork heels that made her legs look fantastic. Yep, that was her outfit all the way. It was very girl-next-door, and she kind of thought he'd be intrigued by that.

Plus, it felt like a very nonthreatening look, just in case a woman answered the door.

She showered, did the hair and makeup thing, then glanced out the front window to see if there was any sign of him. Nothing. And the rear door of the rental truck was still down.

Maybe he was sleeping in. There was no telling how late he'd been out swimming.

Might as well run her errands. She grabbed her purse and the package that needed to be mailed, and off to town she went.

She smiled as she got into her car. Did he sleep in the same outfit he swam in? Maybe she'd ask him when they finally met face-to-face. Wasn't like he'd remember anyway.

In fact, when they did meet, she was going to tell him exactly what she thought about him. Why not? She had nothing to lose.

Something—maybe the coffee, maybe the morning, maybe the never-ending ache of loneliness that permeated her life—had filled her with a greater boldness than usual. If she wasn't going to rob a bank for fun, she was going to tell her neighbor exactly what the sight of him did to her.

Maybe she'd even kiss him. If he seemed interested, of course.

She might be forgettable, but she was not going to be boring.

CHAPTER SIX

Easy had been up since five forty-five. Rising early was a practice he'd picked up in the military and never lost.

Getting up early meant he could get a lot done, so he wasn't eager to lose the habit either.

So far this morning, he'd run a quick 5K through his new neighborhood—no signs of life at Miss Hot-Pink Bikini's house—then back home for a shower and breakfast, which was sadly just a premade protein shake.

Then he poured himself a large coffee and got to work. His office was job one today, and he was making good progress. The dining room no longer looked like a dining room now that he'd added his desk.

Two bookshelves flanked the desk. His planning board was on the wall between the shelves, with all the due dates and deadlines he needed to keep himself on track.

Right now, it was just another reminder of how behind he was.

There was so much house stuff to do, but the writing had to come first, which meant it would take a while to get everything organized. Nothing to be done about that, so it had to be okay.

His office was generally a work in progress anyway. That was his explanation for the permanent state of disorder that existed in his work space.

He stretched. His run had been outstanding today. Maybe because he'd slept like a baby and had hot-pink dreams, resulting in a fired-up mood this morning unlike anything he'd experienced in a long time.

Some of that he'd burned off on the street, but the rest he was channeling into two things. This office, which was getting close to done enough. And his book.

He was going to write today. He was itching to. Whatever had caused that, he wasn't questioning it.

One more box of books got unpacked and put away on the bookshelf, which still left many boxes to go, but it was time to work. He used the eraser end of a pencil to push the power button on his laptop, something he'd started doing since the lightning strike. Maybe it was silly, but he wasn't going to risk a spark erasing his hard work. With the computer humming along, he was ready to make words happen.

He refilled his coffee mug, sat down, and opened up his document. *Long Lone Howl* was his work in progress. If you could call half a chapter *progress*. Which he was sure his editor wouldn't.

He read through the few pages he'd already written to get his head back in the story. At least what was already on the page wasn't complete garbage. He tweaked a few words, rewrote one section to add more tension, then came to the blank page awaiting his input.

A car door shut. Then an engine started up.

He looked up. Sounded like it came from next door.

Miss Hot-Pink Bikini was going somewhere.

He had to have another look at her. Unable to help himself, he got up. The dining room windows allowed him to see most of her driveway.

She was pulling out, the bumper of her Jeep gleaming in the morning light. He couldn't see much of her other than a silhouette behind the wheel, hair swinging.

He smiled. Maybe later, he'd go over and introduce himself. See about that invite to dinner. And a swim.

He laughed and went back to work.

He slipped into the zone, the words flowing, and had managed to finish chapter one and get almost all of chapter two done when the doorbell rang.

Blinking, he looked up from the screen. Almost two hours had gone by. Now that was the kind of workday he needed more of. Too bad life had interrupted him.

Then he realized it was probably Pam, coming to check on him and follow him over to the truck rental place. Although he hadn't gotten a text from her about that.

He got up and went to the door. Maybe he could get another couple of pages done this afternoon. He opened the door, expecting to see Pam.

It wasn't Pam. It wasn't even remotely Pam. He grinned. "Hi."

Miss Hot-Pink Bikini smiled back at him, somehow looking wholesome and wicked at the same time. She was carrying a bakery box in one hand and a to-go cup of coffee in the other. "Hi. I'm your neighbor, Ginny French. I wanted to come over and introduce myself."

"Hi, Ginny. Nice to meet you." So nice that *nice* wasn't even the right word. "I'm Ezekiel Grayle, but most people call me Easy."

Her brows lifted, and the most comical expression bent her mouth. "Oh, really? Easy, huh? There are so many things I could say about that."

His smile was so stuck to his face, his cheeks were starting to ache. "Not that I haven't heard them, but feel free to riff away."

"Not if you've heard them already." She laughed, shook her head, then held the box and the cup out to him. "These are for you, by the way. That's a chocolate cake. A really good one. I hope you like chocolate. And that's coffee in the cup, in case you hadn't guessed. I wasn't sure you'd be able to make coffee yet, although I can smell it now, so obviously you did, but here's some more." Her eyes suddenly went wide, brightening momentarily with a familiar glow. "You're a wolf. I can smell that, too. I'm also one."

He took the offerings. "I am, and I do. Like chocolate, that is." He liked her, too. A lot. Even more now that he knew she was of like kind. "And I could tell by the glow that came and went in your eyes that I'm not the only shifter standing here."

"Nope," she breathed out. "So are the Freemans up on the corner. And the McKinleys who used to live here. I think the town tries to group us together. To be neighborly and all that."

"Well, the town did a good thing, then." He tipped his head toward the inside of the house. "Would you like to come in and have some of this cake?"

"I'd love to." Her eyes narrowed. "Do you have a wife or a girlfriend?"

"Nope. No one to get territorial, if that's what you're asking."

"Sort of." She stepped inside. "The place looks so different without all the McKinleys' stuff in it. Not that I ever really came over here."

"No? Does that mean you only just decided to be neighborly?" He could smell the coffee and the chocolate cake, but he could also pick up the scent of her perfume. A kind of dark floral, but soapy clean that fit her good-girl-who-might-be-a-little-bad vibe.

"No, I, uh…it's complicated." She suddenly glanced down and pulled a vibrating phone out of her pocket. She groaned softly as she read the screen.

"I have to answer this, sorry. One of the images I sent a client isn't right, and they're freaking out."

"No worries." He was happy to stand there and watch her. And her legs, which seemed impossibly long and muscled in a way he found extremely sexy.

What was it about female werewolves that made them so irresistible?

She furiously thumb-typed a message, then hit send and tucked the phone away. "I have to go back to my house to fix this, but then I'll come back and we'll do this all over again. Not that you'll remember."

He wasn't sure what that meant. "Okay. We'll have cake then."

"Yeah, we'll see. Doesn't always work that way." She hesitated, giving him the strangest look. "You're the most gorgeous man I've seen in a long time, by the way. I can't believe you're a werewolf, too. Figures. I mean, really. Your body is amazing. The tattoos are hot, too. Especially the one on your shoulder."

How had she seen that tattoo?

She blew out a breath, eyes glowing hard. "The things I could do to you...with you...oh man."

He just stood there. Mouth open. Female wolves were bold, but this was next-level. No woman had ever talked to him this way before. It was shocking. And possibly the biggest turn-on he'd ever experienced.

Then she raked him head to toe with a gaze that made him feel like he ought to be blushing. Or maybe he was. No telling what was happening right now, except that he didn't want it to end. "Well...I...thank you."

"You're welcome, Easy. I'll see you later, then."

"Okay. Later it is." He was mildly confused in the best possible way. His body temperature had shot up, and every muscle in his body tensed, ready for whatever came next. She was the boldest woman he'd ever met, and surface-of-the-sun hot. Also maybe a little strange. But for this kind of hot, he could overlook the strange.

She held up a finger. "There's just one thing I really want to do before I leave."

He was game. "What's that?"

She stepped toward him, cupped his jaw in her hands, and kissed him, a small snap of electricity biting his lip at first contact.

So maybe he hadn't been ready for whatever came next. He almost dropped the cake and the coffee, then wanted to so he could take hold of her. The heat of her mouth combined with the sheer unexpectedness of her kiss made everything tilt like he was doing ninety-five on a hairpin turn.

He'd only just straightened himself out when she backed away and sighed. "Too bad you're going to forget me the minute I walk out that door."

He frowned. "What?"

She patted his cheek as she headed for her house. "See you later, handsome."

"Bye." He stood there, watching her, still holding the cake and coffee and wondering what in the blazes had just happened. Had he been punked in some way? He couldn't imagine who would do that to him, or how getting a beautiful woman to kiss him was getting punked, but he was too befuddled to think of anything else.

Maybe this was some kind of local pack initiation. If so, his other pack sucked.

A minute passed, and she was out of sight, but he was still standing there, trying to figure out what had happened. And how to get her to do it again.

And maybe how to get this grin off his face.

His phone rang from his desk. He turned, blinking himself back to reality. He put the cake and coffee down and answered it.

"Easy, it's John."

His editor. That snapped him back to reality faster than a bucket of cold water over his head. "Hey, John, how are you?"

"Good. How's the move going?"

"Great. Getting settled in." But he wasn't ready to tell his editor how well the writing had gone today. Just in case it didn't keep going that way.

"Good, glad to hear it. Just wanted to call and let you know that the first two books in the series are going back to print again, and we have some new foreign interest as well. This movie is really heating things up."

"Excellent, uh, news." Easy was still looking out the window, hoping to see Ginny on her way back.

"You sound distracted. Did I catch you at a bad time?"

"Just unpacking. You know how a move is."

"Right, right. Well, let me get to it, then. How's the book coming? I only ask because there's talk of moving the release up and—"

"Moving it up?" Easy's full attention zeroed in on the phone call.

"I know it's a lot to ask, what with the move and all, but we're willing to attach a bonus to it if you can get the book in two months early."

"Two months early." Easy's mouth went dry. That was a pretty major move up. "What kind of bonus?"

"Fifty grand."

Easy's brows shot skyward. "That's quite a bonus."

"Everyone here at Redstone Press is fully committed to making Tomahawk Jones our top priority. We see him as the next Jack Reacher. A kind of ex-military Alex Cross. But totally original, too."

Easy took a breath. Being classed with Lee Childs and James Patterson was enough to make a man need a little air. "That's very kind of you."

"Kind has nothing to do with it, Easy. You're a talented writer, and it's about time the world knew. This movie is just the beginning. You're not working on a book now, you're working on an empire. That's how we feel. Now what do you say? You can do it, can't you?"

He really wasn't sure. But that kind of bonus money was hard to say no to. All of John's flattery didn't hurt either. "I'll do my best."

"I knew you'd say yes. All right, I'll let you get back to it, then. Have a good one."

"You, too." Easy hung up. At the moment, he wasn't sure which way was up.

Between Ginny's crazy-hot kiss and the fifty-thousand-dollar carrot that had just been dangled in front of him, his head was going in a million directions.

Why had he agreed to the new deadline? He hadn't, actually. Because he knew better. He'd never get the book done in time. Not when he was trying to move into a new house *and* find a solution for his shifting problem.

He groaned and ran a hand through his hair, stopping midway to squeeze his skull. The idea of writing that many words in that short amount of time was beyond daunting.

There was only one way to do it.

Everything else had to get pushed aside. Everything. Unpacking the rest of the house. Dealing with his inability to shift properly. Any attempt to join the local pack.

He looked toward Ginny's house. And sadly, whatever might have been with his hot neighbor.

There was no time to properly wine and dine a woman with this new deadline. Just because he didn't want a relationship didn't mean he was interested in a fling instead. Not with the woman he lived next door to.

That could go bad, really bad, way too fast.

He had a couple hours before his car was

supposed to arrive on the transport, and he still needed to get the rental truck returned, but maybe he could squeeze out the rest of that chapter in between all that.

Actually, there could be no *maybe*. It had to be done.

With a deep, beleaguered sigh, he picked up the cake and took it into the kitchen. He left the coffee on his desk. He was going to need that.

And a whole lot more.

CHAPTER SEVEN

Ginny marched across the yard toward her house like a woman possessed. She had never done such an impulsive thing like that in her life. She was shaking, mostly because she didn't believe she'd actually done it.

But also because, wow, she'd just kissed a man whose hotness probably registered on the Richter scale. She'd actually felt a spark when their mouths had touched. Wait. The Richter scale didn't measure the temperature of volcanos. That was for earthquakes. Did they measure the temperatures of volcanos?

Well, whatever, he was lava-hot, and she'd kissed him, so score one for the forgettable Miss French.

Sad that he'd forget that kiss, but whoa, Nelly, she wouldn't. Not ever. Not if she lived to be a thousand years old. Which would probably be awful.

Man oh man, she was wound up. What she needed was a good run, the four-footed kind. No, what she needed was more Easy.

Instead, she had work.

She was definitely telling Aunt Gwen about this, though.

Ginny hit the front porch, went inside and straight to her desk, a little cranky that her client needed this new graphic right away. It wasn't Ginny's fault the woman had decided to launch a new product on such short notice.

There was going to be a rush charge on this for sure.

She sat down and went to work, but Easy's face and body and mouth kept distracting her. She sat back, tipping her head to look at the ceiling. She had to focus, or this job was never going to get done.

And the faster it got done, the faster she could go back over there for cake.

Sure. Cake. *That's* why she wanted to go back to his house.

With a snort of amusement, she put her headphones on, turned up the work tunes, and got creating.

She worked until her stomach growled, then she worked a little longer. But only for as long as it took to finish and get the graphic sent, along with an invoice. Maybe that would keep the woman from making any more changes. Or not. Didn't matter that much as long as the invoice was paid. Happy clients were repeat clients, and that was important.

But Ginny really wanted the job to be done so she could go back to Easy's.

First, she'd need lunch. Or maybe she'd invite him out for lunch. Maybe if she worked really hard on maintaining eye contact he'd remember her. She knew that wouldn't happen, but lunch with him would be so much fun.

She checked herself in the mirror, but nothing was out of place. All she'd done was sit at her desk. Not the most rigorous of activities.

She peeked outside. The rental truck was gone, and another truck was in its place, an eighteen-wheeler with tarp sides. Easy was outside with two other guys. He was signing papers on a clipboard.

And a shiny black Mustang sat in the driveway. Looked new. Maybe not brand new, but close.

He'd had a car delivered. She pondered that for a moment. Made sense. He'd driven the rental truck with the motorcycle trailered behind it, then had his car sent by transport.

She might have done the same thing when she'd moved, except she'd been twenty-six, and everything she'd owned had pretty much fit in her car. What hadn't, she'd sold.

Her little apartment near Shadowvale's library hadn't held much anyway, so it had all worked out.

When she'd bought this house a few years ago, the move had taken substantially more than a single carload. And if she ever moved from here, well, that would take a big truck for sure.

She went back to the kitchen for lunch. Easy was occupied. And there was no telling how much more work he had inside. Maybe she should just let him be today. No doubt he had a ton of unpacking left to do. There'd been boxes everywhere in his house, at least in the living and dining rooms.

Or maybe she'd just leave him alone until this evening. The man had to eat, right?

She fixed herself a sandwich with a side of Green Grocer deli potato salad and a pickle, then grabbed a drink and went outside onto the rear deck. She took her phone out of her back pocket before she sat down. Just because she was going to leave him alone didn't mean she couldn't give him the opportunity to see her and be neighborly.

She sat at her little round glass table, enjoying the day. By the time her food was gone, she'd seen no sign of him.

Busy, she reminded herself. Moving was a tremendous amount of work, and it was exhausting.

What she ought to do was go over and offer to help unpack. But maybe he wouldn't want a stranger helping him.

She slouched down in her chair and stared at the cloud cover. Why was her life so complicated?

Her phone chimed with an incoming email. The graphic she'd just finished was approved and the invoice paid, but now her client wanted a second version in a different color scheme.

Ginny stuck the phone in her pocket, picked up her plate and her drink, and went inside. Might as well work.

And so she did.

She stopped a few times to refill her drink, or get up and stretch, and each time she looked outside, but he wasn't there.

She knew where he was. Working, just like she was. Well, not just like she was, but unpacking and putting things away and all the stuff that went with moving.

But it was odd that in light of that, no stack of flattened boxes grew, awaiting pickup by the recycling truck. No bin filled with the paper used to wrap breakables. He wasn't just letting that stuff pile up in the house, was he?

She was curious. Maybe he had some different unpacking method she'd never heard of.

Or maybe she needed to stop being so nosy and get on with her life.

But he was interesting in so many ways, and her life had lacked something interesting for far too long.

So she was going to indulge herself, and her curiosity in him, and do whatever made her happy. Being forgettable kind of gave her a free pass to do what she liked.

And so far she'd used that free pass only for good.

She straightened. Another forty-five minutes and she'd be done with her work, unless a new request came in, and even then she'd probably put it off until tomorrow. If the man was really working that hard, he had to be in need of something. A drink, a snack, a meal, some help, whatever.

She'd finish her project, and then she would go over there. If for no other reason than to make sure he wasn't buried under a stack of boxes.

At last, the vehicles were taken care of, Pam was gone, and Easy could write.

He sat at his desk, woke up his laptop, and stared at the blank screen for far too long without adding any new words.

Then he wrote a new paragraph. And deleted it.

In the last hour, he'd managed one new sentence that wasn't complete garbage.

It was like the pressure of having to write had sapped his writing mojo. Sure, there had already been pressure because of the original, tight deadline, but now that had been moved up two months, and his editor had reminded Easy of just how much was riding on this book.

An empire. What kind of thing was that to say to a writer? He didn't want or need *an empire*. He just needed to figure out what happened next, then put it on the page.

He sighed and got up for more coffee.

The pot was empty. With a grunt, he got to work making a new one. It was going to be a long night. With no time for a swim. While the coffee started brewing, he glanced at the pool. That swim last night had been great. Maybe he could use the pool as a reward if he hit his word count every day.

He really needed to figure out what that daily goal needed to be. But he was a little afraid of actually seeing that number.

Maybe what he should do was call John back and tell him there was no way he could get this book in that fast.

But fifty grand was a lot of money to walk away from. Too much. He had to at least try.

Too bad he wasn't a better typist. That would help.

He stood there, waiting on the coffee, but feeling guilty about the inactivity. There was no point in going back to his desk. By the time he got his head in the story again, the coffee would be done and he'd just be right back in here.

Five minutes wasn't going to cost him fifty thousand dollars.

But he hated that feeling. That weight of knowing he should be writing. Could be writing. He'd gone through it with his first Tomahawk Jones book after his agent had sold the book on the first chapter. Easy had only sent it to Raina to read and comment on, never thinking she'd end up sharing it with a few editors and starting a bidding war.

Seemed a lot of people in the publishing industry had been looking for his brand of thriller. Which was great. That auction had given him enough seed money to quit his day job at a high-end security firm so he could write full time. Wasn't like he'd been a desk jockey there. He'd been muscle. Part of an elite team hired out when someone with the funds wanted protection.

Basically, he'd been a bodyguard, paid to catch bullets if necessary and make sure nothing bad happened to the client.

He'd been good at it, too. But having a job where the downside was death? That wasn't so hard to walk away from. Not when becoming a full-time writer was the payoff.

Living in the city had meant he already understood how to make a dollar go as far as possible. His tiny apartment had been testament to that. He'd walked to work, or taken public transportation when necessary. So living on that first advance had been tough, but doable.

Now he was three years in and doing really well. Better than he'd thought he'd be doing at this point in his career, that was for sure.

But fifty grand was still too much money to ignore.

Which meant he had to gut it out, deal with the stress, and sleep when he was dead. It was like being back in the Rangers.

The coffeepot sputtered, bringing him back to reality. He turned away from the pool and saw the cake box on the counter.

Ginny. Man, he'd love to go spend the day with her. Or what was left of it. He had to figure out a way to get to know her better while still meeting his deadline. Maybe he could explain everything to her, see if she would be willing to be patient.

But a woman like that... He shook his head. She probably had a pack of guys prowling around her.

Why should she wait for him? He was a pretty good catch, if he overlooked the shifting issue, but he wasn't going to be very available for the next couple of months.

Wooing Ginny would be its own project. A woman like her deserved a man's undivided attention, and his was about as divided as it got.

Then again, she was a werewolf, like he was. Which meant there was very little chance she'd be interested in him once she found out about his shifting problem. Females generally wanted two things in a mate: a good provider and someone with a shot at being alpha.

He had the first one covered. He wasn't even close to the second. And if she was interested in kids, then she'd run in the other direction from him when she found out about his issues.

Whoa. Kids? Where had that come from? He wasn't even looking for a relationship. Or was he? He hadn't been. Until he'd been captivated by her.

But he was damaged goods. He couldn't do that to her. And he needed to stop thinking about her in that way, because it wasn't fair to either of them.

Besides, if the pack's alpha decided Easy was a no-go because of his shifting problem, Ginny would probably stop speaking to him altogether.

With a soft curse, he refilled his mug and went back to work.

This time, he managed to dig in and make some headway. Maybe a fresh pot of coffee was the trick. Or maybe his pep talk with himself. Or the reminder of how much money was on the line. Whatever it was, the switch had been thrown.

He was writing again. Not as fast as he had this morning, but pages were getting done. He was just about to finish chapter two when his doorbell rang.

He groaned. Not a good time. He'd been so close to a great hooky line to close with, and now it was gone.

Reluctantly, he got up and went to answer the door. Whoever it was, neighbors, sales people, Girl Scouts with cookies, he wasn't interested. He had too much work to do. And a chapter that had to be finished.

Honestly, the next one needed starting, too.

He opened the door. It was Ginny. He wanted to ignore all of his work intentions, but he couldn't. He had to get back to the keyboard.

But first, he was going to make a date with her. So he could tell her the truth. And see if at least they could be friends.

That would be better than nothing.

CHAPTER EIGHT

"Hi." Ginny gave Easy a little wave. She was nervous around him this time. That happened occasionally on a second meeting with a guy she found particularly attractive. Which Easy was. In fact, he was possibly the most attractive man she'd ever met.

And it wasn't just that he was handsome and physically fit. There was definitely a little shifter-pheromone thing going on. He was pushing *all* her buttons. Without even trying. At least, she didn't think he was trying.

The nervousness came from her hoping he was going to like her again, but it was compounded by the sense that, having met him already, she didn't want this time to go badly.

She took a breath and spoke. "I'm Ginny French, your next-door neighbor, and I know you just moved in, so I thought I'd come over and see if you needed any help unpacking or putting stuff away or whatever."

He smiled, the simple act weakening her knees a tiny bit. "Hi, Ginny French."

"I brought a cake over earlier." Not that he'd remember. He was probably wondering where that cake had come from.

"Right." He nodded.

Poor guy. Lots of people pretended to remember her. It was some kind of polite, knee-jerk reaction, like how people always answered "good" when you asked them how they were doing. Even if they were crying. She was so used to those kinds of rote answers that it would be weird if someone acted differently.

He glanced back at his desk, then at her again. "I'm kind of right in the middle of something. Maybe you could come back in about an hour?"

"Sure. I can do that." Her heart sank. He was really good at the gracious brush-off. Of course he didn't want some strange woman unpacking his boxes and riffling through his things. "You have a good night."

She turned and went down the porch steps, not waiting for his response.

He called after her. "You, too. See you later."

"Right, later," she answered without looking. She felt like crying, honestly, and she didn't want him to see her face all weirdly screwed up.

Not that he'd remember.

She went back to her house.

After this many years of being forgotten, she shouldn't be reacting like this. Her skin should be thicker. Her emotions should be immune to the disappointment her curse always caused. But she wasn't. Not with Easy anyway. Was that a good thing? That her emotions hadn't grown callous? Maybe. But it sure didn't feel good in the moment.

It felt awful. Like she was trapped in an abyss, and no one could hear her cries for help. She let out a shuddering breath. Now she was just being melodramatic. But trying to make light of the situation wasn't helping all that much either.

She stood in her kitchen, very much at odds with how to deal with the swirling emotions inside her. She wasn't in the mood to make herself some boring dinner and watch some boring show. She couldn't handle another night of that. And that wouldn't take her mind off what had just happened. Tonight she needed something different. Something outside her usual safe routine.

Tonight she needed anything that helped her forget the curse she was living under. There was no way to truly do that, of course, but maybe she could pretend enough to find an hour or two of solace.

She had to get out of the house. Away from the temptation to do exactly as Easy had asked and go back over to his place in an hour. Being forgotten again would only make things worse.

She might break if that happened.

Step one for an evening out and an attempt to have fun was an outfit she felt good in. Not just good, but amazing. The kind of outfit that put an extra strut in her step.

That meant a pair of skintight jeans, her favorite sky-high heels, and a very sexy black off-the-shoulder blouse. After she changed, she took her hair out of the ponytail and gave it a good brushing, then curled it a little.

Happy with that, she touched up her makeup with a darker eye, a slightly deeper-than-nude lip, and a little highlighting.

Simple jewelry, a small purse with the essentials, and she was ready to go. But where? She stared at herself in the mirror. She needed a place where she could mingle, but also a place where there would be plenty of men who could appreciate a woman.

Club 42 was an option, but there weren't many single guys there. Mostly couples. She thought a little more. Maybe the Five Bells. The pub wasn't even remotely as upscale as Club 42, but she didn't need upscale. She needed entertaining.

The pub was never short on men either.

Her destination set, she headed for the door.

Easy finished his chapter with a hook that wasn't quite there yet, but it was good enough for a first draft. It had taken him less time than expected, which surprised him, considering he couldn't stop thinking about Ginny.

She'd reacted so differently when she'd come to the door. Almost like she assumed he wouldn't remember her. How on earth did she think that was possible? They'd been lip-locked only hours before.

And that kiss was the most memorable thing that had happened to him in a long time.

Right in front of the bonus he'd just been promised.

He'd been thinking, too, about her offer of help. If she was serious, that could make his life a lot easier. He just needed to tell her that, until this book was done, he wasn't going to be much in the way of company.

And he had to come clean about his shifting issues. There was no point in leading her on and letting her think he was dating—or mating— material. But maybe she'd be cool with being friends. He'd certainly be able to tell based on how she reacted to his confession.

He hit save on his Word doc, then got up and stretched. He wasn't sure he had enough mental energy to have a big discussion this evening, but he also didn't want any more time to go by without talking to her.

He was far too intrigued by her not to see her as soon as possible. Then it occurred to him that, based on her reaction earlier, she might not want to see him.

Had he said something to offend her? He knew he could be a little short when he was in writing mode. What had he said? He wasn't sure. Whatever it was, he had to apologize.

Even if they were never anything more than friends, he couldn't have the woman next door thinking he was a jerk.

But first, he wanted to make sure he hadn't fermented while he'd been at his desk. He'd been working nonstop all day, whether on the house or the book, and he didn't want Ginny to bear the brunt of that.

He took a quick shower, shaved, brushed his teeth, then dug out a fresh pair of jeans and a clean T-shirt.

It wasn't until he was walking out the front door that a weird case of the jitters hit him. The sensation really threw him. He was nervous. All the things he'd been through in his life, and this was what shook him.

Ginny's potential reaction.

He laughed softly and shook his head. He felt like he was back in high school, about to ask Shauna Perez to prom.

Hopefully, this evening would go better.

He stood on the porch and took a breath. There was no telling, though. He went down the steps and across his lawn toward Ginny's.

Her door opened as he approached, and she came out, dressed to impress. And impress she did. She'd gone from smokeshow to five-alarm fire.

He stopped in his tracks. "Wow."

She turned at the sound of his voice. "What are you doing here?"

Not the reception he'd expected. "I, uh…" He cleared his throat and ran a hand through his hair, undoing the grooming he'd just finished. "What am I doing here?"

Her bare shoulders had knocked the thoughts out

of his head, replacing them with brand-new, and rather inappropriate, ones.

She sighed. "Yeah, I have that effect on people."

"I bet. Especially looking like that."

She smiled. A little. "Listen, Easy, I have to—"

"I'm sorry about earlier. Whatever I said or did to upset you, I'm sorry."

The color drained out of her face, and she stared at him, a mixture of utter shock and disbelief flashing in her eyes. "What did you say?"

"I don't know, but that's part of why I came over here. You looked upset and—"

"No, what did you *just* say? About earlier."

"When you came over earlier, I think I upset you. I'm sorry about that."

She came down one step off the porch, but no farther. "Earlier. You said 'earlier.' I distinctly heard that word."

"Right. The second time you came over."

She looked like she might cry. Crap. He was really bad at this. "The second time? You mean you remember the first time?"

He couldn't help but grin. "Yeah. You, uh, kissed me pretty good. Hard to forget a thing like that."

Her mouth came open, but no words came out. Then her eyes rolled back in her head.

She was going to faint.

With more speed than he'd ever used before, he made it to her just in time to prevent her from cracking her head on the steps, catching her in his arms. She was out cold.

"Ginny?"

Nothing.

He picked her up and tried her front door. Locked. Back to his house, then, because he wasn't about to leave her on her front porch. Or dig through her purse to find her keys.

He carried her to his place, got them inside, then gently laid her on his couch. He stood there for a second, trying to figure out what had just happened, but all he could come up with was that he'd once again said something to upset her.

Enough that she'd passed out. He couldn't recall ever having that effect on a woman before. It wasn't nearly the thrill he'd imagined it would be.

In truth, it was downright terrifying. Whatever had happened to her, he'd been the cause. He'd distressed another werewolf so badly, she'd lost consciousness.

Was this related to his own worsening issues? If it was, he'd have to call John and tell him the book was on hold. Easy couldn't let his problems affect other people.

Especially not Ginny.

He was pacing now, wondering if he should call someone. The only person he knew in town was Pam.

He could take Ginny to the emergency room. He knew there was a hospital in town.

He glanced at her. Still out. He bent and pressed his palm to her forehead. She wasn't feverish.

Although he might be.

He straightened and scrubbed a hand over his face.

This was not how he'd thought his life in Shadowvale was going to start.

CHAPTER NINE

Ginny blinked, opening her eyes. Nothing but a white ceiling in her immediate range of vision.

And then a handsome, pacing man.

Easy.

Was she in his house? Seemed like it. But why was she in his house?

The reason came rushing back to her at a thousand miles an hour. She sat up, swinging her legs off the couch so that her feet were on the floor, heart racing anew like it had before everything had blanked out. "You remembered me."

He was facing away from her, but turned abruptly. "You're awake."

"You remembered me." She repeated the words, the sentence so rare and spectacular that she wasn't sure she believed it herself.

His brow furrowed. "Of course I remembered you."

"No, there is no *of course*. No one remembers me. No one. Except for my aunt. And, well, Seymour, and he's—how do you remember me? How is that possible?"

He shook his head. "How is it not possible? What do you mean no one remembers you?"

"It's my curse. I'm cursed to be forgotten. Ever since I touched a stupid haunted mirror in an old plantation house. No one, and I mean *no one*, remembers me. They do while they're talking to me, but the moment I leave their eyesight, I'm erased from their memory." She snapped her fingers. "Gone. Just like that."

He grimaced. "For real? That's awful. I can't imagine living like that."

"It's…" A lump formed in her throat. "Yeah, it hasn't been great."

"All your life or only recently?"

"Not all my life. But the past ten years. Which feels like all my life sometimes."

He let out a low whistle. "You poor woman."

"Not anymore." He remembered her. She wanted to weep and laugh and dance and—holy smokes. She'd kissed him. And said things to him that she'd never said to any other man. Not in such bold terms, at least. She slapped a hand over her mouth. "I'm so sorry," she mumbled.

"What?"

She took her hand away. "I said I'm sorry."

"For?"

"That kiss. And the things I said to you. I only said them because I thought you wouldn't remember me. Oh my, I might faint again."

He laughed. "I take it that's not your usual greeting when you meet new neighbors?"

"I was…having a bad day. And…" She squeezed her eyes shut. "No, that's not how I normally behave."

"Too bad," he teased. "It's the best welcome-to-the-neighborhood I've ever had."

She dipped her head, putting her face in her hands. "I am so embarrassed."

The cushion beside her moved, and his warmth filled the space next to her. "Don't be. I would have done far worse things in your situation."

"You're just saying that to make me feel better."

"Yes, but I'm also a man, and it's true."

She peeked at him from between her fingers. "I'm still mortified."

"Then I probably shouldn't tell you that I also saw you leaving my house after your *illicit* swim yesterday."

"My illicit—" Her mouth hung open as the memory of the afternoon and the tiny bathing suit she'd had on came rushing back.

He held up a finger. "Before you say anything or pass out again, I have to confess that the vision of you in those little scraps of pink almost made me think I was hallucinating. I couldn't imagine a woman so beautiful really existed."

Her cheeks were getting pink. She could feel the warmth building in them. His words were enough to leave her temporarily speechless.

"Thankfully," he continued, "I realized I wasn't going completely crazy when I saw water by the edge of the pool, then your forgotten towel, and figured out you'd actually been in there and weren't some figment of my mind."

"I'm never wearing that bikini again." She was utterly horrified, but somehow still elated that he remembered her. It was an odd feeling to be so twisted.

"Don't say that. I'm hoping you'll have it on tomorrow at my pool party."

She narrowed her eyes. "You're having a pool party? I didn't realize you knew that many people in town. Wait, never mind. You must be having the pack over, right?"

"No, I haven't met any of them yet. It was just going to be you and me, really."

Caught off guard, she snorted. A most unbecoming sound, but it was too late to take it back. "That's very nice of you to invite me, but that suit isn't really for public viewing."

"I think that cat's out of the bag."

"Oh, no. That cat is in its bag, and it's staying there." She was done discussing her bikini. "Hey, it looked like you were headed to my house when I was on my way out. I think. Were you? What were you coming over for?"

"Oh, yeah, that." His expression turned serious. "I'm not even sure where to start."

She shrugged. "Just jump in."

He sighed. "Right. I was coming over to confess a few things of my own. Namely, the reason I moved here—and the reason I'm not exactly dating material.

I was struck by lightning, and ever since then, I've had some shifting issues."

"You can't shift?"

"No, I can shift." He frowned. "I just can't control what I shift into. Seems confined to animals that are all in the same biological family, but it's not always a wolf."

"Oh." She nodded in understanding. She doubted most of the females in the pack would be interested in a wolf who couldn't guarantee he'd be a wolf when it was time to run. Or reproduce. Actually, she wasn't sure what Rico, the alpha, would think either. "That must be rough."

"Not as bad as what you're dealing with, but it's getting worse. I'm losing control of when and where I shift, too." He stared at his hands. "That's why I moved to Shadowvale. I can't be slipping my human form in the middle of the street."

She gasped. "Did that happen?"

"No. Worse. I turned into a red wolf in the employee breakroom at the Saver's Club."

"Yikes." But the visual stuck in her head. She rolled her lips together, trying to keep from laughing. "I'm so sorry."

"Go ahead and laugh. It's kind of funny."

"It is, but I'm sure living through it wasn't."

"No. What's worse is that the forced shift wasn't something I could just get out of, either. I had to live with it until it had run its course, which took a good five hours. And it was all because I saw a photo of a full moon on a book cover."

"Oh wow. That's crazy. I didn't even know that could happen." If a photo was enough to make him shift, that could cause all kinds of problems. Especially if he had to remain in that form for a while. Most shifters could morph in and out of their animal forms as easily as changing their minds.

"Me either." He nodded, then jerked his thumb toward the backyard. "That's why I thought I was hallucinating when I saw you running away from my pool. I thought it was my problem worsening. Like my mind was going. I mean, anything's possible at this point."

"I'm glad that wasn't the case."

"Me, too. Thanks." He looked at her again. "How come you're all dressed up? You look phenomenal, by the way."

"Thanks. I was going to go down to the pub and pretend I have friends."

The sympathy in his eyes almost undid her.

She shook her head. "Don't look at me that way. You'll make me cry."

"Sorry. Hey, do they serve food? Let's go down there and get some dinner. You look too good not to be seen."

"Really?"

"Absolutely."

"That would be a lot of fun." Her evening was coming together so much better than she'd planned. "I haven't been out with anyone in ten years. You can't imagine how lonely a life it's been." She laughed sadly. "That makes me sound pretty pathetic."

He suddenly took her hand and squeezed it. "Don't say that. It's not like you've been alone because of anything you did, or because you're some terrible person. What this curse has done to you is awful. But don't let it own you like that."

She sniffed, looking at her hand in his. The feel of a man's rough, warm palm against hers was a pleasure she'd forgotten. It was the sweetest sensation she'd felt in a long time. Sweeter, in a way, than her impulsive kiss, because *he'd* taken *her* hand. He wanted to touch her. "Yeah. I try."

"I know it's easier said than done, but I'm here now and—do you think maybe your curse has actually broken? What if everyone can remember you again?"

She lifted her head. "I can't hope for that. The letdown would be too much. But…if that was true, that would mean I was cured."

He stood up, still holding her hand and pulling her along with him. "There's only one way to find out."

She grinned. "Okay, the pub it is. And yes, they serve food, so we can grab some dinner."

"Perfect. Just let me change into something a little nicer, or people are going to think you're slumming."

"People won't think anything. They have no idea who I am."

He winked as he finally released her hand. "Maybe they will now. Be right back."

"I'll be here."

As he left, she did a little twirl of excitement. Was it possible her curse was broken? Or just over? It had been ten years. Maybe that was the curse's life-span, and then poof, it was done. That would be amazing.

Her life would be hers again. She could stop introducing herself constantly. That would be especially nice with the assisted-living people when she went to see Aunt Gwen.

The end of her curse really was too much to hope for, but what other explanation could there be? Easy didn't have any kind of magical powers that would enable him to see her. If such a thing was possible, why wouldn't someone else in town have recognized her by now?

In the early days of living here, when she'd realized how many different kinds of supernaturals and cursed humans resided in Shadowvale, she'd made a point to test her curse on as many of them as she could.

She'd even rung the goblin king's doorbell, only to realize he didn't answer his own door.

No one ever remembered her. Just Aunt Gwen and Seymour. And now Easy. Possibly her goldfish, but the jury was out on them.

She twisted her hands together. She couldn't let herself think anything had changed. It was too much. But maybe if she could figure out why Easy could remember her, maybe that would help her find the key to sticking in everyone else's mind, too.

It was worth a shot. She just needed to spend a lot of time with him and make sure this whole thing wasn't a fluke.

Because if tomorrow came and he had no idea who she was...she was going to be crushed.

CHAPTER TEN

Screw the deadline and the fifty-grand bonus. At least for tonight. He couldn't abandon Ginny at this moment in time. It was too monumental. For her to live with such a curse for so long, then finally find someone to remember her was huge. And he was honored to be that person. Not sure why it was him, but who knew why anything happened, really?

But it had, and here they were. It was obvious that she was hesitant to get too excited. Like she expected him to suddenly look at her and ask who she was. More time together could help her get past that. But he also worried a little that he might abruptly forget her.

If this was some temporary thing, she'd be devastated. And the worst part of it was he'd have no way of knowing, because he wouldn't remember her.

So this wasn't just an evening out, it was an occasion. A celebration. And there was no way he was ditching it to stare at a computer screen.

Plus, the time with her would give them a chance

to get to know each other and for him to explain about his deadline and how he was basically going to disappear into his writing cave until the book was turned in. Now more than ever, she had to know why he was going to be scarce.

In a couple boxes in his bedroom marked Closet, he found a dark gray striped button-down, a black belt, and a pair of black boots. They made a dressier outfit with his jeans than his T-shirt had. He changed, then grabbed his wallet and keys and went back to the living room.

He held his arms out as he walked in. "This okay?"

She nodded appreciatively. "You look great. But you looked great before, too."

"Thanks. You still look phenomenal. Do you mind if I drive? It'll help me get to know the town."

"Nope, good with me." She hesitated. "Wait, do you mean the motorcycle?"

"No, the car. I need to quiet the bike's muffler a bit before I drive it around again. I could tell by the looks I was getting it was a little too loud for some folks."

"Yeah, it's loud." She shrugged. "But people can learn to live with it."

"Better if I fix it. I don't want to be the annoying neighbor." He got the door for her, then locked it behind them.

Once in the car, she gave him quick directions. He'd been downtown before, but didn't remember the pub. After her directions, he realized that was because the pub wasn't on the main drag, but sat on a street right off Main.

He drove a little slower than he might have otherwise, mostly so they could talk. "What kind of work do you do?"

"I'm a graphic designer. Email seems to be about the only way I can communicate without being forgotten. Thankfully. It would be really hard to earn a living without it."

"I bet. You must be pretty artistic, then, and have a good eye for what works."

She shrugged, but a smile was on her face. "It's what I got my degree in, so I do okay. I could always have more work, though." She patted the Mustang's dashboard. "My Jeep is a lot older than this beast."

"I like your Jeep. That's a great vehicle." He grinned. "But what can I say? I like fast machines with a lot of muscle."

"I noticed. What do you do?"

"I'm a writer."

"Really? Of what?"

"Books."

"That's cool. Are you published? What kind of books?"

"Yes, and military thrillers."

"Wow." She bit her bottom lip. "Can I read one?"

"You really want to? Or are you just being polite?"

She laughed. "I want to. I read constantly. And I read everything." She pulled out her phone and started tapping the screen. "What's your pen name? I'm going to look you up right now."

"No pen name. I write under my real name. Well, my initials. E.Z. Grayle."

She typed his name in and tapped the screen again. For two seconds, she was silent. "Holy. Crap. You're the guy behind Tomahawk Jones?"

With a slightly nervous laugh, he nodded. "Guilty. You've heard of the books, I take it?"

"Heard of them? I've read both of them. E.Z. Easy. Why did I never make that connection? What's the Z stand for?"

"Zachariah." He shook his head. "Family names. My brothers got stuck with Malachi and Caleb."

"Those aren't so bad." She shook her head. "How about that? I live next door to a real-live famous person."

The nervous laugh slipped out of him again. "Not really famous. But I might become a little better known when the movie comes out—"

She shrieked. "There's going to be a movie?"

He glanced at her to make sure she was all right. "Yep. It's in production."

She was staring at him now. "I might faint again."

He snorted. "All right, settle down over there."

"So when's the next book out?"

"About that…it's one of the things I wanted to tell you about." He couldn't have asked for a better segue. "My publisher just moved my deadline up by two months. I agreed to it, but it means I'm going to disappear for the next couple months, because writing twenty-four seven is the only way I can meet that goal."

He slanted his gaze at her, to see how she was reacting.

She frowned. "Don't they know you just moved? How are you going to write and get unpacked and do all the house stuff that goes with moving?"

"I'm pushing it all aside, that's how. There's a big bonus attached to turning this book in early. Too much for me to ignore. So if I have to live out of boxes for the next couple of months, so be it."

"Well, I understand that. Money is a big motivator." She crossed her arms. "My offer to help still stands, you know. With the house stuff, I mean. I'm not so busy that I don't have a couple hours a day to lend a hand. You'd be amazed at how not having a social life frees up the day."

"I can't ask you to do that. We just met. That would be taking advantage of your generosity."

"I'm offering, though. That kind of negates the taking-advantage bit."

"Even so." He turned toward downtown. "I could pay you. What's the going rate for an assistant? I can swing that."

"Then you'd be my boss. That might be weird." She went silent for a moment, and he looked over only to see the most curious expression on her face. "You know, like if I wanted to kiss you again."

He almost ran the car off the road. "Yeah, no, that wouldn't work. I mean the boss thing. Not the kissing thing. The kissing thing was good."

He snuck a look at her in time to see her cheeks going pink.

He took a breath. "I would love the help. But I don't want you to do it for free. There has to be something I can do for you in exchange."

"Let's see how the first day goes. I might make you crazy. Not that I plan to, but you never know."

Oh, he knew. She did make him crazy. In the best possible way. "I kind of have a feeling it's going to be fine."

"I won't bother you while you're writing. I promise. I don't like to be bothered while I'm working, so I get it. Disrupts the creative flow. I'm sure writing is like that, too."

"It is." He pulled into the pub's parking lot and found a spot. Looked a little busy. "That's what happened the second time you came over. Why I asked you to come back in an hour. I was trying to finish up a chapter."

"Sorry about that."

He parked and turned the car off. "You didn't know. And I'm sorry I brushed you off. C'mon, let's get some grub."

They got out, and he waited for her at the rear of the car. When she joined him, he clicked the key fob to lock the car, taking a moment to admire how gorgeous she was. "I hope you don't cause any fights looking like that. I haven't knocked a guy out in a long time."

She laughed. "Now who needs to settle down?"

He took her hand. He loved the feel of her skin. Soft and silky and warm and female. Heaven. And although the wolf in him loved it, he realized he might be overstepping. Even if she had kissed him. "Is this okay?"

She glanced at their intertwined fingers, still smiling. "Yeah, it's okay."

They walked like that until they reached the door, which he opened for her, then let her go in first.

The place was exactly as he'd expected. Dark wood, some brass, lots of televisions playing all kinds of sports: British football, rugby, a cricket match, and one even showed curling. Baseball and bowling were on a few more. The crowd was more male than female, which gave Easy some insight as to the kind of attention Ginny had been looking for.

He understood. Nothing picked up the ego like getting noticed by the opposite sex. And the way she looked, it would be impossible for that not to happen.

The small hairs on the back of his neck prickled with protective energy. Normally, he'd tell himself to get over it, that he had no right to such feelings, but there was clearly chemistry between them, and they were both wolves.

Human rules didn't apply.

Ginny might have been floating for all the lightness inside her. Easy was being incredibly sweet. Holding her hand, getting the door, complimenting her. She was enamored, and not just because he was a big, famous author. That had nothing to do with it, although it certainly added to his cool factor.

She wanted to think her feelings were because he was such a gorgeous guy who also happened to be a werewolf like her.

But maybe it was also a little bit because he remembered her. More than a little bit, if she was being honest.

There was no way that wasn't causing some of her feelings. How could it not? But then, how would she know otherwise when she'd been in a ten-year drought? It was a lot to think about, but she wasn't going to think about it too much tonight.

Tonight was for being normal. Being out on a date—was this a date? It sure felt like one—and being happy and not having to reintroduce herself every time someone turned around.

She almost wasn't sure she remembered what that felt like.

As they walked in, the lights flickered.

"That was weird," she said.

"Not really," he answered with a perturbed look on his face.

"What do you mean?"

He just shrugged. "I'll tell you later. Let's find a table."

The pub was fairly crowded and a little raucous thanks to the sports on the various televisions, but she'd wanted to come here because of the testosterone, not in spite of it. Now she wasn't sure that had been such a good idea.

But the pub did have great food, and she'd never had an issue coming here before. Besides, she was with Easy now. Shadowvale's citizens were a decent bunch. No one would bother her with him at her side.

Shifters generally had a code about that sort of thing, and other supernaturals rarely got in the way of shifters.

They found a booth on the opposite side of the bar and settled in. It was a little quieter over here. More people eating than drinking and cheering. He put his keys and wallet on the table near the wall, so she added her small handbag to the mix.

A server came by pretty quickly, dropping off menus and two glasses of water. "I'm Lyra. I'll give you a minute to glance at the menu. We've got shepherd's pie and haddock and chips on special tonight for our entrees and a special appetizer of honey ghost pepper hot wings. Not for the faint of heart." She grinned. "I'll let you ponder and be back in a jiff."

As she left, Easy picked up his menu. "I'm definitely getting those hot wings. But I don't know about the entrees. Both specials sound good."

"They are." Ginny folded her hands over her menu. "I'm getting the haddock and chips. And I'm happy to watch you eat the wings."

He put his menu down. "Then I'm getting the shepherd's pie. I'm a meat-and-potatoes kind of guy, so I'd probably be good with either one."

"I've yet to meet a werewolf who didn't like a good steak now and then."

He nodded. "Yeah, I grilled some last night."

"I know. The smell woke me up." She pretended to be interested in the menu again so she didn't have to look him in the eyes. Not while the image of him skinny-dipping filled her head. She smiled, unable to stop herself.

"I guess that was kind of late to be grilling, but I'd had a long day. What's funny?"

She pursed her lips in an effort to kill the grin, but the memory of him was stuck. "Nothing."

He narrowed his eyes, clearly amused. "Liar."

"The smell woke me up. And I, uh…wanted to see where it was coming from." She pressed her lips together while she waited to see if he'd figure it out.

"Oh. *Oh.*" A slow smile turned up the corners of his mouth. "And did you? *See* where it was coming from?"

"I did." She drew a line through the condensation on her water glass. "But I didn't linger. Once I realized you were, you know, not properly attired, I went right back to bed."

He snorted. "It's my pool. I think I get to decide what's proper attire and what's not."

"True. The pool owner makes the rules." Her cheeks were heating up again, but since he didn't seem too bothered by it, she wasn't going to be either.

He leaned in. "That reminds me. You can come over and swim whenever you want. Especially since you already have a towel at my house."

With a little snort, she cocked her head to one

side. "Is this the part where you tell me my tiny pink bikini is the only thing you'll recognize as proper attire?"

"No, but that's a great idea."

She laughed. "I do love to swim. And I should get my towel. But I don't want to bother you. Not with all the writing you need to get done. Besides, I can go to the lake anytime. That's where I used to swim before the McKinleys moved. Sometimes the community pool, but that tends to be the same crowd, and having them think I'm a new person every time I go gets old."

"Next door is a lot more convenient."

"True, it is."

"How about I text you when the pool's open?"

She nodded. "That would be great. And if you happen to be in it, too, then even better."

He smiled. "You know I'm going to need your number for that to work."

"Oh, right. You should have it anyway. In case of emergency or whatever."

They got their phones out, swapped numbers, then Ginny scooted toward the edge of the seat. "I'm going to run to the ladies' room. If she comes back, would you order the fish and chips for me?"

"Sure thing."

"Thanks." She headed through the pub and into the bathroom. A big corkboard inside the door was covered with flyers announcing all kinds of events. A Howl and Prowl singles meet-up, a Full Moon Party, Wing Night, a live acoustic duo on Fridays.

She smiled. They were all things she and Easy could do. Once his book was turned in, of course. She was still reluctant to make too many plans or look too far into the future, but it was hard not to when she'd suddenly been given this chance to rejoin society.

He wouldn't mind going out now and then, would he? He seemed like a pretty sociable guy.

She laughed to herself as a new thought came to her. She might prefer staying in with him, too.

CHAPTER ELEVEN

The server came back two minutes after Ginny had left, so Easy ordered, then sat back and took the place in.

He liked the vibe here. He could see it becoming a hangout. When he had time to hang out again.

At some point, he was going to have to look up the alpha of the local pack and let the man know about his issue. Easy loathed the very idea of having to expose himself like that to the alpha, but being a lone male wolf in a town that had an existing pack could be considered a threat.

That was the last thing Easy needed. He figured Ginny wasn't a member of the pack either, but she was female, so the same rules and constraints didn't apply to her.

Which meant she'd been running alone for the last ten years, too. Or maybe with her aunt. Even so, two wasn't much of a pack.

Well, no more. They could run together. A pack of three, as it were. So long as Ginny and her aunt didn't mind running with whatever he turned into, which he didn't think they would.

And surely the alpha would understand they weren't out to challenge him by starting a new pack or anything like that. There just wasn't another way unless the alpha explained their special circumstances to his pack, which Easy doubted he would. But then, he was assuming Ginny would give him permission to tell the alpha about her curse, too. If she did, that should be enough to get them a special exemption.

But what difference would an exemption make for Ginny? If they couldn't remember her, nothing would help.

He sighed, starting to understand the weight of what she'd been living with for so long.

Ginny returned to the table. "Did the server come?"

"Yes. I ordered. Did you want anything else to drink?"

"No, water's fine. Thanks."

Easy rested his elbows on the table. "Do you know who the alpha is in town?"

"I do." Her gaze shifted to the bar area. "Rico Martinez. Nice guy. That's him in the black T-shirt with the long black hair with a silver streak. He's had that streak since he was born. It's a birthmark. His mother always told him it meant he was destined to be alpha. But then, don't all wolf mothers tell their sons stuff like that?"

"Pretty sure they do." Easy stopped looking at the man to stare at her. "How on earth do you know all that?"

"I'm a great listener. It's about all I can do most times. And I don't forget much. I'm only forgettable to other people, not as a character trait."

He grinned. "You'd make a great writer. Being observant can really help." He shifted toward her in a conspiratorial manner. "So…who else is in here that I should know about?"

She looked around. "Okay, the two other guys that Rico's talking to? The one that's built like an armored car is Oluf Erikson. He's a genuine Viking berserker. He's a time refugee. He got caught in a time slip and hasn't been back to his own year since he landed here. Not sure he ever will get home. So far, on every occasion he's slipped into another year, he's always ended up back in Shadowvale."

"Wow."

"Exactly." She tipped her head at the trio. "The other guy, that's Deacon Evermore. Town peacekeeper and raven shifter. He and Emeranth Greer are an item. She's the barista at Black Horse Bakery, where that chocolate cake I brought you came from. Em is Amelia Marchand's niece, and Amelia is the witch who created this town."

Ginny looked at him again. "Big magic. *Big*."

He made a point to remember that name. "You really do know these people."

"I have nothing but time." She sipped her water. "Those three guys all play rugby, but on different teams. Well, Oluf and Deacon are on the same team, but Rico's team is strictly werewolves from the pack. Oh, and the guy joining them is Shepherd Evermore.

Shep is Deacon's older brother and also the fire chief."

She glanced toward the door. "I'd expect the third and youngest brother, Bishop, to show up any second. He runs a tree-trimming service in town."

"Good to know." Easy let his gaze wander. "Who's the older woman with the navy blue helmet hair and orange jeans?"

Ginny laughed. "I don't even need to see her to answer that one. Has to be Della Kittridge. Her twin sister, Stella, owns Stella's Bargain Bin here in town. Hands down my favorite place to clothing shop. It's a secondhand store, and it is loaded with gems. Great prices, too. Della works part time there."

He shook his head. "You're amazing. You're like a walking Wikipedia of who's who in Shadowvale."

She grinned. "I'm glad you think so. It's not information I've ever had a use for before. Or anyone to share it with."

Lyra returned with their food. She faltered at first when she looked at Ginny. Easy assumed it was because the server didn't remember her. To Lyra's credit, she covered up her confusion with a smile and set their food down.

The dish of shepherd's pie was enormous, and the plate of haddock and chips was spilling over. The wings, also plentiful, were in a paper-lined basket, and the ghost pepper was so strong, it was already prickling his senses.

"Now that's a serving." He picked up his fork, ready to dig in.

Lyra nodded. "Most of our clientele have big appetites and high metabolisms, so we try to cater to their needs. Also, save room for dessert. We have blackberry crumble with homemade honey vanilla ice cream, a chocolate bourbon pecan pie that's made grown men cry, and our traditional sticky toffee pudding served with custard."

"I'm in." Easy looked at Ginny. "What about you?"

"Heck, yes." She laughed.

He nodded at Lyra. "Thank you. We'll definitely be getting one of those."

"Great! I'll let you two eat and swing back around later. Just wave if you need anything."

She headed off to her next table.

Ginny's expression bore an edge of weariness. "You saw that, right? How she looked at me?"

He nodded. "She didn't know who you were. That's what it's always like, huh?"

"Yep." She picked up her fork. "But let's not dwell on that, okay? I'd much rather enjoy this evening and this food."

"You got it. I think this is my new favorite place to eat." Easy stuck his fork into the cheesy mashed-potato-topped casserole and lifted out a big bite dripping brown gravy.

Ginny was sprinkling vinegar over her fish and fries. "You haven't actually tasted the food yet."

"No, but I can smell how good it is."

"All I can smell is how hot those wings are." She broke off a piece of the giant battered filet covering her plate and held it out to him. "Try this. It's the best fish and chips I've ever had."

He took the piece and bit into it, crunching through the coating. "Outstanding," he mumbled around the mouthful. He swallowed and pushed his plate toward her. "Have a bite."

"I've had it. I know how good it is. And you look hungry."

"You want a wing?" He took one from the basket.

She shook her head, brows raised like he was crazy. "Those are all you."

He popped it into his mouth and stripped the meat off it, setting his mouth ablaze with the intense pepper heat. "Wow. Hot," he wheezed. "But good."

She laughed. "Yep, all you."

They ate and chatted, and she continued to point people out to him, telling him the little tidbits she knew. By the end of the meal, he felt like he knew half the people in town.

When Lyra came to clear their plates, which they had polished off, they decided on a sticky toffee pudding and the blackberry crumble.

Easy's mood was about as good as it had been in a long time. He'd even been able to momentarily ignore the burden of his deadline. "I'm having the best time. With the move and my book and my other issue, it's been a while since I've done anything really fun. I needed this distraction."

"I'm glad to hear that." Her smile was infectious. "This has easily been the best evening out I've had in the last ten years."

He laughed and lifted his water glass. "Here's to more of those."

She clinked her glass against his. "Absolutely."

He took a sip, then set the glass down. "Be right back. I need to wash my hands before I forget and get ghost pepper in my eyes. Don't eat all the sweets without me."

She put her hand to her heart. "I would never."

"Don't talk to any strange men while I'm gone either."

"They're all strange men in this town." Then she lifted one shoulder and said teasingly, "But we'll see."

He laughed as he got up and made his way to the bathroom. He went straight to the sink, turning the faucet on before getting some soap. He was falling for this woman. And that scared him a little.

He had to remind himself that his plans didn't include a relationship, not while he was incapable of shifting properly. And as much as Ginny might say it didn't matter, things changed when people got serious.

That's where this seemed like it might be headed. Somewhere serious. Somewhere permanent. It might be the earliest stages of anything close to a relationship, but wolves had a way of knowing when they'd met the right person. And Ginny felt very right. At any other time, he would have been happy about that. Thrilled, really.

Another guy came in, giving Easy the standard *what's up* nod.

Easy nodded back as he finished lathering. What was up was too complicated to even imagine.

What if she wanted kids? He'd love to have kids, but not with how screwed up his shifting was. No way did he want to pass that on.

He rinsed the suds off his hands, lingering under the hot water. It was way too soon to have that discussion, and yet, if he didn't bring it up, he was going to feel like he wasn't being completely up front with her. She had to understand that wasn't something he could do right now.

The guy who'd come in left.

Easy grabbed some paper towels, lifting his head to stare at himself as he dried his hands.

The reflection of something in the mirror caught his eye, holding his gaze even as he wanted for all the world to turn away.

A flyer on a bulletin board behind him advertising a Full Moon Party. With an enormous picture of a full moon front and center.

"Not now," he whispered. "Not here."

But already, the rush of the change coursed through him. His pulse quickened, and the ache started in his bones.

He couldn't do this here. He was too exposed. But he had no choice. As his body began its transformation, he slipped into one of the stalls and locked the door.

*

The lights flickered again like when they'd first come in. Weird, Ginny thought. Shadowvale wasn't known to have electrical problems.

She stared at the desserts that had just arrived via a food runner. Not eating them was getting harder with each passing second. Ginny looked at her watch. Easy had been gone for quite a while. Longer than she'd realized, actually.

He'd been gone long enough that she was now worried.

She couldn't call him. His phone was on the table.

With a sigh, she scanned the pub again to make sure she hadn't overlooked him talking to someone. Maybe she should get up and walk around. There were parts of the pub she couldn't see from the booth.

She waited another ten seconds or so, then decided she had to do something. She waved the server down.

Lyra came over with a quizzical look on her face. "Can I help you?"

"Yes. Could we get some boxes for these desserts? We have to leave sooner than we expected. And bring the check, too. I'll take care of it."

Lyra looked at her, then the table, then back at Ginny again. "There were people sitting here."

Ginny bit back a smart retort. She was used to this, but also so over it. Now was not the time to alienate this woman, however. "Yes, and I was one of those people, along with a dark-haired man. He had the shepherd's pie, and I had the haddock and chips."

"Right." Lyra nodded, but Ginny knew all the girl remembered was Easy and the order. "Okay, I'll grab some boxes and the check."

Ginny didn't want to wait for her, but leaving might make the poor girl think her guests had dined and dashed.

Thankfully, she returned quickly with the boxes and a bag. Her curious expression told Ginny she'd been forgotten again.

Ginny made herself smile brightly and took the easy route. "Hi, I'm going to pay this tab for my friends. They had to leave. If you could box up those desserts for them, that would be great."

Lyra nodded. "Okay."

Ginny dug enough cash out of her purse and dropped it on the bill, then took the bag with the desserts, along with Easy's wallet, phone, and keys, and slipped out of the booth.

He'd gone to wash his hands, so if he wasn't anywhere in the pub, she'd assume he was still in the bathroom. But what could have happened?

She stopped suddenly in the middle of the bar area, a terrifying thought overtaking her. What if he'd forgotten her? What if whatever magic that made him remember her had worn off? He would have gone home.

But no. She was just panicking based on past history. His keys were in her hand, along with his phone and wallet. He might forget her, but he wouldn't forget them. And he couldn't leave without his keys, so he was here somewhere. She tucked all three into her purse, then blew out a breath and told herself to calm down. This wasn't about her, this was about Easy.

So what would keep him away?

There was only one other explanation that she could come up with. He'd shifted against his will. But how could that have happened in the pub when there was no—it hit her. The flyer on the bathroom wall.

The Full Moon Party, illustrated with a bright full moon. If the men's bathroom had a bulletin board that matched the one in the women's room, Easy could have seen that and gotten himself into trouble.

Ginny swallowed. This was not going to be fun.

CHAPTER TWELVE

She didn't want to barge into the men's bathroom. That could cause all kinds of new trouble. Instead, she hovered near the door until someone came out. "Excuse me, sir?"

"Me?" The man turned.

She recognized him. Jerry Washington. Owned the dry cleaners. Troubled by the occasional white-hot halo of fire that surrounded him. She didn't know what flipped the switch that turned that particular curse on, so she did her best to be as pleasant as possible.

"Yes," she answered with a smile and gave him the simplest story she could come up with. "Sorry to bother you, but my brother wasn't feeling well, and I think he's in the men's room. Was there anyone else in there? I'm worried about him."

His brows scrunched like he was thinking. "Nobody else in there that I was aware of."

"Okay, thank you. He must have gone outside."

"Sure thing." Jerry walked away.

This was her chance. Ginny took a breath and darted through the door. "Easy? Are you in here?"

A soft, pitiful woof answered her.

"Oh boy, it was the flyer, wasn't it?"

Another woof.

"Don't worry, we'll figure this out." She bent down to look under the stall doors. No feet. He must be sitting on one of the johns. "Which one are you in? The acoustics in here are making it hard for me to tell."

Two yips this time. They came from the second stall. Yips? That wasn't a wolf sound at all.

She put the bag of desserts on the counter, then went into the first stall, stood on the toilet, and looked over into the second one.

She bit the inside of her cheek to keep from laughing. "Oh my."

The cutest, most adorable Yorkie looked up at her.

Do not laugh, do not laugh, do not laugh. "You're, um, you're not a wolf."

The Yorkie snarled.

"Hey, don't shoot the messenger."

He let out a sad, apologetic whimper.

"Okay, hang on, I'm coming over." She secured her purse across her body, then pressed herself up, vaulting easily over the dividing wall, and dropped to the floor. Heels and tight jeans didn't really make for her best bathroom stall-climbing outfit, but she'd managed.

She held her hands out toward Easy. "I have to pick you up, but if you bite me, you're in big trouble. Got it?"

A soft, more repentant woof answered her.

She scooped the Yorkie into her arms, smiling as soon as Easy couldn't see her. He was so cute she wanted to talk baby talk to him and kiss his little face all over, but she had a feeling they'd never go out again if that happened.

Actually, he might stop talking to her altogether. She controlled the urge. "Let's get you home."

She shifted Easy to one arm, then unlocked the door, grabbed the bag of desserts, and strode out of the bathroom with her head high just as Deacon Evermore was on his way in.

"My mistake, sorry." She picked up speed before Deacon could say anything, hightailing it for the parking lot.

She got the car unlocked and put Easy on the passenger seat, then slipped the takeout bag behind the seat and went around to the driver's side. She slid behind the wheel and started the car.

With a not-so-subtle thrum, the engine came to life. She could see why he liked driving this machine. She grinned. "Nice."

Easy, in his Yorkie form, was standing on the seat, staring at her. And if Yorkies could look cranky, he did.

"Sorry." Now was probably not the time to be admiring his ride.

He woofed. Apology accepted, she assumed.

She looked him over. "I feel like you should be buckled in, but obviously there's no way to do that. I'll drive carefully, though. Not just because you're unbuckled, but because this is your car, and I don't want anything to happen to it or you."

He turned three times, then sat down, making little grumpy dog sounds that were absolutely flipping adorable.

She was going to laugh. It was coming on like a sneeze and felt about as unavoidable. She looked away so he wouldn't catch the amusement on her face. Biting her tongue helped quell the urge. She pulled out of the parking lot and headed for home. "It's okay, you know. We'll figure this out."

No response.

She glanced over. He'd lain all the way down, facing the door. Maybe he was embarrassed. She understood he must be feeling awful, but it wasn't like he'd had any control over what had happened.

She let him be, focusing on getting them home safely. He didn't budge either, staying that way for the entire ride and getting up only when the car stopped. He stared outside for a second, then barked.

At her.

"Sorry, I don't speak dog." She opened the car door and got out, but before she could open his door, he jumped out after her, then ran straight up to his front door. She grabbed the desserts before following him.

He circled once in front of the door.

She fumbled for his house key. "I don't know if it's a good idea for you to be alone like this. I mean, what if you have to go out?"

He growled softly.

She put the key in the lock and turned. "I'm not saying you can't take care of yourself, but you're so…little."

With a defeated whimper, he sat.

She pushed the door open, letting him go in first. She walked in behind him and went right to the kitchen. She put the bag of desserts in the fridge. "How about if I stay here with you?"

A little doggy sigh came out of him, then she swore he shrugged.

Poor guy. "Listen, if you really want to be alone, I'll go. I just thought…" She exhaled and looked around. "Don't do anything dumb. Like go out that big doggy door and fall into the pool and drown, okay?"

He glanced at her.

"I know you can swim. It's just that the pool is so big, and you're so little—"

Another soft snarl.

She didn't know how to read his expression, but she understood snarling. She held her hands up in defeat. If he wanted to be alone, that was his prerogative. "Okay, going home. See you tomorrow, I guess. Or text me later if…whatever." She turned toward the door.

He ran past her, yipping, and stood in front of the door.

"Are you saying you don't want me to go?"

He yipped—one short, quick bark.

"Then I'll stay." She smiled. "We can eat the desserts. If you want. Or save them until you're you again. Whatever."

She went back into the living room and sat down on the couch, kicked her shoes off, and lay back. She glanced at the enormous television leaning against the far wall awaiting hookup. "Too bad that's not working. We could watch a movie. I could hook it up. You'd be amazed how much you learn on your own in ten years."

There wasn't much else in the room. A coffee table, a recliner, and a floor lamp, also not plugged in. Plus a lot of boxes. A lot. "This place could use a woman's touch. Just saying. An area rug and some throw pillows never killed anyone. A piece of art, maybe. A potted plant. You know, home it up a little."

He jumped up onto the couch next to her feet, sighed, circled three times, and lay down by her calves.

She looked at him, wondering what he was thinking. He closed his eyes. Maybe intent on sleeping it off. Mercy, he was adorable. With nothing else to do, she got her phone out of her purse, pulled up her reading app, and opened the mystery novel she was halfway through.

A couple of chapters in, Easy let out a long sigh, rolling over on his side.

"I can make more room." She turned onto her side a little, too.

He adjusted, moving a little closer to her knees.

She went back to reading, but woke up a few minutes later, having dozed off.

Easy was still a Yorkie, but he was now curled up against her stomach. And snoring slightly. She gently brushed her hand down the silky fur on his back, doing her best not to rouse him, but dying to touch him. He was still the cutest thing she'd ever seen.

There was no leaving now either. If she moved, she'd wake him. She read a little more, then finally gave in to the sleep tugging at her.

Easy woke up to darkness outside his windows and Ginny in his arms, the two of them sprawled in a tangle on his couch. She was asleep, head nestled against his chest.

At any other time in his life, he would have been thrilled.

As it was, he was mortified by what had just happened a few hours ago. A Yorkie. He'd turned into a frigging purse dog. Thank the powers of the universe that Ginny's purse hadn't been big enough for him to fit into, because if she'd done that to him...

He took a breath. He owed her. She'd gotten him out of that bathroom with no one being the wiser, at least not that he was aware of. She hadn't freaked out about it either.

He squeezed his eyes shut in humiliation. If the alpha had found out, Easy might have been permanently blacklisted from the pack.

But then, Ginny's curse had already done that to her. And if she wasn't part of the pack, he didn't want to be either. He opened his eyes and pressed a soft kiss to the top of her head. She'd rescued him. And hadn't made him feel like a fool once.

He let the shame of the situation go long enough to appreciate the incredible woman in his arms. To feel the softness and warmth of her body against his. He would be honored to have a woman like this at his side.

But tonight had highlighted just how unsuitable a mate he was. No doubt she'd pitied him, she'd just been good at hiding it.

Or maybe she was willing to overlook it because she didn't have any other options.

What was worse? Someone settling for you? Or someone pitying you?

He wasn't sure. Both were awful. Either way, he couldn't see a way forward for them romantically. As incredible as that would have been, she deserved better, and he didn't want to be someone's choice because he was her only choice.

That would end badly. There was just no other way for it to go.

He sighed, ruffling her hair. He glanced behind him to the microwave in the kitchen. Almost three in the morning. He was torn whether to wake her up so she could go home to her own bed, do nothing and continue enjoying the moment, or get up, let her sleep, and try to knock out a few pages.

Considering that he was never going to be this close to Ginny again, he decided on not moving. At least for a few minutes more. He wanted to soak up this feeling for future reference.

Truth was, she might be the last woman he held in his arms for a long time.

But he fell back to sleep, and when he woke the second time, it was because Ginny was moving.

"We fell asleep," she whispered.

He smiled. "I know."

She sighed a happy, sleepy little sigh. "No couch should be this comfortable."

And no woman should feel this good in his arms. Especially not a woman he couldn't have. He eased his arms out of the embrace, rolled to his side, and stood. "Hungry?"

He could at least make her breakfast. That would give them a chance to talk, and for him to give her the friends-only explanation.

She stretched and sat up. "I could eat. But all I really want to do is go home and change into something comfortable. These jeans weren't really made for sleeping." She smiled at him. "Nice to see *you* again."

"Yeah, when the change is forced on me like that, I can't just shift right back out of it. Thanks for being so understanding. And for getting me out of there."

"It wasn't a problem. I had a great time last night, regardless of how it ended."

His mood crashed. "About last night." He gathered his words. "I don't want to talk about it except to say it proves my point. I'm not dating or mating material. I like you, Ginny. But I'm not in a position to like any woman as more than friends."

She stared at him like she wasn't quite understanding what he was saying. "Wow. That's not where I thought that was going at all." She stood up. "Do you really think I'd hold it against you that you can't control what you shift into? I don't know who you've dated in the past, but I'm not looking to find my mate anytime soon. I realize a lot of female wolves are built that way, but I have a curse to deal with that kind of puts that on the back burner."

"But how could you look for a mate when you haven't had the opportunity? How could anyone find you when no one remembers you?"

"True, but..." The light of realization shone in her eyes. "You think I'm interested in you just because you're the first guy who remembers me? I mean, sure that's part of it, because I can actually have a conversation with you that doesn't involve introducing myself over and over and over, but wow."

This wasn't going the way he'd expected it to. "No, look, I just think I need to be up front with you. I know what matters to pack females. Even if you say it doesn't matter to you, it will eventually. And I'm not that guy. I just don't want you to pin your hopes on me and then—"

Anger glazed her expression as she held up her hand. "I'm *not* a pack female, in case you forgot. I'll

127

never be a pack female, at least not until my curse is resolved. Which might not be ever. And how about a little credit for the fact that I saved your Yorkie bacon last night, huh? A pack female probably would have left you there."

She wasn't wrong. "Ginny, I didn't mean—"

"Nope, I got your meaning loud and clear." She grabbed her purse, dug into it, then tossed his wallet and phone onto the coffee table and stormed toward the door. "You know, for a writer, you suck at words."

"Ginny, wait."

She opened the door, finally looking at him again. "You're welcome for last night's dinner, too, by the way. There's a doggie bag in the fridge with the desserts we never got to. Hope you enjoy them."

Then she strode through the door, shutting it firmly behind her.

He groaned, cursing the lightning that had struck him and screwed up his life. But this wasn't the lightning's fault. This was his.

He figured she was going to need a little time to cool off. That was good. Because he wasn't sure how much groveling it would take to get Ginny to forgive him, but he guessed he was about to find out.

CHAPTER THIRTEEN

Within ten minutes of walking into her house, Ginny had ditched her heels, shucked her jeans and top in exchange for yoga pants and a T-shirt, then scrubbed off her remaining makeup and knotted her hair into a messy bun atop her head.

She'd also started a load of laundry and fixed herself a giant cup of coffee. Somehow, both of those made her feel a tiny bit better.

Now she stood in front of her aquarium, getting ready to feed her fish. She set her coffee down and lifted the hood lid. The goldfish hovered near the surface, mouths gaping. She picked up the canister of food. "You have no idea how hard life is for humans. You guys are living the dream. You really are."

She sprinkled flakes in, watching Bob, Comet, and Sparky go crazy.

She sighed and put the lid back on the food canister, then closed the hood on the fish tank. Her stomach growled. She needed to eat something, too, but she didn't have much appetite. Unless it was for that sticky toffee pudding she'd left at Easy's.

That wasn't truthfully what she wanted, though. She glanced toward the side of her house that butted up against Easy's property. She wanted *him*. The man she'd had dinner with last night, *not* the one she'd woken up next to this morning.

Not the one who thought he knew what was best for her. Typical, egotistical male wolf. Except, he wasn't really like that.

And having his arms around her had been heaven. But that was before he'd woken up with all those dumb ideas about what would work and what wouldn't.

She was mad at him for letting his weird shift affect him so deeply. But she was also mad at herself for not being more compassionate.

Clearly, turning into a Yorkie had taken a real mental toll on him. Male werewolves had a lot of testosterone, and giant egos to match, which was why most of them grew up thinking they were going to be alpha one day. Even if that wasn't the case for ninety-nine percent of them. They were just built with that kind of drive and confidence.

Easy must have realized after last night's crazy shift that he was never going to be alpha. Not until his situation got resolved, and what hope did he have of that happening? Probably not much when he saw Ginny working on a decade of being cursed, with no relief in sight.

She sighed. "Bob, don't be a piglet. Let Comet eat, too."

Easy had been trying to spare her. She understood

that. He was also right about most pack females. In general, they picked their men based on who had the strongest bloodlines, who was a good provider, and who had the best potential to be alpha.

Easy wasn't that guy. He couldn't be. And even if Ginny wasn't part of a pack, why would he think she'd want anything different in a mate?

If she wanted a mate.

Which…she kind of did. She sniffed. For the brief time it had lasted, being around Easy had been wonderful. She'd almost forgotten about her curse. Because she'd had a taste of what it felt like to live again.

To be remembered again.

And now that they'd had this fight, or whatever it was, she was on her own again. She smiled sadly at her goldfish. "Not that you guys aren't great, but Easy was a different kind of great."

The kind of great she could have gotten serious about.

So why had she reacted to what he'd said like that? Why had she gotten so mad? Maybe she didn't know how to be around people anymore. Maybe her solitary existence had changed her in ways she didn't realize.

Last night had to have been devastating for him. She tried to imagine what it would feel like to be a virile, full-grown werewolf who'd suddenly shifted into one of the smallest, cutest dogs on the planet.

She grimaced. It would probably feel like you didn't know who you were anymore. Like everything you thought you knew about yourself had been erased. Like you might become the laughingstock of your entire race. Like you just wanted to be left alone.

She pressed her hand to her forehead. He had to have been torn up inside after last night, and yet, the first thing he'd done was put her interests ahead of his.

He might have been wrong about those interests, but he'd still made her a priority. When had that ever happened to her before?

She glanced toward his house again. She was a terrible neighbor and a worse friend. Had she really just yelled at him, then walked out in a huff?

She groaned. While other people were forgetting her, she'd apparently forgotten how to be a decent human being.

She had to go back over there and apologize. And then she'd tell him about the magical curse-lifting book in the enchanted forest. Just because she'd never found it didn't mean it might not offer him some hope.

Some days, hope was all that got her through. Easy deserved to have that lifeline, too.

Yoga pants and a ratty T-shirt wasn't the right outfit to apologize in. She needed to look like she'd exerted some effort. And also cute enough so that he'd at least let her in the door, because she wasn't sure he would. Whatever advantage she could find, she'd take.

As she headed back to the bedroom to change, she heard the familiar rumble of Easy's motorcycle.

She ran to the front windows in time to see him driving out of the cul-de-sac.

Well, the apology would have to wait until he got back. Until then, she'd figure out what she was going to say and how she was going to convince him that they were better as a team. Even if that team was strictly platonic.

Because no one should go through such an intense problem on their own. In the day and a half that she'd known him, she'd learned how much easier it was to bear a burden with someone who understood by your side.

Now she just had to hope he'd feel the same way.

*

Falling back on the clichés of flowers and chocolates seemed like a pitiful way to apologize, but Easy wasn't sure what else to do. He needed to make the right impression, and flowers and chocolates would at least help in that department. They were classics for a reason, right?

If he and Ginny had been dating for a while, he would have splashed out on some pricey bling, but at this stage of their fledgling relationship, that didn't feel like the right way to go. Not after one date. An expensive piece of jewelry now might come off as so over the top she'd think he was a nutjob.

Which she probably already thought, so no need to confirm that.

It went without saying that, besides the gifts, he

was going to tell her how wrong he'd been to guess at what she wanted or needed or deserved. He'd pour his heart out until he'd explained himself better.

And until she understood that what he really needed was her.

But the flowers and chocolates ought to help show how sorry he was. And until he knew her better and knew what her favorite things were, they were safe bets.

The only problem was, he didn't exactly know where to find those things. The Green Grocer had a floral department, but this was not a grocery-store-flower-arrangement occasion. This was the moment for something big and custom and showy.

As for the chocolates, well, no preboxed selection from the drugstore was going to cut it here either.

He drove for a bit and found himself on Fiddler Street. The shops here looked more focused on handcrafted items than some of the ones on Main, so he slowed and started scanning both sides of the street for stores that sold what he was after.

The Chocolate Dragon sounded promising, and the window display had the most elaborate chocolate fountain he'd ever seen, so that was a good sign. He parked and went in. The smell of chocolate was instantly overwhelming, in a good way. He smiled. This looked like the kind of place he needed, especially since there were chocolates in the display cases, along with some other items he wasn't as sure about.

At the jingle of the bell above the door, a man

came out from the back. He looked to be only a few years older than Easy and had the rangy build of a distance runner, but there was a preternatural gleam in his eye that seemed to signal he wasn't entirely human. Whatever he was, he either had a very high metabolism or never ate much of what he sold. "Hello there. Anything I can help with?"

"I need some chocolates."

The man smiled. "You've come to the right place. Special occasion?"

"I screwed up, and I need to show her how sorry I am."

"Ah," the man said with an understanding nod. "Apology chocolates. We can fix you right up."

"Great. What do you suggest?"

"The Ruby is a nice place to start." He walked over to a section of the display case that held a variety of scaled eggs in all colors and sizes. Sort of like Easter eggs that had been laid by mythical creatures.

Easy frowned. "Those are chocolates?" He swore he could see individual scales on each one.

"Yes. Chocolate dragon eggs filled with individual chocolates. The Ruby is the one I always recommend for expressing love or seeking forgiveness." He pointed to one of the eggs in the case.

The egg was about eight inches tall, a deep metallic scarlet with a burnishing of gold and touches of purple, and a chocolate medallion on the front embossed with a heart. A smaller version was in front of it and a larger one behind it.

Easy looked closer. "That's really chocolate?"

The man nodded. "Completely edible."

"Amazing. How do you get into it? Just crack it open?"

"Absolutely. Each egg comes with a wooden mallet and chisel to help with the process."

The shop got more impressive by the second. "What kind of chocolates are inside?"

"An assortment of chocolate truffles, some cordials, and berry creams. Very high quality and all delicious, I assure you. Would you like to try one of the truffles?"

"Thanks, but I trust you."

The man smiled. "We pride ourselves on using only the finest ingredients."

"Judging by the way it smells in here, I have no doubt that's true." But would Ginny like such a thing? It *was* impressive. "Women usually go for these things?"

"They're very popular with everyone who gets them." The man tipped his head. "Do I know the woman who'd be receiving this gift? If she's a regular here, I might be able to tell you what she prefers."

Easy shook his head. "No one knows her. That's her curse. Long story."

"I see. A shame, that."

"It is." Easy looked at the egg one more time. "I'll take the big one."

The man pointed to the largest of the three eggs. "The Ruby Grand?"

"Yes."

He smiled as he lifted the egg out of its display nest. "She's going to be very impressed with how sorry you are."

"Let's hope." Easy got his credit card out. "Is there a florist nearby?"

The man's brows lifted slightly. He was placing the egg in a wooden box filled with black shredded stuff that looked like the green grass that went in Easter baskets. "Flowers, too? I won't ask what you did. Yes, one street over. Flora's Blooms. Tell her Charlie Ashborne sent you."

"I will. I'm Ezekiel Grayle, by the way. Just moved to town."

"Nice to meet you, Ezekiel. Wolf, correct?"

Taken back a bit, Easy nodded. "Yes. You must have a great sense of smell."

"I do. All dragons do." Charlie smiled. "We mythical shifters have a little advantage over you ordinaries."

Easy laughed. "Only in a town like this could being a werewolf make a person ordinary. Nice to meet you, Charlie."

Charlie put the box, now sealed with ribbon and a hot wax stamp, on the counter. Easy nodded in appreciation. This was a good gift. Charlie rang the egg up.

Easy started to pick up the box, then looked back at where his bike was parked. "You know, I don't think this is going to fit in my storage well. I came by motorcycle. Wasn't thinking. Can you hold it for me while I run home and get my car?"

"No problem. Happy to do it."

"Great. Just give me a few minutes. I don't live far."

"Stop by Flora's before you go home. Then she can make up your arrangement while you're traveling."

"Good idea. Thanks." Easy went back out to the street, feeling much better. That egg was pretty cool. Ginny couldn't stay mad at him with a gift like that, could she? With flowers, too? Impossible.

At least he wanted to think that.

He got on his bike, drove to the next street, and found Flora's.

The flowers on display were abundant and beautiful, but he wasn't about to pick out each one. With the help of the woman at the counter (not Flora, but an employee named Carena), he ordered a giant bouquet in reds and purples to match the egg, then paid and drove home to get his car.

He practiced his speech all the way home and all the way back to the Chocolate Dragon. Then he practiced it some more after he picked up the very impressive bouquet and drove home again.

Even with all that practicing and the flowers and the chocolates, he was still nervous. The kind of jittery that came with a task that really mattered. Rejection was something he'd grown accustomed to as a writer, but this was different.

This wasn't about having an editor like some story he'd made up or some fictional character. This was about him. His life. His personal happiness.

His future.

He recognized that it was crazy to think that way about a woman he'd just met, but so what? In the military, he'd jumped out of airplanes trusting that the forty-odd yards of fabric in his parachute would prevent him from dying.

So why shouldn't he jump at this chance?

The rewards would be so much greater. So long as Ginny felt the same way.

He pulled into his driveway, his gaze on her house.

Her Jeep was in the drive, so she was home. Maybe even watching him right now. Probably still fuming at him.

He took a breath. He could do this. He'd done much harder things.

They'd just never felt this important.

CHAPTER FOURTEEN

Ginny had no idea what Easy was up to, but he sure had been busy since she'd stormed out of his house. Out on the motorcycle, then back and out again in the Mustang.

Whatever. He certainly didn't seem bothered by their argument. Or her hurt feelings.

She sighed at her own mood. Her crankiness was only because she'd been all set to try to fix things between them, but then he'd left, making that impossible.

Which basically meant she was upset because she hadn't gotten her way. She rolled her eyes at herself. More proof that she'd lived this solitary existence far too long.

Whatever he'd been doing, it had to have been important. Probably house stuff. Something she'd promised to help with, and now...who knew?

The doorbell rang.

She almost jumped out of her chair. Easy? But no. Why would he be at her door? The ink cartridges she'd ordered, more likely.

Even so, she was glad she'd changed out of her frumpy yoga pants and into cute shorts and a tank top.

She went to the door. Opened it. And inhaled a little gasp. "Hi."

Easy smiled tentatively. "Hi."

She almost couldn't see him through the enormous bunch of flowers. He also had a large box in the other arm that looked very much like a crate from the Chocolate Dragon. Her heart was racing. He was *here*. "I'm sorry."

It wasn't the big apology she'd planned on, but she had to say something.

"Me, too. Really sorry. I shouldn't have said the things I did. I was…" He took a breath and seemed to be searching for the right word.

"Freaked out?"

He nodded. "And, truthfully, a little scared. Last night was bad for me."

"I know." Her heart went out to him. "I'm sorry you had to go through that. What happened to you last night, it doesn't change how I feel about you."

He stared at the ground between them, the muscles in his jaw tensing. "I don't know how that's possible."

"Because I know better than anyone else that your curse doesn't define you. Nor should it."

He looked up. "I suppose you do."

She smiled at that. But she had more to say. "I shouldn't have snapped at you the way I did. I reacted poorly."

"I shouldn't have presumed to know what's best for you. I was wrong to do that." He held out the flowers and the box. "These are for you."

She stepped back, opening the door wider. "Why don't you bring them in?"

As he entered, he seemed to exhale with the kind of relief she was feeling, too.

She took the flowers. "These are beautiful. I'll go put them in water. Thank you. You didn't have to do all this."

"I did." He looked at her with the haunted expression of a man with a lot on his mind and heart. "I like you, Ginny. A lot. I know we've only just met, but last night made me realize how compatible we are. Things are so easy between us."

She nodded. There was no denying the chemistry they shared.

He went silent for a moment. "Then I shifted, and it threw me. Hard. Reminded me that I shouldn't be dating anyone right now."

Despite his words, joy spilled through her. All because he'd called last night a *date*. Which meant it *was* a date. And that they were dating. Even with all that rising bliss, she managed not to grin or squeal or clap while he was still pouring his heart out. Instead, she just listened, intent on his words.

He hesitated. "I don't feel like I'm enough for any woman right now. Not just you, but especially not you. I hope that makes sense."

She nodded, overwhelmed by emotion to the point that she did the only thing she could think of to answer him with some kind of reassurance. She leaned in and kissed him softly on the mouth, crushing the bouquet between them and sending a heady floral perfume into the air. "What makes sense is we both have issues. But I think…I think those issues would be easier to bear together than separately."

Gratitude filled his gaze. "Yeah. They would. But it's not going to change my issues."

"It's not going to change mine either, but why don't you let me decide what kind of man is right for me?"

The smallest hint of a smile bent his mouth. "Okay."

"Great. Now can we pretend this morning didn't happen?" She went into the kitchen for a vase. She'd never gotten flowers from a man, but this bouquet made up for that.

He followed her, still holding the box. "Yes and no."

She got a vase down out of a cabinet. "What does that mean?"

"It means we put the bad feelings behind us, but we need to talk about what happened. About the expectations we have for each other. About where this is headed."

She laughed softly as she filled the vase. "Really? That's not at all what I thought you'd want to do."

"Why? Because men don't like to talk?"

"That's part of it. But another part is I haven't had anyone to talk to in so long, I think I've forgotten a little bit how people deal with things like this." She untied the paper from the flowers and arranged them in the water. She looked over her shoulder at him. "These are so beautiful. Thank you."

"I'm glad you like them." He shrugged as he set the box from the Chocolate Dragon on her kitchen table. "There's too much at stake here to brush this under the rug. Does neither of us any good."

"I agree." She turned to face him, thankful he was so willing to talk and pushing her to do the same. She was out of practice, but that was no excuse not to. "And I think it's wise. There's something I want to talk to you about, too."

"What's that?"

"Hope." She smiled. "But first, I could really use some breakfast. Can we talk while we eat?"

"Sure. Where do you want to go?"

"Nowhere. I'll make breakfast, if that's okay with you."

"Absolutely. But just so you know, I'm happy to take you out anytime you want to go. Just say the word."

"That's very sweet." She was mad about him. Crazy. Deep. Mad. "But you have a book to finish."

"True. But then I am taking you somewhere special. The best place this town has to offer. You shouldn't have had to pay for that meal last night."

"I didn't mind." Her gaze shifted to the box he'd set on the table. "That's from the Chocolate Dragon, isn't it?"

"It is. Is that a good thing?"

"That's a very good thing. Their chocolates are amazing. And from the size of that box, you bought them all."

He laughed, a sound sweet to her ears. "No, it's one of those big chocolate eggs they make."

Her eyes widened. "Really? Those are gorgeous. I've never had one. Just the chocolates." The eggs were also very expensive. Easy had really set out to make a point with his apology. She shook her head, a little dazed by his earnestness. "You really didn't have to do all this to say you were sorry."

He broke into a full-on smile. "I felt like I did. I was sure I'd really messed things up."

"I felt the same way."

"Plus, I owe you."

She made a face. "What do you owe me for?"

"For getting me out of the pub last night."

"You would have done the same for me. Right?"

"Damn straight."

He stared at the box of chocolates for a long couple of seconds, then back at her. "I'm glad this morning wasn't the end of us."

"Me, too." She went to the fridge and got out eggs and milk. "Pancakes okay?"

"Sounds great."

"You want coffee?"

He laughed. "Almost more than I want you, and that's saying something."

His words sent a tingle of pleasure through her, causing more blushing.

He shook his head like he'd just realized what

he'd said. "Sorry if I embarrassed you. I sometimes say things that are better left as thoughts in my head. Comes from talking to myself. All that solitary time as a writer."

"I know all about solitary time." She grinned, not quite able to look at him. "But I guess that makes us even for the first time since we met since I basically said things to you better left in my head."

He was still grinning. "It was nice to hear them."

"Um, so about the coffee." She used her elbow to point to the Keurig, since she was cracking eggs. "You know how to use one of those?"

He looked at the machine. "I can handle that. You want one?"

"I'd love another, but you make yours first." She got the pancake mix out and went to work on the batter while he made coffee.

In no time, she had a griddle sizzling with pancakes and a fresh cup of coffee at her side.

He was at the table, drinking his. "So what's this hope you mentioned?"

She turned and leaned on the counter so she could face him. "I don't know if you've heard about it already, but there's a local legend about a book somewhere in the enchanted forest here. A book that, if you can find it and write your name in its pages, will take away whatever curse you're living under."

He was about to take a sip of his coffee. He paused with the mug halfway to his mouth then, after a second, took a drink and set it down. "But it's just a legend?"

"I'm not sure. I've looked for the book since I've lived here and obviously haven't found it, since I'm still forgettable. But recently, the Evermores' little sister, Gracie, has been out and about more than was typical for her. And from what I've overheard, it's because her curse was lifted."

He seemed to ponder that. "Interesting. You want to go look?"

"I was thinking we might have better luck together than I've had alone."

"Makes sense." He nodded, but he didn't look nearly as excited as she'd expected.

"You don't love the idea. Why not?"

"I do love the idea. It would be great to put myself back to rights that easily. But I don't have the time right now. Not with my looming deadline."

"Your book. Right." She'd kind of forgotten about that. "Well, as soon as it's turned in, then. Speaking of…I still want to help you unpack."

"That's a lot of work."

"And you don't have time to do it."

He sighed, but there was warmth in his eyes. "No, I don't. I would really appreciate the help. I can't find anything in that house. It's all still in boxes."

"I can start this afternoon. I have one job of my own to finish, then I'll be over."

"I'll leave the front door unlocked."

She checked the pancakes. They were bubbling at the edges, so she flipped them. "What's your goal for today on the book?"

"A chapter at minimum. If I can do a chapter, chapter and a half, a day, I'll be in good shape."

"Excellent. Pancakes will be done in a minute."

"They smell great." He stood. "I should set the table."

"Thanks. Cabinet over the dishwasher and drawer to the right of it."

He got out plates and silverware. "This is nice. It's been a while since I've had a home-cooked meal I didn't make myself."

"In that case, I wish it was fancier." She loaded a plate with pancakes, grabbed the syrup from the pantry, and came to the table.

He brought her coffee over, then took his seat next to her. "No, this is perfect."

So was he. She nodded. "Good. I'm glad. It is nice."

They helped themselves to the stack of pancakes, the butter, and the syrup, then started eating. It took one bite for Ginny's appetite to come back.

Easy helped himself to another pancake with two still on his plate. "These are great."

She laughed. "I'm glad you think so. I'm a decent cook, but not a great baker. Pancakes are the closest I get to cake."

He smiled, then his expression turned serious again. "Do you really think that book exists?"

She took a breath before answering. "I want to believe it does."

"Then maybe I need to work harder on the book and make time to visit that forest."

CHAPTER FIFTEEN

Having someone in the house might have bothered him under any other circumstances, but since that someone was Ginny, he felt completely at ease. A little guilty, maybe, about her doing so much for him, but he'd already made his mind up to repay her in some way.

At the moment, that way was going to be by making time to search for the magic book she'd talked about.

He'd seen the excitement in her eyes when she'd brought it up. And as much as he couldn't afford the time, he'd have to find a way. Sleep less. Write more.

Something.

Because he didn't want to disappoint her. Even if it seemed like a pretty farfetched idea to him. Sure, this town was all about farfetched, but a book that could remove your curse just by writing your name in it?

That was hard to buy into. Even for a fiction writer.

She was working in the kitchen, unpacking boxes and putting stuff away and generally trying to make it functional. He'd given her full control, told her to set it up however it made sense. He pulled his headphones away from his ears for a moment, listening for her.

He smiled. She was singing. He didn't recognize the song, and she didn't seem to know all the words, but the sound was sweet and happy.

It gave life to a feeling he'd been working hard to suppress. That feeling of need that his father had explained to him a long time ago. How someday, he'd meet a woman, and the wolf in him would want her. Not in an ordinary way, but in a way that was all about the wolf. And the desire to protect and possess a woman. To make her his mate. To make them a family.

Easy took a long breath, then blew it out slowly.

He didn't want that feeling. Not now. Not when he couldn't do anything about it. How could he in his current condition?

He tipped his head back against his chair and stared at the ceiling like it might suddenly provide the answer.

After a moment, he shook his head, told himself to focus on what he could control, the book in front of him, and got back to work.

Progress was slow. Each word was a slog. Each finished paragraph a genuine victory. In an hour, he managed two and a half pages.

Finally, in frustration, he took his headphones off

and got up. He needed a short break. Something to distract him from how badly the word count was going.

He went into the kitchen, leaning against the doorjamb to enjoy the sight of Ginny, up on her tiptoes on a stepstool, stretching to put a stockpot on the top shelf of a cabinet. Her shorts had ridden up a little, showing off her very curvaceous backside. She was still singing.

Silently, he padded up behind her, trying his hardest not to give in to his wolf and take a nibble of the tanned thigh now at eye level. "Need some help?"

She yelped and jumped and almost fell off the stepstool. The pot clattered to the floor as she turned.

He grabbed her, pulling her into his arms before she really did fall. "Sorry, did I scare you?"

"Yes! Bad wolf." She smacked his shoulder, but the sparks in her eyes weren't angry. "You're supposed to be writing."

"I know, but I need a break. I'm having a hard time finding my zone today." She was still in his arms, warm and pliant and seemingly uninterested in changing her current position. "So I thought I'd see what you were doing."

She shook her head, her tone thick with pretend scolding as she said, "This is not the plan, Mr. Grayle."

He ran his tongue over his teeth. "No, it's not. But sometimes the plan changes."

"I'm not done with this kitchen."

He couldn't take his eyes off her. "Looks done to me."

She grinned. "What kind of break do you have in mind?"

"How about…" He tried to think of something that wouldn't get him slapped. "A swim?"

"I don't have a suit."

"That's not a problem."

"Oh, sure." She snickered.

"I meant because you live right next door. Get your mind out of the gutter, Ms. French. I know you'd like to see me skinny-dipping again, but I'm not that kind of wolf."

She giggled. "Yeah, right. Okay. I'll go get my suit."

He started to put her down, then swung her back into his arms again. "Unless you'd rather go for a drive out to the enchanted forest."

Her lips parted, and a little gasp came out. "I'd love to. But that's too long of a break. That could be the whole rest of the day. I think a quick swim is better. Then we can both get back to work."

"I had no idea you were such a taskmaster." He put her down, but on the counter so she was facing him and he was standing between her knees. He pulled her close, threaded his fingers into her hair, and kissed her. "I like that about you."

"Thanks." Her eyes flashed with a wolfy gleam. "I could be harder on you, if you want."

A low growl slipped out of him as their banter heated him up. "Don't play with me, woman. I will bite you."

She shrieked and slipped off the counter and out of his grasp, laughing. "I'm going to get my suit. I'll see you in the pool."

When she got back, not wearing the tiny pink bikini, but a suit that covered slightly more and had one strap safety-pinned in place, he was already in the pool, swimming some laps and trying to work out the rest of the chapter that needed writing.

She came down the steps into the water. "You look like you're somewhere else."

He swam toward her, putting his feet down as he reached the shallow end. "Trying to figure out what happens next. What took you so long?"

"I had to find a safety pin to secure the strap." She tipped her head. "Wait. Trying to figure out what happens next...with us?"

He smiled. "With the book. I think I know what happens next with us."

"You do, do you?"

He nodded and took her hands, pulling her deeper in. "Yes, but I can't tell you, or that would ruin the ending."

She stuck her tongue out at him. "Back to the book, then. What's happened so far?"

"You want to hear all this?"

"Yep. Lay it on me."

He wasn't used to brainstorming with anyone. He took a breath and mapped out the plot as it stood so far. "And now he's standing on a cliff with a horde of villagers coming after him and only half the map he needs to find the girl."

She thought for a few seconds. "He should jump."

Easy's brows shot up. "To his death? I don't think my editor or my readers would like that."

"No! He should have one of those little parachutes tucked away in his backpack. Or one of those flying-squirrel suits, whatever those are called. Then he could glide to safety, which would only seem like safety until the next bad thing happens."

"Huh." He let that roll around in his brain. It was certainly a very Tomahawk Jones thing to do. "I could make that work. Maybe not the wing suit, but the parachute. Especially if I changed a few things in the previous chapter. I don't know why I didn't come up with something like that."

"Too much other stuff on your mind, maybe. You would have thought of something eventually."

"Maybe. But I prefer sooner rather than later. Thanks, Ginny." He grabbed her and pulled her in for a short, hard kiss.

She grinned when he let her go. "You're welcome. I guess swim time is over, then."

He sighed. "Yeah, sorry. It is for me. I need to get this written before—"

"Don't apologize, just go get your words done. I might swim a few laps, though, seeing as how I just got in."

"Go for it. You've earned it." He stole another kiss on his way out of the pool. Once out, he grabbed his towel, dried off briskly, then wrapped the towel around his waist, pulled his T-shirt on, and went back to his desk, still wet. There wasn't time to change, not when this new idea was driving him to write.

Time and the outside world disappeared. He was back on track, deep in the story, and making progress. When he hit save and looked up, the purple filter of twilight had cast everything in gloom.

He took his headphones off. No singing. He got up and walked to the kitchen. It was spotless, not a box in sight. He opened a few drawers and checked a few cabinets. Everything was neat and organized.

"Wow." He breathed out the word in sheer awe of what Ginny had accomplished.

It would have taken him at least two days to do what she'd done today. Instead, he'd made good progress on his book. Enough that he was going to sleep well tonight. He was starting to think he should have bought her jewelry after all. The woman was a gift he'd done nothing to earn.

He wasn't even sure when she'd left, because she hadn't interrupted him to say goodbye.

There was a note on the counter.

Hope you got a lot done. I'm pretty much finished with the kitchen. I'll probably start on the living room tomorrow. Text me if you need anything.

PS. I'm ordering pizza and plan to eat at eight if you decide to take a break. And I will be cracking that egg for dessert. Hah!

XOXO,

G

He grinned that she'd signed it. As though someone else could have been in his house. She was adorable.

He checked the time. Seven forty-five. He grabbed his phone and sent her a text. *Still want company?*

Her reply came quickly. *Yes! Pizza will be here in five.*

So will I.

He was starving, and pizza sounded great. He changed out of his swim trunks, put on jeans and shoes, tucked his phone and wallet in his pocket, and walked over.

She was on the front porch, waiting. What a gorgeous sight to cap off a great day. He smiled at her. "Hi there, beautiful."

"Hi." She grinned. "How'd it go? Did you hit your goal?"

"I did. Surpassed it by a bit, too. Thanks to you. The kitchen looks great, by the way." He climbed the porch steps. "I can't believe how much you got done."

A car parked in her driveway, and he turned to see who it was.

"Fritzi's Pizza," she said.

Easy dug out his wallet. "I've got this. It's the least I can do."

The delivery guy walked up with the hot bag in one hand, meeting Easy at the base of the steps. "Evening. That'll be thirty-two fifty."

Easy glanced at Ginny. "Is there gold on this pizza?"

She laughed. "I got two large Meat Lovers. I thought you might be hungry. I am. And this way, there's a chance of leftovers."

"Starved," Easy answered. He gave the kid two twenties and took the pies in exchange, carrying them into the kitchen.

She had plates out. The television was on in the living room, the screen paused. "You want to watch a movie? I figured it might be a nice mindless thing to do after the long day you put in."

"I'd love to. I don't even care what it is."

"Well, it's *Dark Passage*." She shrugged. "I like old movies. Especially a good comedy or a dark film noir."

"You're a constant surprise, you know that? I've never heard of the movie, but I'm happy to watch it." He piled three slices onto his plate.

"You've never heard of it? Humphrey Bogart and Lauren Bacall. Plus, Agnes Moorehead, who everyone knows as the mother from *Bewitched*. You'll love it. It's one of my favorite noirs." She held up her plate. "Come on, you'll see."

An hour and forty-six minutes later, he was convinced. "That wasn't something I ever would have picked, but that was great. Bogart and Bacall. What a pair, huh?"

"Told you." She grinned. "I'm glad you liked it. Glad you took the time to come over, too. But I know you have another long day ahead of you—we both do—so it's okay for you to say good night and head home."

"Kicking me out, huh?" He winked. "Yeah, you're right, though. I should go." He leaned in. "Can I kiss you good night?"

"I'd be mad if you didn't."

CHAPTER SIXTEEN

They spent each of the next five days almost exactly the same way. Easy writing, Ginny visiting Aunt Gwen first thing, then back home to get her work done, then the rest of the day at Easy's house sorting out another room. They spent the evenings together watching a movie or something light on television over a dinner of takeout. Dessert was the chocolate egg or its contents, every bite of which was out-of-this-world delicious.

Sometimes, they'd swim and brainstorm during the day. Sometimes, they didn't speak a word until he was done writing.

She loved the relaxed rhythm they'd fallen into. The way they worked around each other, giving each other the space they needed to get their jobs done. It was comfortable and domestic without being too heavy. She loved being able to help him. Loved having his presence in her house afterward.

Loved how sweet and appreciative he was. Loved how he never forgot her.

Loved him, if she was being honest. But that

wasn't something she was going to tell him. She knew the feeling was a by-product of having been alone for so long, and because of that, she was able to keep it to herself. Well, she'd hinted to Aunt Gwen about how she felt, but that had been on one of her aunt's not-so-great days, and she probably wouldn't remember. It had been nice to tell someone, though.

Not him, obviously. Telling him would only scare him away, this amazing man who thought he wasn't enough for any woman.

Speaking those words to him could potentially destroy the happy little routine they'd developed.

And losing Easy would be far worse than living a life of unrequited love.

She didn't even mind that much not telling him. She knew he liked her, knew he cared for her. She didn't need him to love her.

Not really. Not at this stage of things anyway. She'd survived ten years of life essentially alone. She could spend a few more keeping her feelings to herself so long as he was in her life.

She hit send on her current project, and off it went for client approval. Now she'd head over to his house and do a little work in the garage. He'd given her a general idea of where he wanted things. She just had to unpack and organize.

Then the house would pretty much be done.

As would her time there. That made her a little sad. Even if they were doing their own things, she'd grown used to the presence of another person who knew her. Heady stuff for a woman who'd been known by no one but her aunt for so long.

But there was no reason he couldn't still come over after his writing was done for the day. She knew she'd still see him. She just wouldn't be as close.

After the book was done, maybe that would change. He'd have more free time, to some extent. She knew he'd be starting another book. That's what writers did. They wrote. But he wouldn't have the same intense pressure.

Then maybe they could take a little time to look for another, even more important book. One that could change both their lives.

She got that he didn't really believe in it. After ten years of looking, she struggled with that, too. But hope was hard to give up on. Until Easy had arrived, the hope of that book had been the only reason she'd gotten up some mornings.

Tomorrow, while he was writing, she was going to visit Seymour. It had been a week since she'd taken him pies and enjoyed his company. Then she'd go see Aunt Gwen again. Maybe take her up to Nightingale Park for some fresh air and sun.

But today she was going to get Easy's garage straightened out. As much as she could anyway. Organizing an entire garage in one day seemed like a monumental task. From what he'd told her, he'd paid extra for the privilege of having a single-car garage when he'd lived in the city, so maybe there wasn't that much stuff.

She walked over to his house and let herself in through the back door by the pool. She'd been coming in this way all week to keep from interrupting him, but he was in the kitchen.

"Hey." She smiled. "Late lunch?"

He nodded, sandwich in his hand and mouth full.

"I had the leftover pork lo mein from last night."

He swallowed. "I ate my leftovers for breakfast."

She grinned. "How's the writing going?"

"Really good. I can't tell you how much it helps that you've taken care of the house. Not walking through the clutter of boxes has taken a weight off my mind. I think it's actually freed up brain space for more book stuff. Brainstorming with you has been great, too."

"I'm really glad to hear that. I'll be done with the house today after I get the garage sorted out."

"Already?" He leaned on the counter and sighed. "That kind of sucks." He laughed softly. "I've always thought I preferred solitude for writing, but having you in the house has been really nice. Comforting in a way."

"I feel the same way." His words warmed her heart. "I'll still be right next door if you need me."

"You know, you could bring your laptop over here and work. But I guess it's presumptive of me to ask you to do that. I could just as easily take my laptop to your house and write. Except…"

"Except what?"

He shrugged. "I haven't been invited."

She made a face at him. "Why don't you bring your laptop to my house and work? There. Now you have."

"We could try it, you know. Maybe start with one day a week and see if we drive each other crazy or not."

"True. But not tomorrow. I have errands to run. Groceries, post office, a visit to my aunt." And Ginny's favorite lake monster. "Do you need anything? I'll be in town."

"I have errands, too, but I'm not asking you to do any of that." He ate another bite of his sandwich.

"Well, if it's mailing stuff, I'm going to be there anyway."

"Okay. I have one package to go out."

"No problem. Leave it on the counter, and I'll—"

"I don't want to write anymore today."

She stared at him. "But you have to."

"Not really." He shrugged. "I've been up since five. Couldn't sleep, for some reason. It happens. Anyway, I finished yesterday's chapter, then wrote another and am halfway through a third. I'm now a chapter and a half ahead of where I need to be. I'm doing great."

"Wow. Good for you. If you want to take the rest of the day off, then I think you should. Do you want to swim? Or do something else?"

He smiled. "Something else."

He looked like he was up to something. She smiled back. "Like what?"

His eyes lit up. "I thought maybe we could take a

little drive out to this place I've heard about. The enchanted forest."

She sucked in a breath. "And look for the book?"

He nodded. "And look for the book."

She clapped her hands. "Yes! Let's go. As soon as you're done with lunch, that is. I'll go change while you do that."

"Into what?"

She glanced down at her shorts and tank top. "Into jeans and a T-shirt. Maybe a long-sleeved overshirt that I can tie around my waist. It can be a little chilly in the forest. Not a lot of sun out there."

He frowned. "There's no sun anywhere here."

"Well, there's even less in the forest. You'll see."

"Should we bring flashlights?"

She hesitated. "We could, but the forest makes its own light. You'll see that, too."

"All right. I'll go put on jeans as well. See you in a few minutes." He started on the remainder of his sandwich.

"You come over to my place. We'll take my Jeep. Better-suited."

He chewed thoughtfully. "Are we off-roading?"

She laughed. "No. But we'll have to park on the side of the road." Then she left the way she'd come in, practically running back to her house to change.

She'd never had any luck looking for the book, but then, no one had remembered her this past decade until Easy had come along. She hoped he'd change her luck with the book. She just knew he would. She felt it.

Today was going to be the day that things changed for the better.

Easy leaned back in the Jeep's passenger seat, letting the warm breeze flow over him. It was a beautiful day, as overcast days went, with the golden hint of sun that was never going to show its face. Perfect for a trip to the forest.

Sure, he could have written more. But Ginny was pretty much done working at his house, and that had been bothering him so much that he'd barely slept from thinking about it. The thought of not having her around made him feel like he was about to lose a very important part of his day.

Silly. She was going to be right next door. But that no longer felt close enough. Not for this amazing woman he was crazy about. So crazy, that he'd filled pages in his journal about her. At least one every day. Part of that was security, in case the worst ever happened and her curse caused him to forget her again. He figured this way, he'd have proof of what had already passed between them.

But part of it was that they were too early in their relationship for him to tell her how he really felt.

Instead, he journaled, page after page of scrawled writing about how wonderful she was. What they'd done that day and evening. Details of what movie they'd watched, what they'd eaten, what she'd worn...memories. But also insurance.

But journaling hadn't helped him go back to sleep in the early hours this morning, so he'd gotten up, gotten to work, and come up with a plan. If they went to the forest today, that would mean she'd have to come back tomorrow to finish the house.

It wasn't perfect, but it would buy him another day.

And today was shaping up to be a good one. Words done, he could relax a little and enjoy the time with Ginny.

He wasn't convinced the magical book existed, but there were worse things to do than hike through an enchanted forest with a beautiful woman at his side. And it would make her happy, something that mattered very much to him.

He liked putting a smile on her face and making her laugh. This was something she really wanted to do, and she'd been working so hard to help him that it seemed like a no-brainer to give the book hunt a shot.

It was the least he could do until he figured out how to repay her for her kind help. He glanced over at his wolfy beauty queen. Did she have any idea how crazy about her he was? How much weight her help had lifted off his shoulders?

He was dedicating this book to her, that wasn't even a question. In fact, he'd written the dedication yesterday.

To my dearest Ginny,

If there was only one person in this world I could remember, I'd want it to be you.

He hoped she liked that. Because in a couple months, when the book was out, he was going to present her with a copy open to the dedication page, and after she read it, he was going to get down on one knee and make things permanent.

It might be too soon now, but it wouldn't be by then. Wolves moved faster than humans, and as he'd thought a thousand times, human rules didn't apply. And if she still didn't care about his shifting issue at that point, he wasn't going to let it stop him.

Ginny looked over. "You look happy."

He nodded without taking his eyes off her. "I am. Very."

"Needed a little time off, huh? You have put in a lot of hours on that keyboard this week."

"Yep. Thanks to you making it possible."

"Nah." She grinned. "You still would have written. You'd just be living in a box canyon of chaos."

He laughed. "True."

She turned off the main road and onto a new one that split a thick, forested area in two. The growth was so dense that the golden light of day turned green as it filtered through the trees. Her speed dropped, making it easier to study their surroundings.

He sat up a little straighter, the magic so present here it was almost like smoke in the air.

"Feel that?" she asked.

"Yeah, I do." He watched the forest go by with a whole new respect. "I didn't think it was going to be so strong."

"It's the meridian lines. Apparently, larger shifters like us are especially sensitive to the magic that leaks out of them. Maybe because we're sort of forest creatures in our own right."

"Seems possible. Where are we going to start looking?"

"I don't think it matters." She pulled off onto a wider section of the shoulder and parked, then turned to grab her backpack from the back seat. "I have a theory. I've been through more miles of this forest than anyone I know, and this is what I've come up with. If the book doesn't want to be found, it won't be, and you know why?"

He shook his head.

"Because I think the book is the seat of the town's magic. All of it. The source of it." She pulled her keys out of the ignition and zipped them into one of the pack's pockets. "I'd bet my entire bank account that Amelia, the witch who started this town, knows exactly where the book is. Not that she'd ever tell anyone. But someday, hopefully today, we're going to find it. And we're going to get rid of these curses."

"Is there any section of the forest you haven't searched?"

"The Dark Acres, but I don't think the book would be there." She paused. "Although that would be a good place to hide it."

Easy had no idea what the Dark Acres was, but to his writer's brain, it sounded like the area had been named to keep people out. "Then let's go there."

CHAPTER SEVENTEEN

Only Easy's presence made Ginny agree to search the Dark Acres. It wasn't the kind of place she'd ever wanted to go alone, even if she was a werewolf. But having him at her side made her feel safe.

What a nice thing to feel after so many years. She glanced at him as they began their trek. "Thank you for doing this with me today. I know you could have gotten more done on your book."

He smiled. "You're welcome. And I could have, but sometimes a break like this really refills the well, you know? Creatively, I mean."

"So you think you might have Tomahawk Jones battle giant spiders?"

His smile disappeared, and his brows shot up. "Are there giant spiders in this forest?"

"Not in this part and maybe not *giant*, but when we get to the Dark Acres…" She shrugged. "The Dark Acres wasn't named Happy Fun Land for a reason."

"Great. Large spiders. Awesome." He snorted.

Ginny couldn't help but tease him. "If you feel the need to shift for protection, go right ahead."

"I'm good. With my luck, I'd probably turn into a corgi."

She laughed. "I'm going to keep my comments to myself on that one. But corgis are adorable."

"Thanks."

They pressed on through the dense woods. Ginny loved the enchanted forest. In her wolf form, she'd run through here many times. Even though the magic was thick and tangible, it wasn't uncomfortable. Maybe it would be for other kinds of supernaturals, but to her it seemed to increase her sense of belonging. Even more so when she was a wolf.

Now that she was here with Easy, she tried to see the forest through his eyes. She pointed out some of the more interesting things around them, like the sprite moss that brightened the darker parts of the forest, or how you could tell if a nymph inhabited a tree by the face visible in the bark.

He took it all in, genuinely appearing to enjoy it. Maybe because, as a writer, he had a thirst for learning. Or maybe he just wanted to get to know this part of his new hometown a little better. Whatever the reason, the time passed quickly, and they made good headway into the forest.

It wasn't long before their surroundings started to change.

Ginny brought them to a stop. "We're getting into the Dark Acres now. It'll be easy to see soon. All the trees will get darker, almost burnt-looking, the light will fade, and there will be new flora and fauna around us. Most of it more dangerous than what we've already passed. Mind it, and it will mind you."

"Got it. You make a pretty good field guide. I appreciate the info."

"I've just been here long enough to know this part of the woods is not a place where you want to drop your guard. Not that I think anything is going to happen. It's just smart to keep your eyes open."

"As we used to say in the Rangers, keep your head on a swivel."

She smiled. "Tomahawk Jones says that in every book."

"I suppose he does." Easy grinned. "He gets it from me. Lead on, Lara Croft."

With a little laugh, she started walking again. The trees and undergrowth grew thicker, making their path a ragged one. She did her best to lead them through the most open spots so they could avoid brushing up against too much foliage.

He followed close behind. "What are we looking for in terms of this book? Are there any signs as to where it is?"

"Not that I know of. I think we'll just know it when we see it. I mean, a book in a forest isn't a typical thing, so…"

"Right. I was just wondering if it's in a knot in a tree or positioned on a rock or on its own little stand or what."

"Good question. I wish I had an answer."

"Maybe it'll have a magical glow around it."

"Could be." She nodded. "That would help, actually."

"Do you think it's like Excalibur? Only the worthy can open it?"

She blinked at that thought. "I hope not. I'd hate to actually find the thing, then not be able to open it to write my name inside."

"You'd be worthy. That's not something you have anything to worry about. Me, on the other hand, who knows?"

"Nah. You're one of the good ones. You'd be able to open it, too. No problem." She gave him a wink over her shoulder.

He smiled. "Thanks."

They walked in silence a little farther, the crunch of the forest floor and the hum of insects the only real sounds.

When the crunch softened slightly, Ginny realized Easy had stopped walking. She turned to see what had caught his attention.

He was staring off to the right. "I think I see a glow."

She went very still. Because of the trees, she couldn't see what he was looking at, but anything was possible in this place. Could it be the book? It was too much to hope for, and yet hope filled her like helium filling a balloon, lifting her with a lightness she couldn't resist. "Do you think it's the book?"

"I don't know. It's…moving. Like it's beckoning me to go after it." He started forward. "Hang on. I'm going to see what it is."

She backtracked around a large, sooty oak, reaching the place he'd been standing, then cut through the brush to go after him. He'd almost disappeared into the trees. She went faster, trying to catch up, but got snagged on some brambles. "Be careful," she called as she freed herself. "Not everything that glows in here is friendly."

Actually, nothing that glowed in the Dark Acres was friendly. Nothing she could think of anyway. The realization spurred her on. Sure, it could still be the book, but it could be a whole host of other things, too.

The glow came into view in a small clearing up ahead. Easy blocked her view. She stepped to the side to see around him.

The light was red and pulsating where it covered the side of a trunk. Not the book at all. Her breath caught in her throat as she realized what was giving off that light. "I don't think this is a good idea. I doubt this has anything to do with the book."

"Are you sure?"

"No, but call it a gut feeling."

He took one step deeper into the clearing and went still. "What are these things? Maybe the book is nearby."

She stayed where she was and kept her voice even. "Lightning bugs. Don't disturb them. I've never seen them clustered like that. They might be protecting their queen or something. If the book is nearby, we'll find it another way. Move slowly back toward me."

He took one step back. Then another. Then he stepped on a twig, cracking it. The horde lifted off the tree, the sizzle of electric stingers buzzing like mad.

"Easy, *run*."

But it was too late. They swarmed him, a bright cloud of light and pain. Sparks cracked against his skin. He jerked and twitched at the stings, the image of his wolf flashing on his face as he tried to shift but failed. He swatted at them as best he could, but the attack was too much.

With a snarl of pain, he dropped to the ground.

"Get off him, you wretched things. Leave him alone." She let out a sob, her hands itching to touch him, to pull him to safety, but if she went for him now, the insects would sting her, too. There was one way she could give herself a little protection.

She shifted into her wolf, growling and snapping as she charged forward to drive them off.

The lightning bugs rose, a few angry sparks cracking the air. She stood over Easy, protecting him from any further attack as best she could. A few dived at her, but her thick fur prevented her from getting more than a minor zap. At last they drifted off, leaving the acrid smell of ozone behind.

She waited as long as she dared, long enough to be sure they were gone. Then she returned to her human form.

"Easy, I'm here." She knelt on the earth beside him and checked his pulse. He was alive. Covered in tiny, jagged red welts, but breathing. If he'd survived being struck by lightning, surely he could survive the stings of these creatures.

At least that's what Ginny chose to believe.

She looked around one more time to make sure the bugs were really gone. She had to get him out of here. Out of the Dark Acres and back to a safer part of the forest. There was no telling if the lightning bugs would return.

He moaned. His head rolled to one side.

"Shh, it's okay now. The lightning bugs are gone. But we should get out of here in case they come back."

He groaned something unintelligible.

"Don't worry, I got this. Just don't fight me, okay?" She got him to a sitting position, pulled his arm around her shoulders, put her arm around his waist, then lifted him to his feet. "Good grief, you weigh a lot."

His only response was a grunt that might have been a yes.

"I know, it's all those muscles."

The banter was for his sake, to keep him engaged and hopefully prevent him from passing out completely again. He was a dead weight like this, lost to the pain of being stung so many times and in no position to help her move him. But she was a werewolf, and she was strong enough to carry him out like a baby if she had to.

Hopefully, it wouldn't come to that.

Holding on to him tightly, she got him moving. He shuffled like a sleepwalker, somewhere between consciousness and incoherence. Beyond an occasional groan or grunt, he said nothing.

"Please be okay," she whispered over and over.

He never lifted his head, never responded. Maybe being semiconscious was the only way his body could deal with the pain. If so, that was okay with her. She just hated not knowing how he was doing.

The trek back to the Jeep was a long one, but somehow he held on until she got him strapped into the passenger's seat. She patted his chest. "You rest now."

He looked at her, and she thought he might say something. Then his eyes rolled back, and he passed out.

She took a deep breath. This was her fault. Hers and that stupid book's. She shook her head, mad at herself. The book probably didn't even exist. This whole dumb trip had been pointless.

"Hang in there, Easy. Please. We're on the way home."

She jumped into the driver's seat and turned the car around. Her gaze was divided between him and the road. She had no idea what the treatment was for lightning bug stings. She wasn't sure if she should take him to the hospital or not.

Better safe than sorry.

She turned toward Shadowvale General. "Sorry, not headed home after all. I think a trip to the ER is a better idea. Just in case. Don't worry, though, they're fully equipped to handle all kinds of supernaturals and all kinds of emergencies. You're not the first person that's been stung either, so they'll know what to do."

She drove as fast as was prudent, parking in front

of the Emergency Room's automatic double doors less than ten minutes later.

She ran inside. "My friend was stung by lightning bugs in the Dark Acres. A swarm of them. All over. He's passed out."

The nurse behind the desk looked up. "Lightning bugs? Not much we can do for him here. We can admit him, but all he needs is a day or two of rest. Wait. Is he human? Because if he is—"

"No, werewolf."

"That's good. It might not take him a full day to recover. I'd say let him sleep it off. He'll be sore when he wakes up. Might have a little double vision, too. But all he needs are fluids and some aspirin. Not ibuprofen, aspirin. If the welts bother him, use hawthorn salve. You can get it at Spellbound on Main Street. They always have some made up."

"Really?" Ginny knew she had a skeptical look aimed at the nurse, but so what? "That's it?"

The woman smiled. "I promise. We can check him in if you want us to, but it'll be an automatic overnight stay."

"No, that's okay. I'll take him home." Easy probably wouldn't enjoy coming to in a hospital bed. A forced day of rest when he could be writing? She didn't want to be the cause of that. "Thanks."

"Sure thing. Take care. If his condition worsens, don't hesitate to bring him back."

Ginny jogged back to the Jeep. Easy was still passed out. "All right. Home it is. I hope this is the right call."

No response from him as she got behind the wheel and pulled away from the hospital. Well, if he didn't wake up in a couple of hours, she was ringing up Rico Martinez. Actually, she might do that anyway. He didn't know her, but once she explained what had happened, he'd at least offer her some suggestions, wouldn't he?

If anyone knew what to do about a werewolf getting stung by lightning bugs, it had to be the alpha of the pack.

But then, what if that conversation led to more about Easy than was her right to share? If Rico found out there was a new male wolf in town who hadn't introduced himself, that might create trouble for Easy.

Easy probably didn't want to meet the pack alpha until he could be sure the creature he shifted into was definitely a wolf.

Ginny loathed the thought of creating trouble for him, so calling Rico was out. Easy had enough on his shoulders without her adding to the weight.

She checked on him. Still passed out.

Eyes back on the road, she sighed. "I guess we have to get through this together. Just the two of us. But I swear, if you get any worse, I'm taking you back to the hospital and you're getting checked in."

Even if she had to introduce herself a thousand times to get him help.

CHAPTER EIGHTEEN

Easy opened his eyes and saw two of everything. He blinked a few times, and the repeats started to fade. He was in his own bed. He felt like a pallet of bricks pressed him down, making it impossible for him to move, so he didn't.

How had he gotten here?

It took a moment for his memory to return.

A dark forest. A red glow. Bugs. Drawn to him. Zapping him with electricity. He'd tried to shift, to run, but each sting had frozen him in place. The pain had been excruciating to the point that he'd passed out. Worse than being struck by lightning, because it had lasted longer. He winced at the memory.

But now he was here. In his own home. He had no recollection of how he'd gotten here. Had he been out there alone? A moment of hard thinking told him no, but he couldn't recall the person he'd been with.

Whoever it was, they had to be who'd saved him. He owed them.

He lay there a moment longer, trying to shake the lethargy clinging to him.

The shades were closed, but there was no light coming through them, and it felt late. Probably why the one bedside lamp was on.

He tried to sit up, and the pain exploded through him, every nerve in his body going white hot with electric fire. He grunted, almost passing out again, and fell back to the mattress. He snarled at the bother of it all.

He didn't have time for this. He had a book to write.

"Easy?" A voice called out to him, followed by a woman coming into his bedroom a few seconds later. "Hey, you're awake."

"Yes." He frowned. "How long was I out?"

She looked at her watch. "Almost twelve hours. It's nearly four a.m., but that's pretty much what the ER nurse said would happen."

"You took me to the ER?"

She nodded. "I did. I wasn't sure what else to do. You were out cold. And I was worried. But the nurse said there wasn't really anything they could do for lightning bug stings and just to bring you home and let you sleep it off. She did say you might have some double vision and that you'd be in a lot of pain. She said aspirin and fluids would help, plus hawthorn salve for the welts, which I went and got."

"I do have a little double vision. And every inch of me hurts." More pain than he'd had in a long time. Since the lightning strike.

She pointed toward the side of the bed. "The hawthorn salve is in that jar on the nightstand. I can help you with that if you want. But first, I'll go get you some painkillers. Be right back."

Before he could say another word, she was out the door. He saw the jar of salve, but hurt too much to attempt putting any on. He closed his eyes. The pain permeated every inch of him, but he felt himself drifting back to sleep.

"Here you go."

He opened his eyes. A woman stood over him with two bottles, one of water and one of pills. She put the water on his nightstand, then twisted the top off the aspirin and tapped two out into her palm.

He blinked, thinking he'd passed out again.

She held them out to him. "You need help taking these?"

"No."

"You could take more. The shifter metabolism can certainly handle it, but let's start with two and see how they work."

"Okay." With great effort, he took the pills from her, lifted his head, and tossed them back. The pain from the movement was unbelievable. He breathed openmouthed, trying to get through it.

She handed him the water bottle with the top off.

He took a slow, careful drink and swallowed. Yep, everything hurt. He handed the bottle back.

She took it and replaced the cap, then set it on his nightstand. "I guess maybe try to sleep some more if you can."

"Yeah, I think I will."

"Do you want me to put some of that salve on you?"

"No, I'm okay." He hesitated, studying her face. "Did you, uh, get me out of the woods?"

"I did. Memory a little fuzzy?"

"Not really, I just…" He stared at her pretty face a little longer. She had kind eyes. She was beautiful in a very pure, natural way that made him want to keep staring. "I just don't know who you are."

She went pale as her mouth fell open and her eyes widened. Almost like she'd been struck. When she spoke, her voice was choked with emotion he didn't understand. "I'm Ginny. Your next-door neighbor. Your friend."

"You live next door?" That was a bonus.

She nodded. "Yes. I've been helping you all week get your house unpacked and things put away so you can write."

"You have? That's nice of you." No wonder there were no boxes in the bedroom.

She took a long breath and swallowed as she knit her fingers together. Her hands were trembling. "You don't remember me."

"No, I don't."

She bit her bottom lip and looked like she might cry. "Excuse me."

She walked out and down the hall. Maybe into the…into the…he blinked and couldn't remember what he'd been thinking about. That it was dark outside?

A few soft sobs came from deeper in the house. His whole system went on alert. Someone was in his house. Someone who was…crying? Who would be in his house crying? And why were they crying?

Was he…going to die? Were lightning bug stings fatal?

A pretty woman came into his room. Her eyes were a little red. She must have been the one he heard crying. "Anything?"

"Anything what?"

"Do you remember anything?"

"I remember being stung. But not how I got home." He peered at her. "Who are you? My nurse?" But even saying that, he knew it wasn't right. He just couldn't place her.

"I'm Ginny. Your neighbor. I brought you home. And I have been playing nurse a bit, so…" Her voice cracked, and she swallowed and looked at the floor. Like she was trying to find strength. Then she took a ragged breath, lifted her head, and smiled weakly. "I guess it was inevitable."

He didn't know what she meant by that. "What was?"

"This. You forgetting me. Don't worry about it. There's nothing you can do." Her throat worked. "Nothing anyone can do."

What was going on?

Her brows lifted. "Is there anything I can get you before I leave? You've already had two aspirin. Maybe I should write that down for you."

He didn't want her to leave. But he didn't know why. "Have you been here the whole time?"

"Yes. I didn't want to leave you alone in case you got worse. The woman at the ER made it seem like that was a possibility, so…" She shrugged.

"You took me to the ER?"

She just nodded, then took a breath.

"That was kind of you." As neighbors went, he'd hit the jackpot. Beautiful, kind, and nurturing. Wasn't much more he could ask for.

"That's what friends do."

"We're friends?" That implied they'd known each other for a while, not that they'd just met. So why couldn't he remember her?

"We are. Or we were. I've been in your house all week, getting you unpacked so you could work on your book."

"You've been here the whole week unpacking my house?"

She swallowed like she was trying to keep her composure. "You moved in last week. That's when we met. The day you arrived. Then your publisher moved the deadline of your book up with the promise of bonus money, and I offered to help you with the house when I wasn't working on my own design stuff."

"You know a lot about me." He hadn't told anyone else about the deadline change or the bonus money. There wouldn't be any way for her to know, except that he'd told her. That made him think everything else she was saying was true, too.

"Do you remember all of that, then?"

"I do. Not the parts about you. But the book stuff."

Her smile wavered, nearly going flat. "I have a curse that makes people forget me. For a whole week, you didn't. It was really nice. I shouldn't have expected it to last. That was my fault. But at least I have the memories."

"That sounds terrible."

"It is." She looked away. "Although I'm not sure if having those memories is a good thing or not..." She blew out a breath and laughed, an odd sound that held no mirth.

"Tell me your name again?"

"Ginny French. I live right next door. We've gone swimming in your pool together. Gone out to the pub in town."

"The pub..." Something came to him. An elusive memory that had no form or substance, but the feeling that he'd been to such a place seemed real.

"Do you remember that?"

"I don't know. Sort of. But not. What did we do there?"

"Had dinner. Then you had a little...problem."

He frowned. "What kind of problem?"

"You saw a flyer on the bathroom bulletin board announcing the pub's Full Moon Party, and you shifted. Do you remember that?"

He squinted, trying to see into the past. The memory was a slippery eel of a thing, slithering out of his grasp just when he thought he had it. "Not fully."

"Your curse took over. You turned into a Yorkie. I got you home."

That unlocked something, and memories came tumbling through. He groaned and closed his eyes, humiliated all over again. "I remember."

"You do?" The excitement in her voice made him refocus on her.

He grimaced. "I remember turning into a Yorkie. But I don't remember you. I know I was there with someone, but every time I try to fix on their face—your face, I suppose—it's a blur. It's the same as when I think back to being in the forest, right before the swarm attacked me."

The hope in her eyes died. "That's my curse erasing me from your memory. Listen, I'm going to go. I need to get a little sleep before I tackle the day's work that's waiting for me. My number is in your phone under Ginny. Call or text if you need me." Then she snorted and shook her head.

"What?"

"You're going to forget me again once I walk out that door, so really, having my number isn't going to help because you're not going to have a clue who it belongs to." She tipped her head back for a second, as if she was petitioning the heavens for help. Then she looked at him again. "I'm going to write a note and leave it on your desk. Maybe that will help."

For reasons he couldn't name, he wasn't ready for her to leave. "So…last week I was able to remember you?"

"Without a hitch." She pondered that. "I wonder if this is just temporary, then. Maybe…you'll remember more as you heal." Her smile returned, a little forced. "That would be nice."

"It would be." And he meant it. Not remembering her made him sad, and there was no logical cause for that except that he must have known her.

She stood there a second longer. "Okay, I'll be next door. I'll put that in the note, too. I hope the pain isn't too bad."

"Thanks. And thank you for everything. Even if I don't remember it." He wouldn't really forget a beautiful, kind woman like this. Would he? All because of some curse? That seemed impossible.

Her smile widened for a moment. "You're welcome."

Then she was gone.

As he lay there, he tried very hard to keep her in his mind. He whispered her name over and over, "Ginny French, Ginny French, Ginny French, Ginny—"

The back door shut, breaking his concentration.

What had he been thinking about? Forgetting something…foreign? What a weird thought. There wasn't anything on his mind. Was there?

He couldn't answer that. And the uneasy feeling that had just come over him added to his distress. What was going on? Something was missing.

Something that had just been here.

Hadn't it?

He'd been struck by lightning once, and because of that, he could no longer trust his ability to successfully shift into a wolf.

Now he'd been stung by lightning bugs, and he felt like he could no longer trust his mind. He closed his eyes and tried to work out what was happening to him, but no answers came.

He didn't like this off-kilter feeling at all. He already hurt head to toe, he didn't need to lose his mental capacity, too. He groaned. Sleep would probably be a good thing, but it wasn't what he felt like doing. He glanced at the bottles of water and aspirin on his nightstand. Where had those come from?

Regardless, he should probably take some.

Gritting his teeth, he forced himself upright. He leaned against the headboard, panting hard against the pain the exertion had caused.

If he ever saw a lightning bug again, he was going to grind it into a stain under his heel. The pain subsided enough for him to attempt moving again. He took two aspirin and washed them down.

Twenty minutes passed with him leaning back, waiting for the pills to kick in. They did, too, taking enough of the edge off that he could move without wanting to scream.

Slowly, using the walls for support, he made his way out of bed. He wore only his boxer shorts. Which meant someone had not only gotten him home, but undressed him, too. But who?

With that on his mind, he went down the hall and into his office. He flipped on the light, a little spark of static electricity biting his skin when he touched the switch.

Apparently, being zapped by lightning bugs hadn't cured *that* problem.

As he sat in his desk chair, he realized too late he should have brought the aspirin with him. In a werewolf's system, they'd last for maybe half as long as they would for a human. Well, he'd be sure to be back in bed before the meds wore off.

He held out his arms, turning them for inspection. He was in bad shape.

Jagged red welts covered every inch of skin he could see. Damn bugs. But he'd been through worse in the Rangers.

Well. He'd been through rough spots that were pretty bad, but he'd never quite experienced pain on this level before.

Doing his best to ignore it, he used the eraser end of a pencil to power up his laptop. Better safe than sorry about a random electrical charge causing the computer's memory to go bad.

While he was waiting for the machine to start, he noticed a folded piece of paper on top of his story notebook. His name was written on it in handwriting he didn't recognize.

He opened it up and read.

Hi Easy,

This is Ginny, your friend and next-door neighbor. I'm the one who brought you home from the woods, but you won't remember me because I'm cursed to be forgotten. All you need to know is I'm next door if you need me. My number is in your phone under Ginny.

Don't be a stranger.

- Ginny

PS. You had two aspirin around 4 a.m.

He read the note a second time, trying to put a face to her name, trying to remember who this woman Ginny was who'd saved his life. He couldn't. That bothered him. A lot. He went to check his phone for her number, but realized he didn't know where his phone was. In the bedroom, maybe?

She'd brought him home from the woods, and she'd given him aspirin. Was she also the one who'd undressed him? Probably. Why couldn't he remember her? Was she young or old? Could a curse really wipe a person from memory?

"Ginny, Ginny, Ginny." He repeated the name, hoping it would jog something loose. It didn't.

His laptop came to life. He logged in and double-clicked on his Word document to open his book. He didn't think there'd be any answers there, but it felt like the right thing to do. And digging into the story might be enough of a distraction to take his mind off the pain.

Probably wouldn't be, but anything was worth a shot.

But before he could write, he had one more thing to do. He opened his desk drawer and pulled out his journal. He wrote in it every morning, and today would be no exception. He thumbed through to the next blank page, catching sight of a name in the scribblings.

Ginny. Over and over.

He absolutely *had* known her.

He went back to the day he'd moved in and started reading.

CHAPTER NINETEEN

In the past week, Ginny had forgotten how it felt to be lonely. Not anymore. She remembered the sensation very distinctly now. It was *all* she could feel.

No. That was a lie. She also felt desperate and sad and like a sucking pit of grief was about to swallow her whole.

She sat on her couch, the only light the soft blue glow of the fish tank, and wept. She didn't like to cry. It was too much like giving in.

Allowing herself to feel the utter despair of her curse led to dark days. The same kind of place she'd been sliding toward before she'd met Easy.

But what did giving in matter now? Easy had looked at her like she was a complete stranger.

Because once again, she was. The man she was crazy about, the only man who'd remembered her, no longer had any idea who she was. Just like every other person in this messed-up town.

How could she be anything but miserable?

Sobs racked her body, but she was powerless to

stop them. Didn't even try, really. Wave after wave of incredible hurt washed over her until at last she lay down, spent and exhausted.

She'd never been suicidal, and she wasn't now. She wasn't going to leave Aunt Gwen on her own, that was for sure. But being dead would be easier. She hurt so much, anything would be better than this.

Except dead.

After a few more tears, she sighed and sat up. She had to get past this, because it wasn't going to change. She was destined to be alone.

Not exactly words that made her feel better, but the truth was often a bitter pill, and accepting the truth, especially when she couldn't change it, had to happen if she was going to move forward.

She put her head against the back of the couch and stared at the ceiling. She was being overly dramatic. Well, maybe not overly—this was a horrible, awful, sucky situation—but she had to get a grip on things before she spiraled into that dark place.

She tried to think of something positive. She was a werewolf and had all the perks that came with that. She made decent money. She had a nice little house. Bob, Comet, and Sparky might not be the cuddliest of pets, but they were still good company. Seymour seemed to know who she was. So did Aunt Gwen on her good days. Ginny was pretty healthy, too.

Other than the curse.

She sniffed. That wasn't helping. "C'mon, focus."

Her mind returned to Easy, replaying the moments after he'd woken up. Had there been even the slightest glimmer of recognition in his eyes?

Sadly, there hadn't been.

But maybe as he healed, his memory would return. Maybe the pain was blocking her out. Or maybe being shocked by the lightning bug stings had erased whatever glitch had allowed him to remember her.

She wanted to see him again. To watch his face when he saw her, to look for any sign that she still existed to him.

But if that didn't happen, she'd be crushed. Again.

Still, if there was the smallest hint that he knew her...then there *was* hope. They could get to know each other again. Maybe eventually, he'd even remember the time they'd already spent together.

But if he didn't, they'd just move forward in whatever way they could. She'd introduce herself every time she saw him. And she'd pray that someday his memory of her would stick. After all, it had happened once. It could happen again. Couldn't it?

What if he *could* remember her again? Would those memories disappear with the next thing that happened to him?

She didn't know for sure why he'd forgotten her this time. Could be due to the lightning bug attack. But it could be some twist of his curse. Or hers. There was no way of knowing.

A fresh tear spilled down her cheek.

It was too much to figure out. And she was too sad to give hope any room. Not right now. Right now, she just had to get through the pain of being forgotten again.

She lay down and drifted off, exhausted by the events of the day and the ache in her heart. She dreamed of Easy. A happy, sweet dream where nothing had changed.

And when she woke, a new feeling filled her. A determination to make that happy, sweet dream a reality. She sat up and scrubbed her hands over her face.

It was light outside. A new morning. She clung to the feeling that everything was going to be all right. No idea how, but that feeling made it possible to breathe.

She got up and walked to the fish tank, switching the blue moonlight LEDs to daytime and flooding the tank with light. "Morning, guys."

Bob made fish faces at her, and Sparky wiggled his little fish butt. Comet was in the rock cave. She sprinkled a few flakes in, causing a small aquatic riot. "I can't let this beat me, you guys. I like him. A lot. I'm not giving up on us that easily. He's worth fighting for."

She watched the goldfish, happy in their insulated fifty-five-gallon world with their bubble maker and plastic plants and fake rock cave. That was the life right there.

"I can't rush it, though. And I can't force it. What's going to happen is going to happen. I just have to hope that what happens is really good. Like the first time we met. I have to hope for that."

Hope. Funny word. Four letters that made the future seem bright even when the past was dim.

She put her finger on the glass. "I think I just have to accept that we're starting over and..." She stared into the water as it blurred away, lost to the new thought in her head. "We need to start over. *I* need to start over."

She blinked, focusing on the fish again. "You guys, that's what I'm going to do. I'm going to repeat the first day I met him. Sort of."

Sparky's little mouth rounded into an O.

She nodded. "I know. Brilliant."

What time was it? A little after nine. So she'd gotten some sleep. It would have to be enough. And with the new surge of energy running through her, it felt like it would be. She'd probably crash later, but for now, she had a plan to execute.

Work first. She checked her email, answered the most important ones, did a quick change on one project, made notes on another, then jumped into the shower.

Hair and makeup, done. Cute outfit on (white jean shorts, top with black and white polka dots, black wedges). Breakfast eaten (a handful of truffles and a big piece of the Chocolate Dragon egg, but still). And she was out the door. She had a package to mail, so an actual errand to run, and she really needed to see Aunt Gwen, but the rest of the day was going to be a repeat of when she first met Easy.

After getting her package taken care of, she went to Deja Brew and had an iced coffee. Partially because she needed the caffeine and partially because it was what she'd done the morning he'd moved in. As she drank it, she watched people go by and thought about her life before Easy, then how wonderful it had been with him in it and how wonderful it would hopefully be again in the future.

She smiled, still filled with the belief that good things were going to happen. That she was going to make them happen. She clung to the thought, pushing it out into the universe with a fierceness that defied failure.

She finished her coffee and got a second one to go. Aunt Gwen loved iced coffees.

Ginny drove straight to Emerald Manor. Drink in hand, she strode in and went right to the reception desk. "Good morning. Ginny French to see Gwen French. She's in Suite 19."

Cathy, the receptionist, smiled. "Sure thing. Let me just pull up her file...there you are on the visitor list."

Cathy stared at her computer screen, then glanced at Ginny.

Ginny knew what the issue was. Same one she almost always had. Cathy could see that Ginny was a regular visitor, but she didn't recognize her.

Ginny relied on her old standby. "I used to be a blonde."

Cathy, happy for the easy out, smiled and

laughed. "Who hasn't, right? Are you taking her out today?"

"Not today."

"All right. Go on through and enjoy your visit."

Ginny walked past the family recreation area and the main dining room, then down a long, bright hall. As assisted-living places went, this side of Emerald Manor was more high-end resort with great medical than nursing home.

Her aunt's suite had all the comforts of a condo, including amenities like the pool, the exercise room, spa facilities, a beauty parlor, library, twice-daily trips into town, planned activities... The residents probably led more-active lives than Ginny did.

At least now anyway.

She knocked on her aunt's door. "Aunt Gwen? It's your niece Ginny."

A moment later, her aunt opened the door. A familiar uncertainty filled Gwen's once-bright hazel eyes. "Hi."

Ginny smiled and lifted the iced coffee and gave the ice a little rattle. "I brought you your favorite. Iced vanilla latte."

"How nice." Gwen opened the door a little more. "Why don't you come in? Ginny, right?"

"Right. I'm your niece. Robert's daughter. You remember your brother, Robert?" Ginny held out her wrist so Aunt Gwen could see his ID bracelet.

Gwen looked at it and nodded. "Yes. Terrible thing. He died many years ago. He and his wife. Left their three-year-old daughter behind. I raised her, you know. Wonderful little girl..." She stared at Ginny, her gaze so intense Ginny thought she was seeing the past and not the present.

"Ginny," her aunt whispered. "Is that you?"

Ginny's heart constricted with love and happiness. Today was one of the good days. "Yes, Aunt Gwen. It's me." She held up her wrist. "See? I have Daddy's bracelet."

Gwen touched it lightly, then wrapped her in a hug. "I'm so glad you came to visit me. I love you so much."

The words almost unraveled the emotions Ginny had managed to tie up neatly. Her eyes watered, and she made herself laugh to keep things light. "I love you, too."

Aunt Gwen released Ginny after another second or two. "Let's sit on the patio, shall we? It's such a nice day."

"It is. And that would be great."

"Do you want something to drink?"

"Nope. But you enjoy your iced latte. I know how you love them."

"I do." Gwen took the drink, then headed for the patio.

Ginny followed her out to the little brick-paved area off the living room. They sat in the glider, but there was a chaise out there, too. Ginny knew on nice days, her aunt liked to nap outside. It was a wolf thing. She did it sometimes herself on the back deck.

A tall white privacy fence divided Gwen's side

from the neighbor's side, but Ginny didn't hear anyone next door.

Gwen patted Ginny's knee. "How are things, honey?"

"They're...okay."

"There's a man, isn't there?" She lifted the straw to her mouth.

Ginny looked at her aunt. "How do you know that? Do you remember me telling you about him?"

"No, sorry." She tapped the side of her nose as she finished a long sip. "But I can smell a male wolf on you."

Aunt Gwen's mind might give her trouble, but the rest of her was just fine. "My new neighbor. Bought the McKinleys' place. He's really nice."

"But?"

Ginny told her everything, including all the stuff she'd told her aunt already. From the kiss that should have been forgotten to the lightning bug attack and Easy losing his ability to remember her. "I'm not giving up, though."

"Nor should you. He sounds like a man worth fighting for."

Ginny nodded. "That's exactly what I told my fish this morning."

Aunt Gwen gave her a funny look. "You really do need a man in your life."

"It's been kind of hard, what with the curse and all."

"I know." Gwen sighed. "There's got to be a way for him to remember you. Especially in this town."

"You'd think so."

Gwen set her empty cup on the ground, then crossed her arms. "What about that shop in town that sells potions and things? Spellbound? You know, Lucas swears by their full moon cream."

Lucas Cartwright was her aunt's gentleman friend and a fellow wolf shifter.

"Aunt Gwen! I don't think you should be telling me Lucas's business. I also don't want to know how you know he uses that." For a werewolf, full moon cream was almost the equivalent of a certain little blue pill in unisex form. It enabled a shifter to shift at will, if they couldn't otherwise. No lunar help required.

Gwen laughed. "We're both consenting adults, and we like to go for off-cycle runs occasionally."

Ginny gave her aunt a hard stare. "Are you seeing Lucas? I know you're friends with him, but are you…more than that?"

"I thought you didn't want to know about personal business."

"Aunt Gwen."

The sly smile on her aunt's face was answer enough. "He's a lovely man. He'd make a wonderful stepuncle for you."

Ginny slipped her hand into her aunt's. "I'm happy for you. I really am."

"Thank you. I'm happy for you, too. But I'd like to be happier. Go to Spellbound and ask if they have something that might help you. It can't hurt."

"No, I don't suppose it can. I should have asked when I was there last night."

Aunt Gwen kissed her cheek. "Go on, now. You've spent enough time with this old woman."

Ginny shook her head. "Never." It was especially hard to leave on one of her aunt's good days.

"Lucas is coming over in a little bit. We're going to the spa for a couple's massage."

Ginny stood and held her hands up. "Okay, going. You two have fun. Love you."

"Love you, too, honey. Next time, you bring that young man with you, you hear?"

CHAPTER TWENTY

From Emerald Manor, Ginny went straight to Black Horse Bakery. Spellbound could wait until she was on her way home.

Nasha was at the counter and just finishing up with a customer. Ginny smiled as she got six blackberry pies and one chocolate cake in three separate shopping bags. She loaded the bags into her Jeep and drove to Miller's Lake, turning onto the dirt road that would take her to the old boardwalk and fishing pier. As usual, the area was deserted.

Good. Just like the day Easy had moved to town.

Bags with the pies in hand, she walked out to the very end of the pier, slipped her shoes off, and sat, letting her legs dangle and her toes almost touch the water. "Seymour, you around, buddy?"

Nothing. She scanned the surface of the lake. *Please don't let him have forgotten me, too.* Today was on an upswing. She wanted to keep it that way.

Then the water rippled.

She grinned and gave the nearest shopping bag a little rustle. "I have pie."

His head rose out of the water as he swam toward her. He made his little throat noises of happiness.

All was well.

"I've missed you, too. And a lot has happened since I was here last. Long story. Short version is a lot good, but some bad."

Seymour honked at her.

"You want the whole story?"

He nodded.

"Okay, but I'm still giving you the condensed version, because I don't want to bore you silly, and I know you're waiting for pie. I met a guy who could remember me, a wolf like me, and we were kind of falling for each other, but then he had an accident, and now he doesn't remember me anymore."

Seymour made a sad sound.

"Thanks. I was pretty miserable, but I'm trying to focus on what might still be possible, you know? Think positive and all that. My plan is to meet him all over again and see if we can make some memories that stick. Plus, my aunt said a shop in town might have a potion or something that could help. I have my doubts. It's not like I haven't asked around before. Anyway, I'm kind of hoping that as he heals from his accident that his memories will return. If not...I don't know."

He tipped his head like he was listening, then stuck his face into the water and blew air through his snout, making bubbles.

"No, I can't swim today. I have to take a cake to my wolf friend. It's all part of meeting him again.

But hey, don't you want pie?" She took the first pie out of the bag, got it positioned for flipping, and waited.

Tongue out, he grinned.

"That's what I thought. Ready?"

He swam closer and opened his mouth.

She launched the pie. He caught it with a snap of his jaws, swallowing it down in a couple of big chomps.

"That's not quite what I had in mind when I said you needed to chew more, but I suppose it's an improvement." She laughed. This was exactly what she needed. A great visit with her aunt, then a little fresh air and some time with Seymour, her two constant reminders that she *could* be remembered. Well, her aunt didn't really count as a *constant*, but today, she did.

Ginny fed him the rest of the pies, then bundled up the trash. She stood on the end of the pier and smiled at her friend. "I'll see you again soon, okay? I promise that next time I come, I'll swim. Deal?"

He trilled his answer, then bobbed his head as a fly buzzed around him. It landed on his ear. But only for a second. A little crack of electricity broke the stillness. The fly fell off.

She shook her head. "We really could have used you in the Dark Acres." She wiggled her fingers at him. "Bye, Seymour."

With a burble, he slipped back under the surface as she walked away. The water held only the faintest ripple by the time she got back in her Jeep. The whole interior of the vehicle smelled like chocolate cake, even with the top off.

She smiled. "Time to go meet Easy. Again."

/

Easy woke to the sound of a car door shutting. He'd fallen asleep in his recliner watching ESPN. He blinked a few times, then checked the nearest clock. Huh. He'd been out for a few hours. And he'd been dreaming. About…a very attractive woman in a pink bikini? That was nice. But random.

Or was it?

He rolled his head back and forth. The pain wasn't as bad as it had been earlier, but he'd taken more aspirin before nodding off. His journal was tucked between his leg and the arm of the chair.

Welts still covered him, but he'd slathered on the salve from the jar on his nightstand, and it seemed to be helping. At least they weren't itchy anymore. And they didn't look quite as red.

All in all, he was doing a little better. Thanks to…someone. But who?

No one came to mind. Then he saw a sticky note on the arm of the chair. It just said *journal*.

He pulled his journal out. There was another sticky note on the front of it.

Ginny. Read today's entry.

He couldn't remember who that was, what she looked like, or how he knew her, but he figured the journal entry would help.

He turned to the day's entry.

Ginny is your neighbor and your friend, and until you were stung by the lightning bugs, you were falling in love with her. Even planning on proposing in a couple months. She's that great. She's also an incredible kisser, a kind and generous person, and a beautiful woman with a killer body. And a wolf like you. She knows about your curse. Get to know her again. Do not forget her. You will. She's cursed to be forgotten. But try not to anyway. And write down everything you do with her while you can remember it. You owe her a lot. Read the last week of entries. Or just ask her to explain.

Wow. He read the entry again, hoping it would help him recall what she looked like. It didn't. He scanned last week's entries, getting a bigger picture of what she'd done for him and how he felt about her.

His stomach growled. He sighed and closed the journal. He should get something to eat, but he had no idea what there was in the house. He'd probably have to order something.

His doorbell rang. Had he already ordered something? That would be too convenient. He got up, thankful he'd put on lounge pants and a T-shirt, and shuffled slowly to the door. Moving exacerbated the remaining pain.

He winced but made it to the door before whoever it was rang again. He opened it. "Hi."

"Hi there." The woman smiled. She had a shopping bag from the bakery in one hand, the faint aroma of chocolate unmistakable. And she was the sexiest, cutest thing he'd seen in a long time. "I'm Ginny French. I'm your—"

"Neighbor," he finished. "Wow. *You're* Ginny? This is great."

She gasped. "Do you remember me?"

"No. Well, sort of, but not exactly." He moved back, opening the door wider. "Come in, I want to show you something."

She held up the bakery bag. "I brought you a chocolate cake."

"Perfect timing, I'm starving."

She laughed as she came in. "This might not be the most nutritious thing to eat while you're recovering. Hey, how are you feeling? How's the pain? The welts look a little better. Are you using that salve I picked up?"

"You got me that? Thanks. Yeah, I'm using it. I think it's helping. The welts seem a little better." He held his arms out. "The pain is manageable, but that might be because I'm eating aspirin like candy." He took a good look at her, trying to imprint her face on his memory. "You really are beautiful."

She smiled, then blushed a little. "That's very sweet of you, thank you."

"I know you have a curse that makes you impossible to remember. And I know you know about my curse."

"All true. And excellent that you know that." She canted her head. "But how do you know that?"

"Because I wrote it down in my journal and left myself a note to read it."

"That was a great idea. I take it you got the note I left for you by your laptop?"

"I did." He was afraid to stop looking at her. "Am I going to keep forgetting you?"

"I don't know." The question had brought sadness into her eyes. "I hope not, but more than likely…yes."

"I need to take your picture. I need to take a picture of us together. A couple of them. In fact, I should print some out and put them around the house."

"That's a really good idea, too." She dug into her purse. "I went by the shop where I got your salve, and they sold me this." She pulled out a small brown glass pot. "It's cerebellex powder. You're supposed to mix it with water and drink it while concentrating on the thing you want to remember."

He shrugged, which made him wince. "Anything's worth a shot."

"That's what I figured. My aunt suggested it."

"You have an aunt here in town?"

"I do. I've told you about her, but I'm guessing the memory of her is attached to the memory of me. Aunt Gwen lives at Emerald Manor, the retirement place here in town. They have an assisted-living wing. She had a stroke not long after I graduated from college, and since then she's had memory issues. Not exactly dementia, not exactly senility… just good days and bad days. You'd think that would have prepared me for this curse." She smiled sadly. "It didn't. But today was a good day, and she remembered me. She's the only person who can since you…you know."

"Right. But with any luck, I'll be able to remember you again." He rubbed his hands together. He needed to put all of this into his journal. The more details he had, the harder she'd be to forget. He hoped. "What do you say we have some of that cake and talk some more about the week I don't remember? Maybe take a few pictures together? You have the advantage on me here, since you remember everything."

She smiled. "But I'll be happy to tell you about it."

"Good. I want to hear it in your words." He thought that might somehow make the experiences more real for him. Maybe even help bring some of the memories back.

They went into the kitchen together. He got plates and silverware out while she unboxed the cake.

"You know," she said, "I organized your kitchen for you."

He paused and thought back to his journal, then nodded. "You did the whole house."

"That's right. Do you remember that?"

"I remember an entry from my journal." He shook his head. "You already know what I do for a living, but I journal every day. When I saw your note on my desk, I knew I had to write about what happened to me in my journal. But when I opened it up, I found your name all over the last week of entries. All the things we did together. All the fun we had. How you helped me. Man, you really helped me."

He stared at the counter, the pages of his journal flashing through his mind. "Including during the incident at the pub."

"I did what any friend would do." She sniffed. "I can't believe you wrote about me in your journal."

He nodded, lifting his head.

There were tears in her eyes.

"Sorry," she said. "It's been a very emotional half day for me. Or fourteen hours. However long it's been since we walked into the enchanted forest. I can't believe you wrote about me."

"I did. I'm going to keep doing it, too. With more details. I hope that it might help."

She smiled. "So you didn't have a lot of details in those first pages?"

He wasn't sure what she was hinting at, but he had a feeling. "I had enough."

Her cheeks went slightly pink.

He grinned. "Enough to know what a good kisser you are."

She laughed and shook her head, causing tendrils of silky brown hair to fall around her face. "Yeah, well…you're not so bad yourself."

"Glad it's mutual. I'd hate to find out it was one-sided." He sliced the cake into large pieces.

"Did you write about our little fight?"

He looked up. "We had a fight?"

"After the pub incident."

"Oh. That." He added a slab of cake to each plate. "Yes, I wrote about it. And how I bought you flowers and chocolates."

"The best flowers and chocolates I've ever gotten." She snorted. "Also the only flowers and chocolates I've gotten, but they're amazing."

"I tried to tell you what was best for you." What a fool he'd been.

She nodded. "You did. But you apologized. I was equally to blame, which is why I also said I was sorry. I only bring it up because going forward, when things get hard—and they will, I'm sure of it—I don't want us to go through that again."

"Things are already hard, aren't they?" He slid a plate toward her. "They have to be. For you anyway. You have memories of us that I don't. Sure, I have my journal entries, but right now that's like reading a story about someone else."

"Are you trying to tell me you don't want to try to recapture all that?"

"No, not at all. Just asking for your patience, I guess." He pulled his phone out. He needed photos of them. Lots of photos.

She nodded. "I can do that. I've done it for the last ten years with pretty much everyone around me. But this time is different. This time, I really care about the outcome."

He held his phone up to take a picture of them together and smiled. "Good. Me, too. Now, smile. This is going to be my home screen. Me and Ginny French. World's best neighbor. Maybe also the world's hottest neighbor."

She laughed, and he snapped the picture. If there

was anything he could do to remember her, he was going to do it.

He took a few more pics, then put his phone on the counter. "Now, about that cerebellex powder…"

Chapter Twenty-One

As they each downed a glass of the powder mixed into water (which tasted like a very bitter lemonade), Ginny was struck by Easy's request for her to be patient with him.

Was that really what he wanted? Or was that his way of starting some kind of slow let-down process, preparing her for the day when he'd tell her it wasn't working out?

Maybe she was being paranoid, but maybe she wasn't. If she put herself in his shoes, she understood how strange it would be to be with someone who had completely different memories of your life than you had. Memories that also included emotions you no longer had.

Weird, *awkward*, and *uncomfortable* would all apply here.

Worse, he might feel like he was being forced into something. A relationship, a friendship, whatever it was, and he just didn't know how to tell her he wanted out. He was a nice guy, and the nicest thing was to let her down gently. To ease her into the *it's not you, it's me* speech.

This was the reality that she lived with constantly.

But never in the history of her curse had anyone had notes to look back on. Easy did. And he might have written something in his journal that had made him decide this second chance wasn't for him.

What that thing might be, she didn't know. And she wasn't about to steal his journal to read it for herself.

But the questions were there in her mind now. And would be until she no longer had a reason to wonder.

It took the shine off things, for sure. But she tried to remind herself that she could also be wrong. Very wrong. This might all be some overthinking on her part born out of too many years without much deep human interaction.

And he was clearly going to some effort to remember her. She had to focus on that.

So she smiled and bantered and kept up a good front while they ate their cake and quickly realized the cerebellex powder didn't seem to have any immediate effect. She filled him in on all the little details he hadn't written down, doing her best to focus on the fun, positive stuff and keep things light.

But all the while, a part of her brain was obsessing over how difficult it was going to be having a relationship under these circumstances. Every time he forgot her, he'd lose his feelings for her. Which would be awkward for him. But devastating for her.

Was she up for this emotionally? What if he decided it was too much work? She couldn't let it go, try as she might.

And if he decided that he'd be better if she didn't know about his curse? What if he was embarrassed by the fact that not only did she know, she'd experienced it firsthand?

And what if he came to blame her for the lightning bug attack?

He wouldn't be wrong. She *was* the reason they'd gone into the enchanted forest.

Either way, there was nothing she could do to counteract those things. They were done deals. History.

All she could do was keep moving forward and hope she was wrong. Actually, she'd never wanted to be wrong so much in her life.

"This cake is amazing."

She glanced at his plate. "And almost gone. I guess you really were hungry."

"Still am."

"So have a second piece."

He shook his head. "I need protein. A steak. Or a burger, maybe."

She looked at the clock on the microwave behind him. "It *is* lunchtime. A little past, actually. You want me to go into town and get something?"

"No, I want to go out."

"You feel well enough?"

He stared at her for a moment. "I do. So long as we go anywhere but the pub."

She laughed. But was that a clue about what was on his mind? "Okay. The diner? They have good burgers."

"Let's do it." He licked the remaining chocolate crumbs off his fork. "Then we can come back here and have more cake."

She shook her head, smiling. She was being silly with all this overthinking. Would a man who wanted to be rid of her invite her back to his house? Chances were, he wouldn't. Why was she stressing about this? She needed to stop and let things happen as they were going to happen. Wasn't that the plan anyway?

And if Easy decided at some point that he didn't want to get to know her again, or to see what could be with them again, he would tell her. Because he was a nice guy, but he was also a straight-up guy.

The night they'd gone to the pub, he'd told her about his book deal and the workload that was going to make him scarce. Proof that he wasn't the type to hide what was going on with him.

Easy drove, and at the diner, they settled into a booth and ordered. Burgers for both of them, complete with fries and chocolate malts.

Conversation was light and easy, and halfway through the meal, Ginny felt like things were back to how they'd been before the lightning bug attack. She knew they weren't really, but she could sense what was possible now. See a bright, beautiful light at the end of what had felt yesterday like an impossibly dark tunnel.

Hope grew inside her again.

She picked up a fry. "Are you going to write this all down?"

He nodded, burger in one hand. "Everything. What we ate, where we sat, what our server's name was. The more details the better, I figure."

Yeah, this was not a man about to tell her it wasn't working. This was a man working to keep her. The thought filled her heart with gratitude and happiness. And love.

His gaze narrowed as his mouth curved up. He pointed at her with a fry. "Your eyes are glowing. What are you thinking about?"

She glanced at her plate, suddenly a little shy. "You. And how lucky I am that you're willing to go through all this."

"Willing to go through all—" He leaned forward. "You're the one that has to shoulder the bulk of the burden. The one who has to deal with me not remembering."

"True, but the way I see it, you're the one with the heavy lifting to do. You have to write it all down, reread it all the time in hopes of remembering. Deal with me knowing more…" She shrugged. "I guess we both have our part to play."

He nodded. "We do. But I think it's been so long since you've had real human interaction that you've forgotten the lengths people are willing to go for someone they care about."

He cared about her. All she could do was smile and whisper, "Thank you."

He winked at her. "Thank *you*. I still haven't repaid you for all the work you did at my house."

"You're doing that right now." She picked up her burger again. "Speaking of work, are you getting back on schedule with the writing tomorrow?"

"I have to. But I'm not waiting until tomorrow. I'm starting this afternoon when we get back."

"Good. I'm glad. I don't want you to get behind. Hey, tonight after you hit your goal, you want to come over for dinner? Nothing fancy. I was going to roast a chicken. Make some mashed potatoes."

"That sounds great. I'd love to. It'll be a good motivator to get the words done." He smiled. "I think the more time we spend together, the better."

"Me, too." She took a bite of her burger, happier than she'd thought she could be after everything that had happened.

"What are you doing with your day tomorrow?"

"A little work in the morning, then I'll go visit my aunt, run a few errands, then home to work until it's time to make dinner. Nothing exciting. Oh, you know, I still haven't finished your garage."

He shook his head. "Don't worry about that. Maybe sometime I could go visit your aunt with you."

"She'd like that. She asked me to bring you by."

His brows lifted, and he held a fry midair. "You told your aunt about me?"

"I did."

"Then I really do need to meet her, don't I?"

Ginny smiled, her entire being happy. "You do.

She'd love you. But she's not always completely there. Just so you know. Sometimes she's right as rain, others…she struggles."

Concern and understanding filled his gaze. "My grandfather lost his battle with Alzheimer's a few years back. I know that's not what your aunt has, but I understand what good days and bad days are for someone with cognition problems."

Ginny ran a fry through the dwindling pool of ketchup on the edge of her plate. "Then you know, for sure. It's hard. I hate the bad days. She's the woman who raised me. As much my mother as my real mom was. And all I want is for her to be herself again. The vibrant, funny, wonderful woman who put her life on hold to take care of me."

"If I can get back into a good rhythm with this book and get ahead by a chapter, maybe we could take her to Nightingale Park. It's in my journal that it's a good place to go for sun. If you think she'd like that sort of thing."

"She'd love it. I was thinking about taking her up there anyway." Ginny nodded, so overwhelmed with affection for the man across from her that she thought she might blurt out how she truly felt about him. But now wasn't the time for that. Not by a long shot. "I've taken her up there before, and she's always loved it. I love it. It's funny, after you've lived here awhile, you kind of forget about the sun. But take a day and go above the twilight line, and you'll feel like a switch has been flipped inside you. It's amazing what a few hours of sunlight can do for you."

"Then we'll do it. For sure. More writing motivation for me. And trust me, I need it. The promise of the bonus money is great, but rewards of fun seem to work better." He shrugged. "Not sure what that says about me that fifty big ones don't drive me as much as a picnic in the sun."

She ate her last fry. "I think it says volumes about what an amazing person you are."

Burger finished, he wiped his hands off. "I think you're pretty amazing, too. And as much as I hate to end this lunch, I really should get to work."

"Me, too." She picked up the remaining piece of her burger. "Does that mean you're feeling pretty good now?"

He hesitated, then nodded. "I wouldn't say I'm a hundred percent, but the pain is pretty minimal." He glanced at his arms. "Welts are mostly gone. They still itch a little. Probably a sign they're healing. I have a feeling tonight's going to be an early one, though."

"Then don't worry about coming over for dinner tonight. We've both had a long day. I'll make the chicken and mashed potatoes tomorrow."

"Yeah?" He nodded. "Okay, that would be good. I'm already starting to feel like I could crash."

"Same here. I only had a few hours of sleep."

He paid the bill and drove them back home. He parked in his driveway, then got out and came around to her side to open her door. "I'll walk you to your porch."

She laughed as she got out. "It's not that far. You don't have to."

He reached around her to close her door, putting himself in her personal space. "I want to."

Her breath caught at the commanding tone of his voice. It was as if his wolf was speaking to hers. And hers was listening. "Okay."

They came around the back of the car, went down to the sidewalk, and made the small trek to her front porch.

He put his hand on the small of her back as they went up the steps.

She unlocked her door, but didn't open it. "I guess I'll see you tomorrow. Thanks for lunch."

"You're welcome. And you will see me tomorrow." Then he leaned in and kissed her softly on the mouth, lingering for only a second and zapping her with a little spark of static electricity.

Her breath was stuck again, keeping her from saying anything.

"Too soon?" he asked, eyes glowing.

She shook her head—she could manage that much—and whispered, "No."

"Good. Because I really wanted to do *this*." He threaded his hands through her hair and pulled her close, covering her mouth with his in a kiss that wasn't nearly as soft or gentle as the first one, something she was perfectly happy about.

The kiss lasted longer, too. Long enough to send a shiver of pleasure through her, long enough to raise the hair on her arms, long enough to make her knees melt.

Long enough to erase any lingering doubt about

his commitment to getting to know her again.

She grabbed hold of his waist as his arms encircled her. He was a hard plane of warm muscle, and the low rumbly growl vibrating out of his throat set parts of her on fire.

At last, he took his mouth off hers, but held on to her. "I want to run with you some night soon."

She nodded. "Me, too."

He pulled her hand to his mouth, kissed her knuckles, then released her. "See you for dinner tomorrow, Ginny French."

"Tomorrow. After your words are done."

"Exactly." He went down the steps, but kept glancing back at her. When he hit the yard, he waved and crossed toward his house.

She waved back, but watched him walk away until he was on his own property again, headed for his own porch. Then she went in, closed the door, and leaned against it. Today had started out as a very bad day, but it sure had done a one-eighty.

That was life in Shadowvale, though. You never knew what the day might bring you.

And while she and Easy might not be back to where they were before the lightning bug attack, things were looking good.

Really good.

With a smile, Ginny went to her office to get some work done. She couldn't wait to give Aunt Gwen the amazing update.

Tomorrow was going to be even better. Ginny just had a feeling.

CHAPTER TWENTY-TWO

After walking through his front door, the first thing Easy did was write in his journal. He didn't want to lose a single detail about the afternoon, so he wrote and wrote and wrote. Nothing was too small to include.

He hung on to the memories better than he thought he would, maybe because of the cerebellex powder. Whatever the reason was for him being able to remember her, he didn't waste a moment.

But even as he filled the pages of his journal, Ginny's name and face were being pulled from his memory. He took out his phone and brought up the pictures he'd taken of them, as well as a few he'd snuck of her alone. He made one of them the home screen on his phone just like he'd told her.

The sensation of losing her from his mind didn't go away, though. It was a struggle to keep her there. Even with the pictures and the journal. That made him sad. And angry. After everything he'd read about her in his notes and the great lunch they'd had, he wanted to remember her more than ever.

But her curse had other ideas.

At last, he'd put everything he could remember into the day's entry. He closed his journal, left himself a note to read it, then went to work on his book.

He managed what he could. A little more than half a chapter, which wasn't enough, but by nine he was fading. He popped a few aspirin against the final dregs of pain, eked out one more paragraph, then saved his work and went to crash on the couch and watch baseball.

He was less than an inning into the game when the itching started up again. He slathered on some of the ointment. Relief followed, and he could feel himself nodding off.

Less than an inning after that and he gave in to the urge to sleep. He woke up to light outside the windows and a regional morning news show on the TV.

He rubbed his face. Sleeping on the couch wasn't really his thing, but he felt surprisingly good.

Then it struck him. No more pain or itching. None. He checked his arms. The welts were completely gone. Not a single mark or scar remained.

Outstanding. The day they'd lasted was enough. He sat up and yawned, staring at the news without really seeing it. Amazing the television hadn't woken him up during the night, but apparently he'd been so tired he'd slept straight through. Well, he wasn't tired anymore, and it was time to get his day going.

He turned the television off, then went into the kitchen to start some coffee.

He got a pot going, then stretched. It was good to move without pain. What he needed was a run. In his wolf form, sure, but he knew better than to do that in the neighborhood, no matter how lenient the town might be about supernaturals.

So a run in human form would have to do. It wasn't a hardship. It was how he'd started most of his mornings when he'd lived in the city. While the coffee brewed, he went to the bedroom and changed into shorts and a T-shirt, then tied on his trainers and went back to the kitchen.

He had a feeling he was forgetting something, but then again, he hadn't had coffee yet. It wasn't quite ready, so he went into his office to fire up his laptop and check email.

The light switch zapped him when he turned on the light. He frowned. Man, that was getting old. It was only a small annoyance, but one he'd like to be done with all the same. Like a hangnail.

He sat at his desk and peeled the sticky note off his computer. *Read your journal.*

Why had he left himself that note? He wrote in his journal daily, but he didn't usually read it. He opened the drawer where he kept it and was greeted with another note telling him to read yesterday's entry.

He flipped to that page. And found it was nearly three pages long on both sides of the paper. This would need coffee and more than a minute.

Thankfully, the coffeepot sputtered with the sounds of the brew being done. He took the journal into the kitchen and poured a big mug of coffee, then took both out onto the back patio.

Steam rose off the pool in the cool morning air, giving his backyard a lot more atmosphere than usual. He stretched out on one of the chaises, took a sip of coffee, then with mug in hand, started reading.

Between the coffee and the journal entry, he was well and truly awake.

He glanced from his handwriting to the house next door. Where Ginny French lived. The name was new to him, but at the same time, it wasn't somehow. He didn't remember her, didn't remember the lunch they'd had yesterday, but he wanted to.

He read a little more, discovering he'd taken pictures. His phone. He'd left it on the charger in the kitchen last night and had yet to touch it this morning. He took everything back inside and tapped the screen to wake it up.

A beautiful face greeted him.

Ginny.

Wow. What a knockout. He stared at her until the screen started to go dark again. He touched it to keep it bright. She was beautiful. And a wolf. And apparently, he'd kissed her after lunch. A pretty good kiss.

One he was bummed to have forgotten.

A new feeling settled over him unlike anything he'd felt before. It was longing mixed with a little sadness, but there was also an odd tint of jealousy and, most unexpectedly, some anger. As he studied her face, he tried to unpack some of that.

For one thing, he wanted to remember her and their time together, and he was angry he couldn't. He was also jealous of the version of him that had been with her, held her, kissed her. More than anything, there was the understanding of her curse that kept them apart like this.

But another feeling surfaced, too. The desire not to let the curse win. He smiled and flipped through to the rest of the pictures he'd taken. In one of them, she was gazing at him with an expression that, to Easy, looked very much like love.

Could this woman love him? Even while knowing about his own curse?

He stared at that picture the longest, trying to see the truth. But maybe he was projecting that expression onto her. Maybe he was just wishing a woman this beautiful might fall for a man in his current cursed state.

Of course, if his journal was correct—and why wouldn't it be—he was definitely falling for her. Which meant anything was possible.

He finished his coffee, repeating her name in his head like a mantra. He was going out to run, then he was going to shower and write two chapters.

Then, according to his journal, he was going next door to have dinner with Ginny. He smiled. If that wasn't the best motivation for getting his chapters written, then great motivation didn't exist.

Three and a half miles, one very hot shower, and

a protein shake later, Easy was planted at his desk. He had a fresh mug of coffee, his laptop was humming, his Word doc was staring back at him, and Tomahawk Jones was about to get into worse trouble than he'd been in since the book had begun.

Life was good.

The words came fast, and he slipped into the zone with no problem. Page after page, the story seemed to fly from his fingertips onto the screen. Good words, too. The kind that with a little manipulation could be turned into great words.

Then Easy hit a snag. He needed an old enemy to cross paths with Tomahawk, but he'd already killed that guy off two chapters ago. He'd thought that had felt like it was happening too early on, but he'd ignored his inner editor. Sometimes that happened, where his brain would send him a warning that he wasn't making the right decision for the story. And his brain was pretty much right every time, which meant not listening created more work.

Bringing that bad guy in now would give the reader a real gut punch, but doing that would mean a major rewrite of the opening chapters. And that meant no new words for the rest of the day.

It had to happen, but it felt like a step backward. Right when he'd been making such good progress.

He should have listened to that little voice in his head telling him something was wrong, but he'd plowed forward because he'd been more concerned about putting words on the page. He swore loudly at his own poor planning.

The lights flickered at his outburst, then one of the recessed lights overhead popped and went dark.

He growled. Great. Just what he needed. But the light had to be changed. The dining room had a great view of the front yard, but it was a little dark. And in a town that didn't get any sun, a little dark meant borderline cave interior.

With an exasperated sigh, he got up and went to get the ladder and his rubber utility gloves from the garage. Replacement bulbs were in the pantry. He wasn't sure how they'd gotten there, but he'd seen them this morning when he got the protein shake mix out.

In fact, the pantry was incredibly organized. Something he didn't remember doing at all.

The garage, on the other hand, still looked like a cyclone had hit it. A box cyclone.

He hadn't been out here since he'd moved in, and boxes were everywhere. Why was the rest of the house in such great shape, but this area was still a mess? He felt like he should know the answer to that, but he didn't.

Now wasn't the time to worry about that, though. He had a bulb to change and a rewrite to get done.

The ladder was easy to find. It was resting against the far wall. He took that inside and set it up in the dining room under the burned-out bulb, then went back to the garage. He needed his utility gloves. They had a rubber coating, and ever since the lightning strike, he wore them when he worked on anything electrical.

It was probably overkill, like how he always turned his laptop on by pushing the power button with the eraser end of a pencil, but with the way electricity was always sparking and snapping around him, he was okay with erring on the side of caution.

The stacks of boxes were all labeled *garage*, although a few also said *tools*. None, unfortunately, said *gloves*.

He grabbed the box cutter sitting on the workbench and started opening, but after a few boxes in, he hadn't turned up anything close to gloves.

He didn't have the time for this. He was just going to have to chance it. What was the worst that could happen anyway? He'd get shocked and stop shifting into creatures that weren't wolves?

With a sigh, he went back in the house. He made a quick detour to the pantry to get a new bulb, then went to the dining room. He turned the light switch off, casting the whole room in shadow.

Then, bulb in hand, he climbed up the ladder. He hesitated before touching the bulb, but that was the kind of silliness that made him roll his eyes at himself. "Just get it done. You're wasting time."

He grabbed the bulb. No shock. Breathing out in relief, he braced his fingers around the bulb and started twisting, easing the bulb out of the socket, being careful it didn't slip from his grasp.

Cleaning up shattered glass definitely wasn't on his schedule.

Bulb out, he lifted the new one and seated it, then started screwing it into place. On the second twist, the bulb flashed with a bright flare of electricity.

The bolt shot down his arm and into his body, knocking him back. He fell off the ladder and onto the hardwood floor, forcing the breath from his lungs with the impact.

The bulb that had been in his hand popped, sending glass everywhere. Electrical tremors ran through him. He gasped once for air, then everything went dark.

CHAPTER TWENTY-THREE

Ginny arrived at the reception desk at Emerald Manor at eight a.m., the start of visiting hours. Normally, she would have done more of her design work first, but after handling a couple quick emails, she decided she wanted to see Aunt Gwen more.

Ginny had a lot to tell her. And the emails would always be there. Aunt Gwen wouldn't. Getting here early also meant they could spend more time together. Ginny wanted to take her into town for breakfast, then out to the lake to see Seymour. Maybe they'd even do a little shopping later, depending on how the day went.

Nightingale Park could wait until Easy was with them.

Besides, Seymour would enjoy the visit, and so would Aunt Gwen. Ginny had brought her suit and was hoping, if Aunt Gwen was having a good enough day, that they could both swim.

"Good morning. I'm here to see Gwen French. Suite 19." Ginny slid her driver's license across the counter. It sometimes helped to speed things up.

"I'm her niece, Ginny."

The receptionist smiled brightly. "Good morning." She looked at the license, then Ginny. She handed it back. "First time at Emerald Manor?"

"No. I just don't have a memorable face, I guess." Nothing could destroy Ginny's good mood. She smiled at the folks reading the morning paper in the lobby's tropical lounge area. Emerald Manor had recently installed UV lighting in the space to simulate the sun's rays, and it seemed the residents were enjoying it. Probably wouldn't hurt all the plants the Manor had added either.

The receptionist laughed. "I don't either. Are you taking her out today?"

"That's the plan. Should be back by lunch."

"Sounds good. If she's not in her suite, she might be at breakfast. Enjoy your day."

"Thanks." Ginny headed toward her aunt's suite. If Gwen had already eaten, they'd go straight to the lake. After a trip to the bakery, of course.

She knocked on the door of her aunt's apartment, but there was no answer. Ginny backtracked to the dining room and stuck her head in. Most of the tables were full, and the space was divided into smaller rooms, making it impossible to see the whole place at once. There was an outside terrace, too.

From experience, Ginny knew her aunt would probably be out there. She went in that direction, smiling at the familiar faces. Most of them smiled back even though they didn't have a clue who she was.

She pushed through the door to the outside patio and saw her aunt at a small table with Lucas Cartwright.

Ginny grinned. She didn't want to break up their breakfast date, but from the looks of things, they were just lingering over coffee. She went up slowly, giving them time to notice her. "Hi, Aunt Gwen."

Her aunt looked over with no recognition, and Ginny knew instantly that today wasn't one of her better days. "Hello."

Lucas smiled at Ginny, but his eyes held sadness. He knew what kind of a day Gwen was having, too, and yet he was there with her. Ginny loved him for that. "You must be Ginny."

She nodded. "I am. How did you know?"

"She talks about you all the time." He stuck his hand out. "Nice to meet you."

They'd met many times, but there was no way he'd remember that. Ginny shook his hand. "The pleasure is mine. I'm so glad my aunt's made a friend here."

His smile brightened a bit. "She has a lot of friends here."

Ginny laughed. "Not quite as good as you, though."

He chuckled. "That's probably true. I guess she's told you about me, too, then."

"She has. All wonderful things."

Aunt Gwen frowned at Ginny. "I don't remember you."

Lucas patted her hand. "It's your niece, Ginny. You told me just the other day about how she'd finally met a man." He glanced at Ginny. "Sorry, but it's what she said."

Ginny shook her head. "Sounds just like her."

Gwen looked at her niece. "You're my niece? Ginny? The one I…raised?"

"That's right, Aunt Gwen. That's me." Ginny held out her wrist with her father's ID bracelet. "See? There's your brother's bracelet. Remember that?"

Gwen stared at it for a moment, then nodded. "Robert. He and his wife were killed in that terrible crash." She looked up at Ginny. "That's when you came to live with me."

"That's right." Ginny hated that her aunt's memory of her was so linked to that awful day. Time to focus on something happier. "If you're interested, I'm here to take you out for the day."

"Oh?" She seemed to ponder the idea. "Where?"

"Well, I was going to take you to breakfast and then the lake for a swim, but I see you've already eaten, so if you'd like, we can go straight to the lake."

Gwen's face brightened. "I do like to swim in the lake."

"Would you like to go, then?"

Gwen looked at Lucas for reassurance.

He nodded. "Sounds like a great day out to me. Go on, Gwen. You'll have fun. I have a poker game at nine anyway."

She only hesitated for another second. "All right, then."

"Wonderful," Ginny said. "We'll swing by Black Horse Bakery first and get something for after our swim. Lucas, would you like us to bring you something back?"

"Well now, I am partial to their peach coffee cake." He sat back in his chair, smiling. "Wouldn't turn down one of those."

"Peach coffee cake it is."

Aunt Gwen was staring at her. "You look like my brother, Robert. He died in a car accident more than thirty years ago."

"I know," Ginny said softly. Today was really not a good day. "He was my father."

Gwen blinked a few times before speaking again. "You're Ginny."

"Yes, I am."

Lucas stood and held his hand out to Gwen. "Come on, Gwen. I'll walk you back to your suite so you can get ready for the outing with your niece."

She took his hand. "Okay. That sounds nice."

She stood, and the three of them returned to her suite. At the door, Lucas kissed Gwen on the cheek. "Have a nice time. I'll see you for dinner."

Gwen smiled. "See you then." She unlocked her door and went in, then hesitated. "Do you come to visit me often?"

Ginny nodded. "I do. I was here yesterday, as a matter of fact. But you remembered me yesterday."

Her aunt sighed. "I had a stroke, didn't I? I remember that."

"You did. Right after I graduated college."

"Are you a wolf like me? You'd have to be if you're my brother's child."

"I am. We go running out by the lake sometimes, too, but I thought today we could swim after we feed Seymour some pies."

Her aunt tipped her head. "Seymour. The lake monster. He likes blackberry."

Ginny nodded, a little hope returning. "Yes, that's right."

"I'm sorry I don't remember you."

Ginny shrugged. "Don't be. I'm used to it. And some days you do."

"Well, I'm sorry that today isn't one of those days."

"Me, too, Aunt Gwen. But I'm happy to spend time with you all the same."

Gwen smiled and moved farther into the suite. "I'll put my suit on and throw a sundress on over it."

"Great. I'll just sit in the parlor and wait."

Gwen was quick, returning from the bedroom in five minutes, wearing a little T-shirt dress over her swimsuit and a floppy straw hat. She had a beach bag with a towel in it over one shoulder. "All set."

Ginny got up. "Let's go, then."

"Wait a second," Gwen said. "Look what I found." She took her phone out of the big pocket on the side of the beach bag, tapped the screen a few times, then turned it so Ginny could see. "That's you."

The photo was of both of them from about a year ago when they'd gone to the Creamatorium for sundaes.

Ginny smiled. "Yep, that's us."

Gwen smiled. "I remember you when you were little. You only wanted to wear purple, and you refused to eat Cheerios unless you could have them with a cut-up banana."

Ginny barked out a laugh. "I'd forgotten about my purple phase. Still like it, but I do wear other colors now."

Gwen came closer, cupping Ginny's face in her hands. "You grew into a beautiful woman."

"Thanks, Aunt Gwen."

"Thank you for being patient with me."

"You were patient with me more times in my life than I can count."

With teary eyes, Gwen patted Ginny's cheek. "You're a good girl. I'm glad you have your daddy's bracelet. Your mother gave that to him."

"I know." Ginny sniffed. Bad days were like this. Lots of past memories surfacing, but not much grasp of the present. It was okay. They had a lot of good times to remember, and in that regard, the bad days weren't that bad.

It was just the part where Aunt Gwen couldn't remember her that hurt. That's when Ginny felt the most alone. Especially now that Easy no longer remembered her either.

She could disappear, and no one in the world would ever know.

Despite that sobering thought, Ginny made herself smile. "We should take some more pictures today."

"That would be nice. I could show them to Lucas at dinner." She started for the door, then stopped. "Are you driving? I can't drive anymore."

"I'm driving. I have a Jeep. This time of year, the top is off. Is that going to be okay?"

"I might have to hold on to my hat, but all that fresh air sounds wonderful."

They walked out of her suite, she locked the door, then they headed for the parking lot.

Ginny was glad that her aunt not only wanted to go, but also seemed enthusiastic about it. Sometimes a bad day was *truly* bad. To the point that she wouldn't even agree to see Ginny. But Lucas had definitely helped with that today. "I really like Lucas. He's a very nice man. And obviously sweet on you."

Aunt Gwen smiled. "I'm sweet on him, too. He's a wolf like us, you know."

"I know. It makes me really happy that you've connected with him." *Connected* sound like such an odd way to describe her aunt having a boyfriend, but so did calling Lucas Aunt Gwen's boyfriend. "Maybe some time you could both come to dinner at my house."

They walked out of the building and toward Ginny's Jeep.

"That would be lovely. Lucas drives. He doesn't live on my side of the property. He lives on the retirement side."

"Oh. I see." Emerald Manor's over-fifty-five retirement community was a lot larger than the assisted-living side. Ginny had always hoped Aunt Gwen would move to that part of the community someday, but that seemed less likely all the time. She got the car door for her aunt, taking her beach bag and putting it in the back seat next to her own bag.

Gwen nodded. "There's nothing wrong with that man, I can tell you that. He might be slowing down a little, but he's still fit as a fiddle. Although, he does like that full moon cream they sell down at Spellbound." She put her hand to her mouth as she giggled. "A wolf's gotta run when a wolf wants to run."

"Aunt Gwen, that's an overshare, but I'm glad he's in such good shape. You are, too, you know."

Gwen climbed into the Jeep with little effort. "Except for my mind."

"True. But otherwise, you're perfect." Ginny hopped up behind the wheel. "All right, let's hit the bakery, get our supplies, then head to the lake. At this hour, there shouldn't be too many people there, although we might run into some fishermen. Not sure Seymour will come out if anyone else is there. Maybe, but it's been my experience that he avoids crowds."

Aunt Gwen clutched her hands together. "I'd love to see him. It's been a while for me, hasn't it?"

Ginny pulled out and got them on the road. "Almost three weeks since I took you to the lake."

"Do you think he'll remember me?"

"I do. But I also think having pie for him will help."

"Pie helps everything."

Ginny laughed. "I'm going to get something for myself, too, one of those giant blueberry crumb cake muffins maybe, since I haven't eaten yet."

"I used to make blueberry muffins."

"You did. And they were terrible. Either burnt or underdone. Or both. Once you added salt instead of sugar." Ginny laughed.

Her aunt gasped. "You're right, they were terrible. I remember that now."

"It must be a family thing, because I can't bake either. Cook, yes, but when it comes to baking, nope."

"We used to get cookies from the little place down the street," Gwen said, her voice a little distant as her mind worked to pull memories together.

"That's right. Smith and Sons Bakery. Whenever I had to take baked goods to school, you ordered from them."

Gwen nodded. "I remember that. I just wish I could remember you now."

"It's okay. It really is. It'll come back to you. Maybe not today, but someday. That's just how your mind works now."

"I don't like it."

"I don't either." She pulled into a spot near the bakery, parked, and turned the car off. "But I'd rather have you this way than not at all, and that stroke could have been much worse." She squeezed her aunt's hand. "Now let's go get Seymour his pies, Lucas his coffee cake, and us a decadent snack."

Her aunt opened the door and got out. "I want chocolate."

Ginny joined her on the sidewalk. "We can definitely make that happen."

CHAPTER TWENTY-FOUR

Easy came to, staring at the ceiling, the metal utility ladder, and an empty light socket. He cursed as the memory of what had happened came rushing back. His head was throbbing, but he didn't feel concussed. At least, he hoped he wasn't.

He sat up, gingerly touching the spot on the back of his head that hurt the worst. He had a goose egg back there the size of, well, a goose egg. Shards of broken light bulb surrounded him, glittering in the dull light. He groaned. "I cannot catch a break."

The good news was werewolves healed quickly.

The lingering tingle in his nerves from the shock he'd gotten would soon be gone, but his ability to heal rapidly wouldn't remove his anger. This whole electrical issue of his was nothing but aggravation. If it wasn't the small, constant shocks, it was something larger. Like attracting lightning bugs or getting zapped unconscious. "Wait until Ginny hears about this. She's going to think I need constant supervision."

Of course, there were worse things than having a beautiful woman worried about you or checking up on you. He grinned, thinking about how she'd want to take care of him.

Then his smile disappeared, replaced by a shock of a different kind.

Ginny. His neighbor. The gorgeous werewolf who lived next door, who'd snuck into his pool to swim, who'd organized his house. The woman whom he was falling madly in love with. The great kisser.

He *remembered* her. Remembered their week together. Remembered exactly how he felt about her.

Getting zapped had brought her back. He jumped to his feet, then realized there was still glass everywhere. And he was barefoot.

Carefully, he picked his way around the shards and into the kitchen. Thanks to Ginny's organizational skills, he knew exactly where the dustpan and broom were. In the pantry.

He put shoes on, then cleaned up the glass, folded the ladder and leaned it against the wall. The bulb still needed replacing, but first he was going next door to tell Ginny the amazing news.

Then he'd go to the hardware store and buy another pair of rubber-coated utility gloves. That would be faster than digging through all those boxes in the garage, and he ought to have a second pair anyway.

He ran next door. Her Jeep wasn't in the driveway, but it could be in the garage. He knocked on the door. "Ginny, it's Easy. You home?"

He waited a few more minutes, but she didn't answer. He knew she often worked with her headphones on. He ran around to the side of the house where her office was, but from what he could see she wasn't at her desk.

This news was too good to just text. He wanted to see her face when he told her. Where was she?

Then he remembered she'd said she was going to visit her aunt. Well, what better time and way to meet the woman?

But if he was going out there, he couldn't go like this. He changed his well-worn T-shirt for a clean white button-down, ran a comb through his hair, and put on loafers instead of sneakers. Ginny's aunt was her only family. He needed to make a good impression.

Once in the Mustang, he called up his GPS. He knew the place was called Emerald Manor. He punched that in and found it. Not too far.

Seven minutes later, he pulled into the parking lot, found a spot, and was headed for the front desk.

It was a nice place. Really nice. A group of residents, two men and two women, were sitting in the large lobby next to a waterfall that took up the whole wall. With all the greenery and sunny lighting, it had a very tropical feel. They were playing poker at one of the tables. The man with his back to the water feature gave Easy a nod of greeting as he came in.

Easy smiled back. "Morning."

As he reached the desk, the receptionist greeted him. "Good morning. Can I help you?"

"Yes, I'm looking for my girlfriend." Why not call her that? That's what he wanted her to be. What he hoped she wanted to be, too. "She came to visit her aunt. Gwen French. That's the aunt, not my girlfriend. Anyway, I know she's here. I was hoping to surprise her with some good news."

Great news, actually.

The receptionist tapped a few keys. "Gwen French is indeed a resident here. I'll call her suite for you."

"Thank you." He waited while she did just that.

After a few moments, the receptionist hung up the phone. "No answer. I'm sorry. They could be anywhere on the campus."

"Okay, thanks. I guess I can just call her." He'd be vague, though. Or as vague as he could be without giving away the surprise.

But Ginny didn't answer her phone either. He sighed and walked toward the door, pausing to send her a quick text. *Call me when you get this.*

The card player who'd nodded at him got up from the table and came over. "Did I hear you say you're looking for Gwen French?"

Easy nodded. "Her niece, really. Well, both of them. I have news for Ginny, but I was hoping to meet Gwen, too."

His eyes narrowed. "I don't know the niece. Can't recall her at all, truly. But Gwen went into town this morning with…someone." He shook his head. "I think she was going out to the lake. But they were going to the bakery, too. I know, because Gwen said she'd bring me a peach coffee cake from Black Horse."

The person he couldn't remember had to be Ginny. "Thanks, that's very helpful. Maybe I can catch them there."

The older man smiled, a faint, familiar gleam. "We wolves have to stick together." He glanced at the receptionist. "The humans might know what we are, but they don't know our ways."

Easy liked the old dude instantly. He stuck his hand out. "Easy Grayle. Nice to meet you, sir."

The man's smile widened. "Lucas Cartwright. Nice to meet you, son."

"Do you know if Gwen and her niece have a certain part of the lake they go to? Or is there really only one spot? I just moved to Shadowvale, so I'm not that familiar with the area."

"Oh, no, it's a big lake. Gwen favors the old boardwalk and fishing pier. It's not used as much as the new one, but it's a good spot for swimming or strolling." He glanced toward the parking lot, then back at his card-playing friends. "Wouldn't mind taking a drive up there myself if you want some company?"

Easy nodded. "I'd love some." That was the way with most wolves. Friendly, willing to help, so long as you were part of their pack. And for all Lucas knew, Easy was part of the local pack.

Lucas's pleasure was apparent in his grin. "Lead the way."

Easy started for the parking lot. "I should warn you, I'm a fast driver."

Lucas chuckled. "Son, I was a cop for thirty-five years. I know all about driving fast."

"Good. If I get pulled over, you can talk the officer out of giving me a ticket." He clicked the key fob, unlocking the Mustang and causing the lights to flash.

"Nice ride," Lucas said as they got in.

"Thanks." Easy started the car up. "Let me show you what she can do."

The bakery was a little busy, but half of the customers were in line for coffee, and things were moving quickly. Gwen and Ginny got in line and had their goodies in no time. Six blackberry pies, one peach coffee cake, one blueberry crumb muffin, one Chocolate Reaper cupcake, and a half-dozen day-and-night cookies, just because they looked so good.

Ginny found the chocolate-and-vanilla frosting combination hard to resist. She ate one of the cookies on the way back to the Jeep, finishing the last bite just as they reached the vehicle. They put their shopping bags in the back seat, then climbed in.

Aunt Gwen snapped her seat belt into place. "It's a beautiful day. Great day for a swim."

"It is. And with these pies, Seymour is sure to show up."

"You think so?"

Ginny started the car and pulled out of the parking spot. "He's always shown up when I've had pie. It's only when I don't bring it that he's not come. And even then, it's rare. He likes the company. Especially swimming company. He'll be thrilled."

She drove on to Miller's Lake, enjoying the warm breeze and golden light that almost felt like sun. "One of these days, we need to have a day up at Nightingale Park. We'll have a good run, then a nice picnic. Maybe even a dip in the creek up there."

Aunt Gwen clapped her hands. "That would be lovely. Can I invite Lucas?"

"Of course." Ginny smiled. "I like him a lot."

"I do, too. Very much."

Ginny glanced over. "I don't recall you dating at all when I was a kid. I think when I was a high school senior, you went out with a man. The insurance man, actually. Am I remembering that right?"

Gwen laughed softly. "Yes. Arnold Fuller. He was a nice man, but we didn't have a lot in common."

"Why didn't you date more?"

The distance of memory glazed Gwen's eyes. "You'd already had enough upheaval in your life. You didn't need a parade of men coming and going." She shrugged. "I was content to wait until you were older."

"Really?" The confession tugged at Ginny's heart. Her aunt had done so much for her. Sacrificed so much. "You were an amazing mom, even though you never let me call you that. I hope you know that. I probably should tell you that more."

Gwen smiled. "Thank you. It's nice to hear."

"Why didn't you let me call you Mom?" Apparently, today was the day to ask every question she'd always wanted to.

Gwen stared at her hands for a moment. "You had a mother. A great one. I never wanted to take her place. To me, letting you call me Mom—and you did a few times before I corrected you—felt too much like pushing her out of the picture."

A tear spilled down Ginny's cheek. "I love you, Aunt Gwen. And I know you don't really know who I am right now, so you don't need to say it back, but it doesn't matter, because I already know you love me, too."

"I remember you as a child. I'm sorry I don't remember you now."

Ginny gave her a quick smile before turning down the road that would take them to the lake. "No one does. It's my curse. It's why we moved here. Do you remember that?"

Gwen was silent. Thinking, most likely. Finally, she said, "No. The last memory I have with you in it is…dropping you off at Tulane. I was so proud of you for going to college, but I was so torn up inside to leave you there."

"Really? Because you didn't seem torn up. Just really happy, and obviously proud."

Gwen laughed softly. "I cried all the way home."

"You did? Aunt Gwen! I had no idea."

Ginny turned onto the unpaved road that led to the old boardwalk. "Thank you for all you've done for me."

"You're welcome, Ginny. Thank you for today. I'm having a really nice time."

"Good. I know you don't remember the conversation we had the other day, about the guy I met, but things are going well with him. He doesn't remember me either, but he's working on a way around that. He writes everything down, then leaves himself a note to read it in the morning."

"Maybe I should do that."

"You could, but you have days when remembering isn't a problem for you."

"I wish that was every day."

"Me, too." She parked in the small gravel lot at the end of the pier. It was getting a little overgrown from disuse.

"Why doesn't your curse affect me on the good days?" Gwen asked as they got out of the Jeep and gathered their things.

"This is just a guess, but I've always attributed it to us being blood relatives. Could also be because we've known each other for so long, but I think the blood connection is probably the reason." Ginny hoisted the shopping bag with the pies. "Whatever it is, I'm glad for it. Having you remember me has been one of the main things that's kept me going."

"I'm glad I can do that for you. But you have a lot of reasons to keep going."

"It's been hard at times. Really hard. I get lonely, you know."

"That young man should help."

Ginny smiled. "For sure. Ready to swim?"

"Yes." Gwen hitched the straps of her beach bag higher on her shoulder.

"Good."

They headed out, and as they reached the end of the pier, Seymour surfaced.

"I guess pie did the trick again." Ginny waved. "Hi, Seymour. We're here to swim."

He ducked his head under, then flicked it back up, spraying them with water. They laughed and shrieked.

Ginny set the shopping bag down. "Aunt Gwen, I think he wants us to swim first."

Gwen put her bag down, then peeled her sundress off. "Sounds good to me." She jumped in and started wading through the shallows.

Ginny stripped off her T-shirt and shorts. Despite everything they'd talked about, it was easy to forget her curse in a moment like this, when everything was so good and happy. Even with Aunt Gwen not fully remembering her.

No matter what else happened, she'd cherish the memory of this day. Because the time would come when all Aunt Gwen had was bad days.

A time, Ginny realized, that was coming much too fast.

CHAPTER TWENTY-FIVE

A slow roll by the bakery had been enough to show Easy the women weren't there. Lucas offered to run in and ask after them, but Easy thought heading to the lake would be the next logical thing. If Ginny and her aunt weren't there, he and Lucas could always come back to the bakery.

Easy was still creeping along, looking at his GPS. "Is this the right way to the lake?"

"Yes, but it's not the part we want to go to." Lucas pointed ahead. "Straight like you're going to the gate, but turn right at Lake Road."

Easy snorted. "I probably could have figured out that Lake Road led to the lake."

"Maybe," Lucas said. "But now you won't have to wonder. And you wouldn't have known to take the unmarked road that'll lead us to Gwen."

Easy picked up speed, and a few minutes after he'd made the right, Lucas pointed again.

"Turn onto that gravel road up there. That'll take you to the old scenic walk and pier. If they're not there, I don't know where they are."

Easy turned, slowing down on the road so his tires wouldn't kick up stones. "If they're not here, we'll just go back to Emerald Manor and wait on them."

Lucas gave him a look. "Or we could get something to eat. Have you been to Philly's?"

"I've only been to a few places. Five Bells Pub and the diner. Too busy working since I moved in to get out more than that."

"Then we'll go to Philly's. Best hole-in-the-wall in Shadowvale. A lot of miners hang out there, maybe because it's out by the mines, so it's nothing fancy because they aren't a fancy crowd, but the food is good, and the portions are generous. Cheap beer, too."

"All right, I'm game." Easy really needed to go home and write, but Lucas had been helpful, so he didn't want to ditch the guy. Although he was glad Lucas hadn't suggested the pub. Last thing he needed was to see that Full Moon Party flyer again. "Might be a little early for a beer, even if it is a bargain."

Lucas laughed. "I'm retired. It's never too early for a beer. But I understand you might not feel that way."

"Well, I still have work to do when I get home."

"Understand."

Easy gestured ahead. "Hey, there's Ginny's Jeep." He parked beside it, and they got out. Easy put his hand on the hood. "Still warm, so they can't have been here long."

"We must have just missed them at Black Horse."

Easy peered into the back seat and nodded. "There's a bakery bag in there."

"I hope there's a peach coffee cake in it." Lucas started for the stairs up to the old boardwalk. "They must be down at the end where the pier juts out into the water. They're probably swimming already."

Easy caught up. "Let's go see."

The elevated walkway followed the shore for a bit, then doglegged to the right and disappeared behind the trees. As they hit the bend, Easy went dead-still.

The lake spread out before them, but it wasn't the size or beauty of the place that made his mouth drop open.

Ginny and her aunt were standing in the water about chest high, just talking. Completely oblivious to the danger behind them. Because just a few feet away from them loomed a green-gray monster of mythical proportions. Spines ran down its back. It seemed to be watching Ginny and her aunt, until it saw Easy.

The creature hissed, showing off a mouth filled with needle-sharp teeth, and raised its spines.

Easy let out a curse and went flying forward, every inch of him ready to fight for Ginny's life.

Lucas was on his heels.

"Ginny, out of the water, now," Easy yelled.

"You, too, Gwen. And hurry," Lucas hollered. "I'm coming."

Both men hit the end of the pier at the same time

and dived forward. The creature squealed, the women shrieked, and Easy and Lucas plunged into the water.

That instant, underwater, Easy realized he had no plan. He'd acted on instinct, the pure driving need to protect Ginny. He pushed off the lake bottom, surfaced between the women and the monster, and snarled at it. He planted his feet and waved his hands, trying to scare it off. "Stay away from them."

"Easy, Lucas, no," Ginny cried out. She grabbed Easy's arm. "Seymour isn't—"

The monster whipped its head back, then thrust it into the water inches from Easy. The smell of ozone reached him a split second before the pain did, but he already had an idea about what was coming.

The current cut through him like the bite of a whip. He jerked back, frozen by the electricity running through him. He was marginally aware that Lucas, Gwen, and Ginny were caught in it, too. The four of them were immobilized by the relentless surge: teeth gritted, muscles tensed, nerves on fire.

Steam rose off the water. His eyes started to roll back in his head. Then it ended, and the monster turned and dived, disappearing.

As the current subsided, the tingling was all that remained. Like the worst case of pins and needles possible.

They all gasped, having momentarily been left breathless.

Ginny still held on to Easy, but she turned to look behind her. "Aunt Gwen, are you all right? Lucas?"

"I have her," Lucas answered. He had her in his arms, but she and Ginny were also holding hands.

Ginny let her aunt go to face Easy. "What on earth were you doing?"

"I thought you and your aunt were in danger. That's what it looked like. I was just trying to save you."

"Same," Lucas added.

She glanced at the lake beyond Easy, then sighed in frustration. "Seymour's a friend."

"For one thing, there was no way I could know that." Easy glared at her. "And for another, your friend just tried to electrocute us."

"No, he didn't. He was scared. It's his only defense. If he'd really wanted us fried, we'd be floating facedown."

"That's reassuring."

Ginny pursed her lips. "You scared him. He was just protecting himself. He might be big, but he's harmless."

"Not with that kind of firepower and those teeth." Easy had expected a very different response from her. A much more grateful one. "How was I supposed to know you'd come out here to swim with a monster?"

"You weren't. But you could have asked if we were all right when you saw us in the water with him."

This wasn't going the way he'd thought it would go at all. He frowned. "I could have, but you could have been eaten by then."

She sighed, put her hands on her hips, and stared out at the open water. "Poor Seymour. He just freaked out. He probably thought you were going to hurt him. Or us. He's a little jumpy around people he doesn't know."

Easy rolled his head around. The monster's zap had left him with itchy muscles. "Yeah, I get that way around strange monsters."

Ginny glanced at him, amusement in her eyes. "It *was* very kind of you and Lucas to leap to our defense like that."

"Thanks."

She tipped her head. "What are you doing out here anyway?"

"I have good news. I wanted to tell you face-to-face. I went to Emerald Manor, but you weren't there, but I ran into Lucas, and he said you'd probably be here. So. Here we are."

Ginny nodded and moved closer. "What's the good news? It must really be something if you wanted to tell me in person."

"It is. I got shocked changing a light bulb in my office this morning and fell off the ladder—"

"That's terrible news!"

"It is, but the result of that shock is that I remember you again. All of you. Last week. Everything."

Her eyes rounded. "That's awesome!"

"I thought you'd think so." He looked in the direction that Seymour had gone. "And if I still remember it after that heavy-duty jolt, then I'm thinking it's permanent this time."

She squealed and threw her arms around him. "That's wonderful."

He hugged her. "It is."

She leaned back. "You're kind of wet. And fully dressed."

"Yeah, I am."

"You should have shifted before you dove in."

He made a face. "Not sure your monster friend would have been scared off by a Pomeranian."

"You might have turned into a wolf."

"Maybe." He sighed. "But then again…"

Lucas and Gwen were stopped on their way toward the ladder that led up to the pier. Lucas put his hand up to shield his eyes. "How about we dry off and go eat? Gwen and I are hungry."

Ginny answered, "We have that stuff from the bakery in the Jeep."

Gwen shook her head. "I'd rather have real food first."

Easy nodded. "I could eat. I'd like to dry off, too."

"You can use my towel," Ginny said. Then she spoke to Lucas and Gwen again. "Let's go to the diner. They have breakfast all day."

Lucas gave her the thumbs-up.

Ginny and Easy headed for the ladder.

He placed his hand on the small of her back, even though that part of her was still underwater. She was in the more modest red bikini again. "I'm sorry I scared Seymour off."

"I'm sorry he shocked us."

"Has he ever done that to you before?"

"Once. Accidentally. But this time was a little more intense."

As she started up the ladder, Easy looked out over the lake. "Will he come back?"

"I'm sure. Then I'll explain to him that you didn't know he was a friend."

Easy glanced up, admiring the view right before she climbed onto the pier. "So you talk to him? And he understands you?"

She nodded down at him. "Yep. He seems to."

He climbed up and joined her, her aunt, and Lucas on the decking. "You must be the descendant of a fairy-tale princess. Do bluebirds land on your finger when you're out walking with your herd of pet deer?"

She laughed. "No. Seymour's pretty easygoing. I think he's lonely. As far as I know, he's the only one of his kind in this lake. At least, I've never seen another one like him."

Easy took that in. "That would suck. Being the only one of your kind." Then new understanding hit him. "I can see why you two would be friends."

Ginny smiled at him as she pulled a towel out of her bag and handed it to him. "I know it's odd, but he seems to remember me." She shrugged. "That's hard to ignore in my situation."

He took the towel. "Well, maybe I can come with you sometime and apologize in person."

"That would be nice. I love coming out to the lake for any reason, but that would be a great one."

"We'll do it." He looked around as he did his best to dry off. "Does this place have a boat ramp?"

"Only for nonmotorized boats. Pretty sure the town council knows about Seymour. Motors would be bad for him."

Easy considered that. "They would be. Kayaks would be cool, though."

"They would. Do you have one?"

"No, but if I get this book in on time, maybe I'll dip into that money and buy one. The kind that seats two."

Her smile broadened. "That would be fun."

They walked back to the cars.

Easy stared at his, slowly shaking his head. "I really don't want to sit on that leather while I'm this wet."

Ginny pointed at the towel he was still holding. "Sit on that. I know it's wet now, too, but it's better than nothing. Unless you want to go in mine? I can bring you back later to get your car."

"That's kind of you, but the towel will be fine. So long as Lucas can use your aunt's."

Gwen nodded. "No problem."

"Okay." Easy and Lucas got into the Mustang, while Ginny and Aunt Gwen climbed into the Jeep.

With the top off and the warm air blowing over them, the women were almost dry by the time they reached the diner. The boys were still pretty damp, but didn't seem to mind. Ginny and her aunt put their cover-ups back on in the parking lot, then they all went in and found a booth.

Easy and Ginny sat on one side, her aunt and Lucas on the other. Easy couldn't help but smile. He liked being this close to Ginny. Liked feeling her knee brush his and the warmth of her radiating toward him.

He itched to put his hand on her leg, but wasn't sure if that would be welcomed or not. And after he'd scared away her favorite lake monster, he didn't want to push it.

Today was going really well, all things considered.

He didn't want to do anything to run it off course.

CHAPTER TWENTY-SIX

Ginny had been mad about Easy and Lucas ending the enjoyable morning she and Aunt Gwen were having, not just because time with Aunt Gwen was precious, but also because Seymour had borne the brunt of their enthusiastic defense.

Granted, the big zap he'd given the four of them hadn't been fun, but they'd survived it and weren't the worse for wear. At least not that she could tell.

Part of her wondered if such a zap would have an effect on Easy, seeing as how electricity tended to change things for him. But he still knew who she was and wasn't having any problem remembering her, so the latest jolt didn't seem to have done anything.

With the incident behind them, it was simple to see how Easy and Lucas had misread the scene. Of course, their desire to protect was part of their wolf DNA, but it was also very sweet. Flattering, really. If a little misguided. But Ginny also understood why Easy would be so eager to tell her his incredible news face-to-face.

Being remembered again was everything. It meant he wouldn't have to work so hard to keep her in his mind. That meant a real relationship was possible.

For Ginny, that was life-changing. She was giddy about it. So much so that she reached under the table, took his hand, and laced her fingers with his. She needed to be more than just close to him, she needed to touch him.

He glanced at her, the smile in his eyes filling her with bliss. "Hey," he whispered.

"Hey," she whispered back.

Life was so good right now that she vibrated with the joy of it.

He leaned in. "What's good here? And don't say all of it."

"Everything?" She laughed.

He shook his head, grinning.

"I'm getting the steak sandwich," Lucas announced. He put his menu down, then shifted his attention to Gwen. "What about you, honey?"

She smiled. "I think I'll do the same."

Easy added his menu to the stack. "Sounds good to me."

All three of them looked at Ginny.

"Well, I can't order a salad now." She laughed. "Not that I was going to."

The server came by with four glasses of water, which she distributed as she greeted them, then she stood with her pen and pad at the ready. "What can I get for you folks? We have a buffalo chicken sandwich on special, by the way."

"Aunt Gwen," Ginny said, "you go first."

"I'd like the steak sandwich with fries. And an iced tea."

Lucas and Easy echoed the order, except Lucas got a strawberry shake and Easy got a root beer. Ginny asked for the same as her aunt, iced tea included. The server took their menus and left.

The four sat back to wait.

Lucas shook his head. "This has been quite a day, and it's not even lunchtime yet."

"You can say that again." Easy slid down in his seat a little as if he was worn out. He held on tight to Ginny's hand, though. "This town never fails to amaze me."

Aunt Gwen turned to Lucas. "Ginny and I are going to plan a picnic up at Nightingale Park soon. Would you like to join us?" She looked at Easy. "You're invited, too, of course. We'll go for a run, then lounge around in the sun while we eat. Maybe dip our toes in the creek."

"Sounds great, and I'd love to join you." Easy laughed. "Good to know our daring rescue attempt isn't being held against us."

Lucas nodded. "I'll say." He leaned forward, voice low. "Have you ever seen a creature like that? Or felt such a shock? I swear, my back teeth must have lit up."

"The creature, no. But I've had a worse shock," Easy answered.

Ginny leaned in. "He was struck by lightning."

"No." Lucas's eyes narrowed in disbelief. "Saw

that happen to a man once when I was on the force, doing crowd control at a rally. Big storm rolled in, and lightning cracked a guy holding a sign on a metal pole."

"Did he make it?" Easy asked.

Lucas shook his head slowly. "He was human. Didn't have a chance. But you must have been awful sick from it."

"I was." He glanced at Ginny, like he expected her to say more, but she just sat there, waiting on him. This was his story to tell, and she wasn't going to assume otherwise. He took a beat, gathering his words. And maybe his courage, too. It was a lot to reveal. "Messed up my ability to shift, too."

Lucas sucked in a breath, and Gwen put her hand to her mouth.

"I can shift," Easy continued. "I just can't always control when. And...what I become."

The two older wolves looked at Easy with such concern that Ginny hurt for him all over again. "It's why he moved here."

Easy nodded. "I didn't have much choice. Way too risky to live like that in the human world."

"I'll say," Gwen said softly. "You poor man." Then her face lit up with a luminous smile. "I am very sorry for your trouble, but I'm glad it led you here. And to my Ginny."

Ginny smiled. That was Aunt Gwen. Always finding the bright spot in something.

Easy slipped his hand from Ginny's to put his arm around her shoulders. "I'm glad about that, too."

But the concern had yet to leave Lucas's gaze. "That's going to make it hard on you with the pack."

"I know," Easy answered. "That's part of the reason I've held off introducing myself. The other part is Ginny."

Lucas squinted. "This has something to do with her curse, doesn't it? Gwen told me about that."

Easy nodded, then he blinked, mouth open like he was stuck on a thought and not ready to speak until he sorted it out. A moment later, he came out with it. "Ginny, have you noticed that Lucas hasn't seemed to have forgotten you once since we've been together? Well, since the shock anyway."

She'd been so wrapped up in the joy of the company that she hadn't noticed. "No, but you're right. Aunt Gwen hasn't either, and she couldn't remember me this morning."

Aunt Gwen made an odd face. "Honey, your curse has never had an effect on me."

"I know," Ginny said. "But when your memory issues kick in, it sometimes feels like my curse is working on you. Today was one of those days."

"Oh." She looked utterly forlorn. "I guess I didn't remember *that*. I'm so sorry."

"Not your fault, Aunt Gwen."

"But," Easy said, "you remember her now?"

Gwen nodded. "Without trying."

He looked at Lucas. "And you?"

"Sure. How could I forget her?"

Ginny took that in. "I was thinking the zap from Seymour hadn't had any effect on us, but it's definitely done something. Something good. Could it be that I'm not forgettable anymore?"

"Sure seems that way," Easy answered. "How about that?"

Their server returned with their drinks on a tray. She walked by the table once, giving them an odd look, then came back again and stopped. "Did you just take this table?"

"No," Easy answered. "We've been sitting here. You took our order a few minutes ago. Those are our drinks on your tray. Two iced teas, a root beer, and a strawberry shake."

She put the tray on the table and passed out the drinks. "That's what I have on here, but I don't remember taking your order, and I sure as heck don't remember the four of you sitting here."

The chill that went through Ginny made her grab Easy's leg. She whispered to him, "She doesn't remember us. Any of us."

He nodded, a little paler than he had been a second ago. "Miss, would you mind getting us some napkins?"

"Sure, be right back." The server left.

Aunt Gwen looked confused. "What's going on?"

Ginny shook her head. "I don't even want to put it into words."

Lucas's brow wrinkled in confusion. "Well, one of you needs to, because I'd like to know what's happening."

Easy was watching the server. "She's not coming back." He lifted his hand and got the server's attention.

She came back to the table. "What can I do for you?" Then she frowned. "This is my section, but I see you have drinks already. Did someone else wait on you?"

"No," Easy said. "You did."

It was clear by the look in her eyes that none of this was making sense to her. "I'm pretty sure I'd remember that."

Ginny's heart dropped. "No, you wouldn't. Could you just give us a minute?"

The server left again.

Ginny let out a sigh of despair. "I am so sorry."

"What's happening?" Aunt Gwen asked. "Explain it, Ginny."

"As best as I can tell, when Seymour shocked us, you all got a piece of my curse. That's how you can remember me, but the server doesn't remember any of us. You're part of it now."

Easy didn't want to believe that, because if they'd all gotten Ginny's curse, wouldn't they have gotten his, too? He felt like he'd been punched in the stomach. "If that's true, then…"

Ginny put her hand on his arm. "We could all have your curse, too."

"Yes," he breathed out.

She shook her head. "I don't know. Maybe. There's only one way to find out. And we can't do that here."

The server returned. This time, her tray was loaded down with their sandwiches. She gave them an odd look. "Were you guys here a couple minutes ago? I could have sworn there were different people here."

Ginny sighed. "Welcome to my life."

"We are the same people who were here," Lucas answered. His gruff tone made the server's brows shoot up.

"My bad. Sorry." She handed out their meals, then quickly disappeared.

Aunt Gwen's expression was haunted. "Is this really what it's like, Ginny? Do people forget you that quickly?"

Ginny couldn't even pretend to smile. "Pretty much as soon as they stop looking at me. And yes, all the time."

"You poor thing." She reached out and grabbed her niece's hand. "Well, we're in it together now."

Easy picked up his sandwich, although his appetite was mostly gone. "We should eat, then go back to my house and see what happens when we shift."

"Agreed," Lucas mumbled through a mouthful of food. "Although I'm not so sure I can shift on command. And my full moon ointment is back at the condo. You'll see when you get to be my age."

"We'll figure it out," Easy said.

They ate in relative silence, and it was clear that despite how tasty the food was, none of them was really in the mood for it anymore. Easy had been chewing the same bite of his sandwich for minutes. Ginny and Gwen were picking at their fries.

Lucas, however, had finished half of his plate and all of his milkshake.

He frowned at the rest of them. "It's not the end of the world. Stop moping. Eat your lunch. We need to keep our strength up for whatever comes next. And regardless, we're in this together."

"True," Easy said. "But if we all have both Ginny's curse and mine, that's a heavy burden to bear."

"Heavy is relative." Lucas chomped down on a fry. "There are four of us. All of us strong people. We can handle whatever it is that we've been dealt. I'd venture a guess to say all of us have already been through worse."

Aunt Gwen nodded. "You're right, Lucas. I survived my stroke. I can survive this. Ginny's been dealing with this for ten years on her own. Lucas, you were a police officer for thirty-five years. Easy, you must have been through something harder than this?"

"Yes, ma'am. I was an Army Ranger. Did a tour in Afghanistan." Something he shouldn't have needed anyone to remind him of. But the weight of spreading his curse to others…that was a heavy thing.

"See there? You survived that." She lifted her chin with triumphant pride. "We need to pick our heads up and figure this out, not allow it to get the best of us."

Ginny picked up her sandwich. "You're right, Aunt Gwen. Thank you."

Gwen smiled at her niece. "You're welcome. And you're not alone anymore, sweetheart."

Ginny smiled. "No, I'm not." She turned to Easy. "None of us are. We're all in this together. Now let's eat and get back to Easy's to see just how deep this curse business has gotten."

Chapter Twenty-Seven

They gathered in Easy's living room. The shopping bag from the bakery sat on his kitchen counter, but the sweets might as well have not existed.

All anyone could think about was what their next shift would bring. Ginny could see it on her aunt's face and Lucas's too.

She felt for them. Getting hit with two curses in one day was a lot to deal with. She and Easy had had time to get used to each of theirs, as much as anyone could get used to such curses, but the older pair seemed to be keeping it together pretty well.

Lucas and Gwen sat next to each other on the couch, Easy in his recliner, and Ginny sat cross-legged on the floor near him.

"What kind of uncontrolled shift are we talking about here?" Lucas asked. "What exactly does your curse do?"

Easy's chest rose and fell with his breathing as he seemed to be picking his words. "I haven't seen my true wolf form in months."

Lucas frowned. "Then what do you shift into?"

Easy sighed and glanced at Ginny. "Whatever else is in my bloodline."

"Meaning?" Gwen asked.

"Other kinds of wolves. Foxes." He paused. "Domestic dogs."

Lucas and Gwen looked at each other.

Easy nodded. "Yeah, it's pretty much what you're thinking." He rubbed the bridge of his nose. "Most recently, I turned into a Yorkie in the bathroom at Five Bells."

Lucas grimaced and swore softly.

Gwen laughed, but cut herself off almost immediately. "I'm sorry."

"No, no," Easy said. "I know it's funny."

Lucas hmphed. "Not when it's happening to you, I suppose. How did you get out of that?"

"With Ginny's help," Easy said.

Lucas leaned back and stuck his thumbs in his pockets. "So that's what we're up against. An uncertain shift. The possibility of becoming a poodle."

Easy's nod was slow and steady. "Basically."

Gwen shrugged. "I think our bloodlines are pretty pure."

"I thought the same thing," Easy said. "But you have no idea until this thing kicks in what kind of mating went on in your family."

Lucas's lip curled. "Great. I've heard some rumors about my great-great-grandfather. I guess I'm going to find out if those rumors are true."

A new and very interesting thought rolled into Ginny's head with the kind of insistence that wouldn't allow it to be ignored. She got up, shuffled her feet across the area rug, then reached her index finger toward the nearest light switch.

"What are you doing?" Easy asked.

"I want to see if we picked up the electrical part of your curse." She touched the light switch. Nothing. "I'm guessing not. But just to be sure…" She did it one more time. Still nothing. "Interesting."

"What does that mean?"

She shrugged. "I don't know." She took a closer look at him. "After the lightning bug attack—"

"You were attacked by lightning bugs?" Lucas sat up. "You never said anything about that."

Easy nodded. "We went out to the enchanted forest looking—"

"Around," Ginny interrupted. She made a quick face at Easy, but how was he to know she'd promised her aunt she'd stop looking for the mysterious book? "You know, showing Easy all the sights in Shadowvale."

Aunt Gwen's gaze narrowed. "Were you looking for *that* book?"

"No!" Ginny laughed like that was the craziest thing ever. "That's just a fable."

Easy gave them both strange looks, but went on explaining. "Well, while we were out there, I got swarmed. Apparently, whatever electrical thing I have going on attracted them. They attacked me, zapped me pretty good, and when I woke up, I'd forgotten Ginny."

Aunt Gwen nodded with understanding. "You'd

remembered her before that without any problem. Ginny told me about that."

"Right," Easy said. "Which is why when I got zapped changing the light bulb today and could remember her again, it was really big news."

Another thought popped into Ginny's head. She came over to stand by the recliner. "Did you shift after the lightning bug attack?"

"No. Why?"

"Did you shift after the jolt from changing the bulb?"

"No. Seriously, what are you getting at?"

"Just that you have no idea if you're still cursed. Any one of those jolts, even the one you got from Seymour today, could have set things right for you."

He thought about that. "I suppose that's true. But any one of those jolts could have reset it, too."

She tapped her fingers against her thigh. "But if each of those moments reversed your curse, then in theory, you should currently not be cursed. Right? You started out cursed, then the lightning bugs could have uncursed you, then the light bulb could have recursed you, then Seymour would have uncursed you again."

Lucas slapped his hand to his forehead and looked at Gwen. "Are you following this?"

"Sort of," she said.

Easy made a face. "I get what you're saying, but if that's how getting zapped affected me, Seymour should have knocked out my ability to remember you."

"True. Except you're now as forgettable as I am. So maybe sharing that curse makes you immune to it. Seems to be true with my aunt and Lucas."

Easy scratched his head. "This is complicated."

"You're telling me," Lucas said. He stood up. "I say let's shift and see what happens. If, uh, I can, that is."

"I can help with that." Ginny pulled her phone out of her purse on the counter and searched for a video. When she found the one she wanted, she turned up the brightness on her phone, then faced the group and showed them the screen. "Does this help?"

At the sight of the shining full moon, three pairs of eyes took on the glow that preceded a shift.

"That'll do it," Lucas mumbled.

She nodded. "I thought so." Then she hesitated. "Easy, Lucas, what are your regular wolf forms? Aunt Gwen and I are gray wolves who are actually gray."

Easy answered first. "I'm also a gray wolf, but I'm more brown than gray."

"Alaskan timber wolf," Lucas said. "Mostly white."

"Okay, then. We know what everyone should look like. Let's see what we actually turn into." She propped the phone against the bakery bag on the counter so they could all see it, then joined them. Her body welcomed the change. She dropped to all fours and let it consume her.

In a matter of minutes, their human forms were gone.

But the forms that had taken their places weren't all wolves.

Aunt Gwen was a blue-eyed husky, Lucas was still a wolf, but he was more gray wolf than Alaskan timber. And Easy…Easy was like no wolf Ginny had ever seen, but she knew her canine history.

He'd gone prehistoric. Easy was a dire wolf, an extinct breed considered the grandparents of all wolfkind. So much so that they were commonly called first kin.

They were a breed that, these days, most people thought was born out of the imagination of a popular fantasy writer. But werewolves knew better. Most learned about dire wolves at the feet of their parents. She'd learned about them from Aunt Gwen. Of course, Ginny had never seen one in person. Being extinct as a breed didn't mean there weren't some shifters who still took on the form—Ginny had just never met any.

As a shift went, it was pretty impressive.

Made up for the Yorkie, if he was keeping score. Not that he could see himself.

She couldn't help but wonder what she'd turned into. She let out a woof, but it came out more of a bark. A solid dog sound. She wandered over to the sliders that led to the back patio and had a look at her reflection.

What stared back at her was full-on mutt. A domestic dog with no real discernable breed. A little terrier, maybe? Hard to say. She was all sandy-brown shag and wagging tail. She barked at herself. Regardless, she was forty pounds of cute. There were worse things.

Easy, Lucas, and Aunt Gwen all joined her to have a look at themselves.

Easy snarled at his reflection, but the sound had no bite. He was just testing out this new and fascinating form, that was plain.

They all turned, wagged their tails, barked, and generally put their canine forms through a few paces.

Except for Easy, they'd never been anything but wolves, so seeing themselves as something different was pretty interesting.

Ginny wished she could take a picture of them all, but not having opposable thumbs made that tricky.

A few more minutes passed, then Easy shifted back to his human form. Ginny did the same with Lucas and Aunt Gwen following right after.

He sighed. "I guess that question's been answered. You all have my curse, too."

Ginny tried to offer some comforting words. "But a dire wolf? That was cool. I've never seen one in person."

"Me either, until now." He smiled without much humor behind it. "Sometimes I win the curse lottery, apparently."

Lucas stood near Gwen, the two of them looking very much like a team. "Easy, have you talked to the pack alpha about this?"

"No," Easy responded. "And I don't think it's a good idea. Especially now that he won't be able to remember me, but what does it matter? No alpha is going to want such a cursed shifter in his ranks."

Lucas frowned. "I'm a member of the pack, and I know the man. You're selling Rico short. This is Shadowvale, remember? He knows that. And allowances can be made."

Aunt Gwen shook her head. "But not now, not when Rico won't remember Easy. Or any of us."

The words filled Ginny with such guilt that she wrapped her arms around herself in a lousy attempt to self-soothe. "This is my fault."

Easy turned to look at her. "What? How?"

"Because I made you go look for that stupid book with me."

Aunt Gwen gasped.

"Yes," Ginny said. "That's why we went to the enchanted forest. To find the book to remove our curses. And if we hadn't done that—"

"I told you that book was trouble." Gwen sighed. "Virginia French, you promised me you wouldn't."

Ginny exhaled with all the exasperation inside her. "I know. And I did. And you were right. Nothing but trouble."

Aunt Gwen's frown had yet to disappear. "That book isn't real. I know you want to think it is, you want to have that hope, but it's a cruel trick. If there was anything that ought to be forgotten, it's that book."

"But, Gwen," Lucas said, "it's not a trick. It's real."

The three of them stared at him, but Easy was the first to speak. "How do you know it's real?"

"Because," Lucas said, "I've seen it with my own eyes."

CHAPTER TWENTY-EIGHT

For a moment, no one said a word. Then Easy made a decision. "We're going back out there. Lucas, you're going to take us."

"No." Gwen managed to pack the single-word command with the same fear, anger, and disappointment that filled her stern gaze. "Ginny, you promised me. And, Lucas, you promised, too."

Lucas gave her a pleading look. "Gwen, this isn't some lark. These kids need this. We need it."

Gwen put her hand to her throat. "The woods are dangerous. Look at what already happened to Ezekiel when he and Ginny went out there."

Ginny put her hand on her aunt's arm. "We'll shift as soon as we get to the woods. That's what I did when Easy was attacked, and the lightning bugs couldn't zap through my fur enough to do any damage."

Gwen wasn't convinced. "You're assuming we'll shift into something with thick enough fur for that to work."

Easy sighed. "That's true. But getting our names

in that book is the only hope any of us have for a normal existence now. Living under a single curse is bad enough, but two?"

Gwen took a step toward him, pulling away from Ginny. "And what happens when something else goes wrong out there? Don't you see that Ginny and I come from a cursed family? Her parents died in a freak accident, I had a stroke that left me with memory problems, she touched a mirror that made her forgettable... Why would you want to tempt fate?"

She turned to look at Lucas. "Ginny and I could be putting our lives in danger. And your lives, too, because you'd be with us. If you want to go, you're going without us."

"No, Aunt Gwen." Ginny stepped up beside her. "I'm going. I don't want to live my life like this anymore. I know there's always the possibility that something else could happen, but it's a risk I'm willing to take. Please come with us. We're not a cursed family. We've just had some really awful experiences. But finding that book could change some of those experiences. And our future."

Gwen wasn't persuaded. "Ginny, please don't."

Ginny took her aunt's hand. "Do you think I'd ever ask you to do something that I truly believed was dangerous? Do you think Lucas would? Do you think Easy would want me to put myself in that kind of position? He's willing to go back, and he's already run into trouble in the forest once. This is too good an opportunity to pass up."

Gwen looked at all of them, the fear in her eyes clear. "I understand all that, but it doesn't make me any less scared." Her inhale shuddered with trepidation. "I cannot lose you, Ginny. It would destroy me."

"You're not going to lose me. If this goes well, you're going to gain a new me. A niece that people remember. A niece that doesn't have to explain herself to the reception desk every time she comes to see you. Remember what that was like? Back before I touched that stupid mirror?"

Gwen swallowed. "I do." She cupped Ginny's cheek. "I know your life is hard." A long moment passed, then she nodded. "For you...I'll do this. But at the first sign of trouble, we leave."

Ginny's smile was thin. "I don't think I can promise that, Aunt Gwen. The enchanted forest is full of trouble. Just because something scares us, we can't run." Her smile took on new strength. "The Frenches are made of stronger stuff than that."

Gwen nodded weakly.

"Come on," Ginny said. "This is our chance to prove we're not cursed. This one thing will erase all that. I mean, it's not going to bring Mom and Dad back, but nothing's going to do that. We can't let fear rule us."

Gwen lifted her chin. "You're right. I've done that for too long. I can't say I'm not going to be afraid, but I'm willing to go."

Easy smiled. "You're not going alone. We're all in this together."

"That's right," Lucas said. "Together."

"Lucas?" Easy faced the man who held the key to his salvation. "How did you come to see the book?"

A sly look overtook him. "It was right after I moved here. I wasn't cursed, I just wanted to retire to a place where I could be myself. I used to run solo through the enchanted forest all the time. Loved the place. It was sort of the culmination of Shadowvale to me. All that wild and crazy stuff. And I was too young back then to ever think any of it might cause me harm."

He cleared his throat. "Anyway, I was out running one day and fell asleep during a rest. A voice woke me. A woman. She was talking to someone who wasn't answering back. I didn't recognize who it was at first, but when I got a look, I knew instantly. Amelia Marchand and her tiger, Thoreau."

"Whoa, hold up." Easy stared at Lucas. "She's the witch that started this town, right? She has a pet tiger?"

"That's right," Ginny said. "Amelia created this town. Her magic built it and, along with the meridian lines that run through this ground, helps to keep the town hidden. And Thoreau isn't so much her pet as her companion. Some would probably call him her familiar, but I don't know if she really considers him that."

Easy rubbed the back of his neck. "This town is crazy."

"It is," Gwen agreed.

"Go on, Lucas." Easy nodded at him. "What happened then?"

"Well," Lucas said with a shrug, "maybe it was the cop in me, but I was curious. So I followed them."

They were all silent and still, waiting on his next words.

"They went deeper into the forest than I'd ever been. Into the fairy realm. And that's when I saw it. A grove. With trees that soared overhead and bent together to form a chapel of sorts." Lucas gestured with his hands, making a dome shape.

"And in the center of that grove was a carved pedestal, on top of which sat *the* book."

Ginny sucked in a breath, her mouth open slightly in rapt attention. "Did they go into the grove? Did they touch the book?"

Lucas nodded. "Amelia and Thoreau went into the grove. They were greeted by a band of nymph warriors who suddenly appeared. I think they inhabit the grove's trees. The leader of the warriors welcomed Amelia, they spoke a few words, then the nymphs disappeared, leaving Amelia and Thoreau alone."

Gwen was chewing on her thumbnail, but listening intently. "And?"

Lucas spread his hands out. "Amelia and the tiger approached the book. It was already open. Like it was waiting for them. She patted the page and told Thoreau to put his paw on it."

"Did he?" Easy asked.

Lucas nodded. "He did. But Amelia seemed disappointed after that. I suppose she thought the tiger was under some kind of curse and was hoping that putting his paw on the book would remove it, but it must not have worked. At least not the way she'd thought it would."

"I've always heard you have to write your name," Ginny said. "I can't imagine just touching it would do much good."

Gwen frowned. "Wouldn't the witch know that?"

"You'd think so," Ginny answered. "But maybe she thought Thoreau was some kind of special case."

Easy put his hands on his hips. "How many years ago was that, Lucas?"

"Thirty. At least." The elder shifter's eyes narrowed. "You think I can't remember how to get back there?"

"The thought occurred to me," Easy said. "Not because you'd forget necessarily, but that was a long time ago. And from what Ginny's told me about the forest and what I've seen for myself, magic makes its own rules there."

"True," Lucas said. "But I've been back to the grove since then. Just to see if I could find it again, and I did. Does the grove move within the forest? I don't know. But what I can tell you is that the place has an unmistakable scent that makes it easy to track. Well, not easy. But possible."

Easy smiled. "Then you have my complete faith. Why don't you and Gwen run back to Emerald Manor and change, then come back here? If we go with you, we'll have to go through the whole process of showing ID. You both have your keys, you should be able to walk right on in. Then we'll take Ginny's Jeep to the forest, if that's okay with you, Ginny?"

She nodded. "Perfect."

Lucas shook his head. "One of you will have to drive us. My car is still at the Manor."

Easy grabbed his keys off the counter. "Take my car, then I'll drive you back when we return."

Lucas smiled, seemingly pleased with that idea. He looked at his watch. "Half an hour, then?"

"Sounds good," Easy answered. He would have rather left immediately, but half an hour was no time at all when the payoff could be freedom.

*

Ginny watched her aunt and Lucas leave in Easy's black Mustang. "I can't believe we're doing this again, but even more, I can't believe my aunt is going."

Easy came up beside her, slipping his arm around her waist. "Nervous?"

"Very. Especially for my aunt. She might have put on a semibrave face, but I know her, and she's terrified."

"I wish she didn't have to go, but if she doesn't put her name in that book, she'll be stuck with the curses."

Ginny nodded. "I know. I just…worry."

He pulled her closer. "I give you my word that I will keep watch over her. As I'm sure Lucas will, too."

"I'm sure he will, but he's also going to be leading us in. Kind of hard to do both. So thanks, that makes me feel better knowing you're looking out for her, too."

"And you," he whispered into her ear.

She smiled. "Do you really think Lucas will be able to find the grove again?"

"Do you doubt him?"

"Not him, exactly. But this is the enchanted forest we're talking about. A place I've been searching for ten years without luck. Forgive me if I have some doubts."

"Understandable. But maybe you just never looked in the right place."

"Well, then, I really hope today is different."

"It needs to be. For all our sakes." She sighed and glanced up at him. "Are you prepared for what happens if Lucas can't find the grove?"

His smile was brave and, she had a feeling, entirely for her sake. "He'll find it."

"But if he doesn't. Are you going to be okay with that?"

He looked out the window. "Okay with it? I don't think I'll ever be okay with the burdens we're bearing. Have you been okay with your curse all these years?"

"No. But I've learned to deal with it."

"And that's what I'll do, too. Learn to deal. But even if that's the outcome, and I don't think it will be, we have each other. We might be impossible to remember to the rest of Shadowvale, but there are four of us in this together. We can make it work."

She leaned against him. "Thank you."

His arm tightened around her. "For?"

"For not freaking out about this. For keeping your head level. For being the kind of guy I can lean on."

He kissed the top of her head, making her feel completely safe and protected. "Between the military and writing, there's one thing I've learned. There's always a way through whatever trouble you're in. If you're determined enough to find it, it's there."

"I think we're determined enough."

"I do, too. But we should probably change so we're ready to go."

"Right." She put her finger on the glass. "I just hope the way through our trouble is in the enchanted forest."

CHAPTER TWENTY-NINE

Easy had sat in the back seat of the Jeep with Lucas on the drive to the enchanted forest, and while the ride hadn't been long, there'd been very little said. The importance of their trip weighed on all of them, but it was apparent that Lucas felt it the most.

That weight increased now as they stood at the edge of the road, staring into the depths of the woods while Lucas got his bearings.

Some of that weight was lifted by the strength of the magic in this place. It buzzed over Easy's skin with an energy all its own, reminding him how much power was here.

When they shifted, it would become even more noticeable, especially when they were connected to this ground with four feet instead of two.

After a few more moments, Lucas shook his head. "I have to shift. My senses aren't keen enough in my human form to find the scent trail." He dropped his gaze a little. "I'm not as young as I used to be, but I know it's here. I can almost pick it up, but every time I think I have it, it slips away."

"Hey," Easy said, "there are enough different smells out here to make tracking difficult for anyone." He said it like it was no big deal, which it wasn't to him, but Lucas's trouble picking up the trail clearly wasn't sitting well with Gwen.

Her face showed every worry she felt, but Easy wasn't sure how to make her feel better. He gave her props for coming with them, despite her misgivings. That took courage.

"Yeah," Lucas said. "I suppose."

"Plus," Ginny added, "we're all going to shift anyway."

"I know," Lucas responded. "But I'd hoped to pick up the scent trail first."

Easy shrugged. "I'm sure you will once we're in the woods. Ladies, Lucas will lead, then Ginny, then Gwen, then I'll bring up the rear. Anyone needs to stop for any reason, vocalize once. Softly. We don't want to draw unnecessary attention to ourselves."

Gwen hugged her arms around her torso.

"And when we get to the grove?" Ginny asked.

"We shift back to our human forms and put our names in the book." He smiled at her and gave her a little wink.

She smiled back. "That's the plan, then." She glanced at her aunt. "You good, Aunt Gwen?"

The woman nodded, but her eyes never came off the forest. Her nerves were almost a visible thing.

Ginny stood beside her. "I know you're worried. But it's going to be okay. This is a good thing we're doing."

Gwen nodded, her smile tight. "I know."

Ginny gave her a quick hug. "If you really don't want to do this—"

"No," Gwen said, her smile relaxing a little. "This is our only chance for a normal life. And you deserve that. You've already had too many years of being forgotten."

"Thanks," Ginny said softly.

Easy clapped his hands lightly. "All right. Let's get moving. We don't want to be out here after dark if we can help it."

"Agreed." Lucas glanced at Ginny. "You have that video handy? I put some full moon ointment on back at the condo, but that video worked great last time."

"I do." She pulled out her phone and produced the full moon footage again, showing it to him as it started playing. "Here you go."

He took a concentrated look at it. A few seconds later, his eyes started to glow. Gwen and Ginny followed.

Easy willed the shift to happen. In moments, it began. The familiar but welcome ache took over his body, causing bones and muscles to morph into his most natural form.

He went to all fours, his hands and feet becoming broad paws meant for gripping the earth. His ears elongated, increasing his hearing range. His eyesight became keener, his sense of smell sharpening to the point that he could pick up the scent of a rabbit a mile away.

He stretched his front legs out to get a look at

what he'd become. Maybe not the wolf he really was, but some kind of wolf.

Lucas was a hound, graying at the muzzle, but perfect for tracking. Gwen and Ginny had both become coyotes, although Gwen's was darker, making it easy to tell them apart at a glance.

Lucas sniffed the air, then woofed quietly and started into the woods, nose leading the way.

They were off. They fell into line as Easy had described and kept up a good pace. Nothing too fast. There was too much to pay attention to in the forest to run wild. Too much to be wary of.

Easy had his eyes peeled for anything glowing red. Actually, *anything* glowing was going to get a second look. He wasn't afraid. He just didn't want to derail their plans by getting swarmed again.

The woods thickened, but Lucas kept on, his stride steady. Suddenly, the trees opened up, and a small clearing appeared, the ground covered in moss and a few rocks where there wasn't leaf litter.

Lucas paused, his nose in the air, taking in scents from every direction. He turned south, sniffed again, then whuffed and took off.

A little faster this time, a little more intent, perhaps.

The women followed with Easy close behind. A drox, one of the winged, fire-breathing foxlike creatures the woods were known for, trotted past at a distance. Easy knew about them only because Ginny had told him over dinner one night, and Easy had written about the creature in his journal.

The drox stayed far enough away to see but too

far to catch, should they choose to pursue. Which wasn't something they'd do, but the drox didn't know that.

Easy had a feeling the drox was more curious about them than they were of it. Did the creature know that they were shifters? Could it tell? Would a drox consider Charlie Ashborne kin? The chocolatier was a dragon shifter, and droxes were part dragon.

His mind continued to wander while his senses remained on alert for danger. None, thankfully, appeared. So far anyway.

The woods dimmed, the canopy overhead blocking most of the available light. Clumps of sprite moss began to show up on the tree trunks. An owl hooted. Or maybe it was a meowl, something else Ginny had told him about.

Ginny paid little attention to any of it, but Gwen stumbled once because she was too distracted by what was around her.

That worried Easy a little. This wasn't the place to lose focus.

Mist rose up around them. At first, it clung to the ground, twirling away in little eddies as they trotted past.

Then it grew denser and deeper, reaching almost to their chests. Still, Lucas led them on. Tiny spots of blue light danced at the edges of Easy's peripheral vision. His eyesight was sharp enough to detect the outlines of wings in the orbs of light. Fairies.

An excited burst of energy zipped through him. Lucas had said the grove was in the fairy realm. That meant they were getting closer.

There was no visible sky above them, and no horizon line to be seen anywhere. They had to be in the depths of the forest. Still, the mist rose up around them until all Easy could see was the tip of Gwen's tail.

It wagged nervously. He understood. The chances of getting lost or separated in this foggy soup were high. They'd slowed some, too.

Easy prayed that was because Lucas was being careful, not because he'd lost the trail.

Leaves crunched underfoot occasionally, but soon the ground was all moss, and any sound their footsteps made was swallowed up by the mist.

Still, Lucas plodded on. Slowing a bit more, but going forward all the same. Easy had no sense of time. They might have been in the forest for thirty minutes or three hours. It was impossible to tell. His senses, even as keen as they were, felt muffled by the closeness of the trees and the cover of the haze.

It was like they'd been purposefully blindfolded. Like the path they were traveling wasn't supposed to be memorable.

That creeped Easy out. But it also gave him hope.

Then he walked through a curtain of mist and came into a clearing on the other side without a trace of haze. Lucas and the others had come to a halt, so he stopped, too. As resting spots went, it was a decent one. Better visibility than they'd had in a long while. Even so, he kept a watchful eye on their surroundings until Lucas signaled it was time to move again.

"This is it," Lucas whispered.

Easy turned to see the man back in his human form. Gwen and Ginny were shifting back, too, so he joined them. He shook himself as he became human again, rolling his shoulders. The magic hung on him like a damp blanket.

"The magic is thicker here," Lucas said almost reverently.

Easy nodded.

"I feel it, too," Ginny said. "We all do, I'm sure."

Gwen rubbed her arms. "Too much magic."

Lucas's mouth was a firm line. "It's because of where we are. Some of the meridians spread out from here."

"Where are we?" Ginny asked. "You said this is it, but are we—"

"Turn around," Lucas said.

She, Easy, and Gwen all turned at the same time.

Behind them was the grove.

None of them said a word as they took it in. Easy could only imagine what Ginny was feeling. She'd searched for this place for ten years. To finally be standing here must seem like the answer to a prayer. A dream realized.

He decided in that moment to let her guide them through the next phase of their adventure. After all, they were here because of her in so many ways. Not just because of her curse, but because of her belief in this place, her refusal to give up, her unwavering faith that she'd find a solution.

After a minute or two, she took a single step

toward the circle of trees. "I can't believe we're standing here. It's beautiful."

She reached her hand back toward Lucas, but kept her eyes forward as if looking away might make the grove disappear. "Thank you for bringing us here, Lucas."

He nodded, even though she couldn't see that. "You're welcome. Thank you for believing in me."

Easy went a little closer to Ginny. "This is your show now. What do you want to do next?"

"Okay," she whispered. "I guess…go in?"

"However you want to handle it," he answered.

Her aunt frowned. "I've never felt such strong magic. Do you think we should all go in together? Maybe one at a time?"

"I don't know," Ginny said as she stepped forward. "But this isn't a place to be afraid of. We've made it this far without incident, so we have to believe it's going to continue that way. So long as we're respectful of the power here."

"Exactly," Easy said. But he wasn't so sure he bought that this trip would remain uneventful. His life had taught him there were two sides to everything, a natural balance. If there was good, there was also bad. That symmetry was an intrinsic part of storytelling.

It wasn't lost on him that they were about to trust a *book* to remove their curses. So how could he not wonder what the price of such a gift would be?

CHAPTER THIRTY

Aunt Gwen was right. Ginny had never felt such powerful magic in her life before. It was like walking through warm water and suddenly stepping into a cold current. Impossible to miss. Impossible not to react to.

But as much as Ginny wanted to run into the grove, find the book, and scrawl her name on its pages, she knew that magic could be tricky. There might be a right way and a wrong way to enter this grove. The same went for putting one's name in the book.

And they'd come too far to mess something up now.

She glanced at Easy, smiling. "Thank you for letting me handle this. Doesn't mean I'm not open to suggestions, though."

His gaze narrowed ever so slightly. "We have a saying in the military. Slow is smooth and smooth is fast. I think more than ever, especially when we're dealing with such life-changing power, that's the way to go. Carefully. And with consideration."

"I agree." Ginny took a breath. "I just wish I knew more about magic. About how to approach it. How to stay on the right side of it." She looked back at Lucas and Aunt Gwen. "Any ideas?"

Aunt Gwen put her hand to her mouth. "Just be careful."

"Same," Lucas said. "Whatever you think we should do is fine with me."

"Okay." But the weight of that responsibility only added to the stress of the moment. She could handle it, though. And she would handle it.

She reached out and took Easy's hand. "We all need these curses lifted. I think we should all go into the grove together."

"Sounds logical."

She looked at Lucas and Aunt Gwen again. "Okay?"

They nodded, Aunt Gwen with a little less enthusiasm than Lucas.

Ginny focused on the towering circle of trees. "Let's go. Slowly, with respect, and confidence. We found this place, and we deserve to be here. And we deserve to put our names in that book."

They walked boldly, if not solemnly, forward as a group, slipping through the trunks as they entered.

The book sat in the center of the clearing on a beautiful carved pedestal, pages open and waiting.

They stopped just inside the circle of trees, the book still several yards away. A carpet of blue-green moss blanketed the grove floor. The thick trunks of the twelve trees that encircled the grove rose into the sky, their branches forming a dome with only a circle of midday sky showing through at the center. The book and pedestal sat beneath that. The book was bigger than Ginny had expected and gave off a faint glow.

"You were right, Easy," she said. "It definitely glows."

A sense of calm and sacredness existed within the grove. Like the quiet space inside a grand cathedral, except this one had been grown, not built.

"It's beautiful," Gwen said.

"It is." Ginny took a breath, absorbing the moment.

"Who enters this grove?"

At once, Ginny realized they were surrounded by at least twelve warrior women leveling bows at them. The nymphs Lucas had mentioned. "I...I'm Virginia French. Ginny." Where had they come from? "This is Ezekiel Grayle, Gwen French, and Lucas Cartwright."

The woman in front of Ginny kept her bow steady. The arrow notched into it was tipped with a sharpened flint that looked like it would slice through a body like a hot knife through warm butter. "Why have you come here?"

"Because we have curses we're desperate to remove. We want to put our names in the book." Ginny lifted her chin. They had every right to be here. "You are the nymphs who protect this grove?"

"We are. I am Lylianna, captain of the grove guard, and these are my soldiers."

"Nymphs. Just like last time," Lucas whispered.

Lylianna glanced at him. "This grove is our home, and we are charged to protect it, but also the book that resides within."

Lucas stayed close to Gwen, his hand on her back. "We mean this place no harm. I swear on my wolf."

Lylianna's eyes narrowed as her nostrils flared. "You're all wolves."

"Yes," Easy said. "That's part of the reason why we're here. Our ability to shift into those wolves has been compromised by a curse."

She looked at him. "All four of you?"

He nodded. "But we're also burdened with a second curse that prevents anyone from remembering us."

"And you want that curse removed as well?"

"We do."

She shifted her gaze to each of them in turn before coming back to him. "No."

Panic knotted Ginny's gut. "What do you mean no?"

"There are too many of you," Lylianna answered. "The book must be protected. Only two of you may write your names in it."

The four of them stood there, stunned.

But Ginny's amazement quickly turned to anger. She took a step forward, ending up with the tip of Lylianna's arrow inches from her heart. "That's unacceptable. I've looked for this grove for ten years. Ten years of no one remembering me. Ten years of feeling like a stranger in this town. Ten years of no friends. No neighbors to wave hello at me. No one to nod in greeting as I pass them on the street. Ten years of being alone, except for my aunt, who is only able to remember me occasionally due to her stroke, and Seymour, the lake monster, who mostly remembers me because I bring him pie."

Lylianna blinked. "You dare to argue with me?"

"Yes, I dare." Ginny lifted her hands in frustration. "Did you hear me? My life has been incredibly hard, but the thing that's kept me going is this place. The idea that someday I would be able to get rid of this curse by putting my name in that book." She stabbed her finger at the nymph. "Then you try to tell me I can't?"

"I did not say you can't." Lylianna looked both surprised and astonished to be challenged. "I said only two of you will be granted permission."

"I heard that. And I refuse it. We're all putting our names in the book. All of us. So unless you're prepared to actually put that arrow through me, I'd suggest you step aside."

"Ginny…" Easy's voice was filled with caution.

Ginny held her hand out toward him, a gesture to tell him she had this.

The other nymphs looked shocked. Good, Ginny thought. Let them be shocked. Let them know that she wasn't going to be denied this.

She crossed her arms. "Should I get Amelia Marchand involved in this?"

Lylianna lowered her bow a few inches. "I don't deny your request without reason. The book can only absorb so many curses at a time."

"I understand that. But let me explain it more clearly. We have four people with three curses. Because of an accident, my curse of being forgotten has spread to all of us, as has Ezekiel's curse of not being able to shift into our true wolf forms. My aunt has also been cursed with memory troubles by a stroke. Those are the curses that must be removed. You're the guardian of this place, so you must know how to make that happen."

Lylianna dropped her bow all the way. The other nymphs did the same. "There is a way. But it requires sacrifice."

"What kind of sacrifice?"

"You must balance the bad of your curse with something good. You must offer that good thing to the book."

"I knew it," Easy muttered.

Ginny ignored his comment. "Each of us?"

"The three of you with curses to be removed, but especially you and the young male wolf. You are the originators of the main curses. Only you two and your aunt need put your names in the book."

Ginny pointed to Lucas. "What about him? He has both curses as well."

Lylianna glanced at him. "You bear no curse of your own?"

"No." Lucas's brow furrowed. "Just the two I inherited in the accident."

Lylianna looked at Ginny again. "Then he will be freed when those curses are gone."

"You swear that he'll be curse-free without putting his name in the book?"

"On the tree that gives me life, I swear it."

"Okay," Ginny said. "Then what kind of good thing do we have to sacrifice? We didn't exactly come out here with our most valuable worldly possessions."

"It needn't be something valuable by the world's standards, only valuable to you."

Easy stepped forward as he dug in his back pocket. "I have a challenge coin to offer as my sacrifice. It was given to me by my CO after I completed my last mission in Afghanistan. I went home after that, but he stayed. The next mission was his last." Easy pulled the coin out of his wallet and turned it over in his fingers. "He was killed by an IED. Good man."

After a moment, he held up the coin. "Will this do?"

Lylianna nodded. "Place the coin on the book."

Easy did as she directed, then stepped back.

The book gleamed brightly for a long second, then the coin disappeared into it.

Lylianna gestured at Easy. "Your offering is accepted."

Easy took a deep breath. "Good."

Lylianna focused on Ginny and Gwen. "What will you two offer?"

Ginny bit the inside of her cheek as she glanced at her aunt. "There's only one thing I can think of. And it would be from me *and* my aunt, because it's meaningful to both of us."

Gwen's eyes went wide with realization. "Ginny, no."

"I don't have anything else. Do you?"

Gwen shook her head. "No. But—"

"He would be okay with it."

With only a moment of hesitation, Gwen nodded. "Yes, he would."

Ginny looked at Lylianna again and unhooked her father's ID bracelet from her wrist. The wind rustled the leaves overhead. "This is the most cherished thing I own. It was a gift to my dad, who was also my aunt's brother, from my mom. It was the only personal item that survived the car crash that took their lives when I was three."

She held out the heavy silver bracelet. Her wrist felt bare and much lighter without it. A tear slid down her cheek.

Lylianna gestured toward the pedestal. "Lay it on the book."

Ginny walked over and placed the bracelet in the valley between the pages. The names already written there were a blur, impossible to read no matter how hard she tried to focus. The magic at work, no doubt.

The book and bracelet shone brightly for a moment, then dissolved into the pages.

"Your sacrifice is accepted," Lylianna said. "You may write your names."

Easy held his hand out toward the book. "Ladies first."

Ginny went back to the book. A slim feather pen lay in the same spot where she'd placed the bracelet.

It definitely hadn't been there before. She would have seen it when she'd put the bracelet down. She took the pen and wrote her name on the first blank line.

She stepped back, expecting to feel something. Different, at least. But she didn't. Not even a tingle of magic ran through her.

She held the pen out to her aunt and moved out of the way.

Gwen approached the book and added her name, then handed the pen to Easy. With a great flourish, he signed his autograph.

He put the pen on the book and stepped away. "Is that it? We're curse-free now?"

Lylianna nodded. "You are. Go home. Live your lives in peace."

Lucas frowned. "And what if we aren't curse-free? What if something went wrong? Or the book didn't get it all?"

Lylianna narrowed her eyes. "The book is faultless."

"I hope so," Lucas said. "Because if there's even a hint of curse left, we're coming back here."

"No," Lylianna said. "You won't. The memory of this place will vanish from your minds before morning breaks. You will know that you've been here, but not how to find the grove again." She bowed her head slightly. "Be well."

Ginny's mouth came open. "We didn't agree to a brain-wipe. We've had enough issues with memory to—"

Lylianna raised her hand, cutting Ginny off. "What is done is done." Then she nodded, and all twelve of the women turned and disappeared into one of the grove's trees.

"What is done is done," Gwen parroted.

"Apparently," Ginny said. "I guess we might as well go home."

Chapter Thirty-One

On the way home, Easy sat up front with Ginny. The air flowed over them, warm and sweet. And while hope was strong in all of them that they were free of their curses, a weightier feeling was underneath the hope. A sense of not knowing what had actually been accomplished in the grove until they could test things out.

To Easy, there seemed to be a little sadness in Ginny, too. He put his hand on her shoulder. "I'm sorry you had to give up your dad's bracelet."

"Me, too." She glanced at her wrist. "Funny how you can still feel a thing even when it's gone. But I think he would be happy to know that he could do something like that for me."

Gwen leaned forward. "He would."

Lucas leaned in, too. "Did anyone feel anything when they put their name in the book? I thought there'd be some kind of power surge or something, but then, maybe I didn't get it since I was sort of cured by association."

"No, nothing," Easy said.

"Me either," Ginny agreed.

Gwen tipped her head. "I thought there'd be a physical sensation, too. I hope that wasn't all a bunch of smoke and mirrors."

"Well," Lucas said, "I can't for the life of me pick up the scent of the grove anymore. I mean, it's completely gone. So that part was definitely real."

Easy looked at him. "We need to test this out. Make sure we can be remembered and that we can shift into what we're supposed to shift into."

"Agree," Gwen said. "Because we might not be able to get back to the grove, but we could certainly lodge a complaint with Amelia Marchand if the curse removal didn't take."

"Let's get ice cream," Lucas said.

Gwen snickered in amusement. "You and your stomach."

Ginny nodded, smiling for the first time since they'd left the forest. "I'd be okay with that."

"I'm in." Easy grinned. "I love ice cream."

"Do you?" Ginny asked. "What flavor?"

"Yes," he answered, laughing. "All of it."

"Then you're going to love the Creamatorium."

He made a face. "The what?"

"It's the best place in town to get ice cream," Lucas said. "You'll see."

Easy raised a skeptical brow. "The name is kind of morbid."

Ginny snorted. "Yeah, I suppose it is. But the ice cream is killer. Hey! Maybe that's why it's called the Creamatorium?" She laughed at her own joke.

The sound pleased him to no end. She was happy, and that made him happy. Having the curses removed would be the icing on the cake now.

The fact that he'd had to give up his commander's coin wasn't great, but it was nothing like what Ginny had sacrificed. But he'd do it all over again for her. She was worth it. So was having his curse removed.

He just couldn't get over the feeling that, for her, the sacrifice had been much greater. There had to be a way to help her get over the loss, because it was plain that had been difficult for her.

Of course, now that Ginny could enjoy life, they'd have a ton of fun together. There would be all kinds of ways to distract her. Granted, he still had a book to finish. That hadn't changed.

But without the distraction of his curse hanging over him, he might become a better, and faster, writer.

Time would tell on that front.

He already knew that having Ginny at his side made him a better man. A happier one, too.

Maybe he wouldn't wait until his book came out to make things permanent. Especially if they were truly curse-free.

Ginny pulled into the parking lot at the Creamatorium and found a spot for the Jeep. They all got out and went inside. Lucas and Gwen stood a little ways off, studying the selections.

Easy was in ice cream heaven. The board of flavors was overwhelming. "Okay, just so you know, we're coming back here. It's going to take months for me to try all of these."

She nudged him gently with her elbow. "Then I probably shouldn't tell you the selection changes every month."

He put a hand on his head. "I may never leave."

She stared up at the board along with him. "What are you going to get?"

"I need a lot more time before I can answer that." He read a few of the flavors and descriptions, then looked at her. He was caught off guard by how beautiful she was. And even though she seemed to be dealing okay with the loss of her dad's bracelet, Easy remained deeply sorry she'd had to give that up. It seemed unfair.

In a way, that was his fault. If she'd gone to the grove alone, there would have been no need for a sacrifice to balance things out.

He owed her.

She caught him watching her. "What?"

"Nothing. Just thinking about how pretty you are."

She blushed and poked his arm. "You're supposed to be picking a flavor."

"I want it all." And he realized as he continued to take her in how true that was. He wanted her as his wife. And as the mother of his children. As the woman he'd grow old with. He wanted to share his hopes and dreams with her just as much as he wanted to know what hers were.

He leaned in, nuzzled her neck, and planted a kiss just below her ear. "I love you, Ginny."

Her mouth rounded, and her eyes went wide. "You...do?"

He nodded as he slid his arm around her waist. "Yep. Now, what flavor am I going to get? Decisions, decisions..."

She laughed. "You can't just say a thing like that and then go right back to ice cream."

"I can't?" He tipped his head. "Why not?"

"Because...because that's a big thing to say."

"Not that big. But true."

"And you thought the middle of the Creamatorium was the place to tell me?"

"I thought you should know."

"Well..." The corner of her mouth quirked up in a funny little half grin. "I love you, too."

He grinned and tugged her closer. "Good to know."

"Having said that, don't read too much into the flavor I'm about to order."

"Oh? Which one?"

"Wedding Cake."

He found that flavor on the board and read the description. "Vanilla bean ice cream with swirls of rose-scented buttercream frosting, chunks of wedding cake, and pieces of crystalized violets."

"It sounds a little weird, but it's really good."

His grin widened. "No comment. I think I'm going with Banana Bomb. Banana ice cream, fudge and marshmallow swirls, and graham cracker pieces."

"I haven't had that one." She gave him an optimistic look. "Can I taste yours?"

There were so many ways to answer that, but he just nodded and said, "Absolutely."

They approached the counter to order, meeting Gwen and Lucas there. They put their orders in, found a table, and sat down to wait. And see if they were remembered.

Within minutes, a server approached with their ice cream. She handed out the orders perfectly. Then came back with glasses of water for all of them.

Ginny gasped in obvious relief. Then she went silent as if struggling with emotion. "Wow," she whispered. "It worked. The server knew us. She didn't once look at any of us like she'd never seen us before."

Easy gave her hand a squeeze. "It's over. Your curse no longer exists."

She nodded, smiling and clearly emotional.

Gwen put an arm around her. "It's all done, honey."

Lucas sat up a little taller. "It's a good day."

"That's for sure." Easy let go of Ginny's hand and picked up his spoon. "Now all that remains is for us to shift."

They decided on Nightingale Park for their run. The run wasn't necessary, of course, but Easy had pushed for it. Ginny understood. If his true form was back, he was going to want to run for the sheer joy of it.

And Aunt Gwen wanted to see the sun.

How could Ginny deny her two favorite people? She couldn't, which was why, with a belly full of ice cream, she was driving toward the twilight line.

The ice cream wouldn't matter that much. If anything, it would fuel the run.

A sign up ahead announced the approaching demarcation where the sunless part of Shadowvale ended.

Easy laughed. "Do they really need a sign?"

Ginny glanced at him. "They do after a vampire got lost and almost burned his biscuits."

"Ouch."

"Exactly. That's why they put the speed bump in, too. So there could be no mistaking it." She tightened her grip on the wheel and slowed as the Jeep rolled over the little rise.

Sun spilled over them like warm water. She tipped her head up as much as she could without losing sight of the road.

In the rearview mirror, she could see Aunt Gwen and Lucas doing the same thing. Next to her, Easy had his eyes closed and his face lifted.

"Wow," he breathed out. "I kind of forgot what this feels like."

"I know. Funny how fast that can happen." While her passengers enjoyed the rays, she drove the last few minutes to Nightingale Park and found a place in the lot. Only a few other cars occupied the spaces. She turned the Jeep off and turned to look at Easy. "If there's anything you don't want to take, we can lock it up in the glove box."

"I'm good," Easy said. He got out, looking around. "This is pretty nice up here."

Ginny jumped out, then helped her aunt do the same. "It's really nice. Every time I come up here, I think about how I should come up here more."

Easy looked toward the distance. "I hear water. Did one of you say something about a creek?"

Lucas pointed in the same direction. "There's a good-sized creek that runs down the mountain here. Feeds into the river that runs through the bayou and fills the lake. About a half mile up from the park, there's a nice little swimming hole."

"Cool," Easy said.

"And there's a picnic area here," Lucas continued, "all kinds of trails for hiking, even a playground for the littles."

"See?" Ginny said. "Already, I'm wondering why it's taken me so long to get back here."

Easy nodded. "We should make this a regular outing. When I'm done with my book."

"Naturally. Which you're getting back to tomorrow, right?"

"Yes. Maybe even tonight."

She looked at her aunt. "Ready to run?"

"I am." Gwen smiled at Lucas. "This will be fun. It's been a while."

"It has," Lucas said as he took her hand.

"South trail?" Ginny asked. "It gets the most sun."

"Sounds good," Easy said, and Gwen and Lucas agreed.

They followed the signs to the beginning of the marked trail. Beside the sign announcing the start of the 2.6-mile dirt path, there was a wooden bench. The sign had a small color map on it, showing the route and where it linked up to some of the other trails.

Ginny tapped the sign. "We're the red path."

"Got it," Easy said.

"Okay." Ginny smiled. "Let's shift." She checked on Lucas. "You want me to pull up that video?"

"No." He raised his brows. "I've got this."

Gwen smiled at him, then her eyes gleamed with the start of her own shift. Ginny and Easy joined them. In less than a minute, they were on all fours and ready to run. And they were all in their true forms. Except for Easy.

Who had become a dire wolf again.

CHAPTER THIRTY-TWO

Easy could tell by the look on Ginny's face that something wasn't right. He shifted back to his human form immediately. "What's wrong?"

She shifted back, too. "I don't know that's wrong, exactly, but you went into the same dire wolf form as before. I meant to tell you earlier that you were a dire wolf in the enchanted forest, too."

"That's odd. Since getting struck by lightning, I've never been the same thing and certainly not in three shifts back to back." He ran his hand through his hair. "I don't know what to make of it."

Ginny shrugged. "It's not a bad form to have. It's pretty rare. And well-respected. Do you think maybe you just stuck with the last form you were in?"

"Maybe. If so, I'm glad I wasn't a poodle." He winked at her. "Well, I'm not going to worry about it. Not much I can do at this point. Besides, your aunt and Lucas are waiting on us."

She looked at them, then took a few steps closer to Easy and lowered her voice. "If it makes any difference, my wolf finds your dire wolf very sexy."

The urge to tip his head back and howl was strong. Instead, he grinned. "Yeah, I'm good with the dire wolf, then."

With a laugh, she shook herself and transformed back into her wolf.

A moment later, he joined her, and the four of them took off down the sun-dappled trail.

Just minutes in and he was the happiest he'd been in a long while. He hadn't been for a pack run in a very long time, and while calling this quartet a pack was stretching the definition a bit, it was the closest to that dynamic he'd come since realizing his shifting abilities were iffy.

There was nothing like it, and the experience filled a place in him he hadn't realized was empty.

Ginny was at his shoulder, as beautiful in her wolf form as she was in her human one. The urge to give her a playful bite was strong. He also wanted to tackle her and roll around in the leaves with her. But maybe not in front of her aunt and Lucas.

Although there was no reason not to publicly declare his interest in her that way. Because he was absolutely interested. In her alone.

Maybe at the end of the run.

Behind him and Ginny were her aunt and Lucas, who kept up without issue. That was the beauty of their wolf forms. They aged, but not quite as rapidly as their human ones.

And there was something about the earth under your paws, the wind in your fur, and the sun on your muzzle to bring the joy of life out in you. It just made you feel alive.

The path's incline took them farther up the side of the mountain, then curved around. Easy remembered the route from the map. Any minute, they'd pass a turnoff that connected this trail to the blue one. He'd like to run that sometime with Ginny, but the extra three miles wasn't in the cards for today.

They ran on, driven by the sheer fun of the activity, the endorphins of the exercise, and the rare glimpses of sun. They became one with nature, one with the animal who lived within them. It was freedom that no nonshifter would ever know, a kind of lightness of being and wholeness of spirit that Easy had never experienced in any other part of his life.

The air swirled past them as they ran, scented with a thousand earthy things only their powerful noses could pick up. Birds chirped overhead, insects buzzed by, and a squirrel darted across their path.

Before long, the sound of moving water reached them, and Easy knew they were on the back half of the circuit and headed toward the trail's end. They slowed to a trot as a group, as if none of them was quite ready for it to be over.

As for Easy, he would be back here. Hopefully with all of them. Today had been incredibly hard, but incredibly good, and this run had capped it off perfectly. He glanced around, wanting to imprint his surroundings on his memory so that not a single detail would be lost.

Ginny yelped and skidded to a stop.

Easy looked at the trail's head.

A big black wolf stood in the way, staring them down. Lips curled.

They all stopped. Easy stepped in front of Ginny, and Lucas joined him so that Gwen was behind them as well.

A subtle shift in the air told Easy that Ginny had returned to her human form. She spoke, confirming that.

"You're Rico Martinez, aren't you? Alpha of the Shadowvale pack."

The black wolf stopped snarling and, a few seconds later, turned into the man Ginny had called out by name.

"How do you know who I am?"

"Long story," she said. She put her hand on Easy's back, weaving her fingers into the thick fur between his shoulder blades.

"Start talking," Rico said. "Because I don't know you."

Lucas shifted. "Yes, you do."

Rico frowned at him. "Lucas Cartwright?"

Easy looked behind him. Gwen was shifting out of wolf mode, too. He joined her, taking on his human form to stand with Ginny.

Rico stared them down. "Who are these wolves, Lucas?"

"My friend Gwen lives at Emerald Manor like I do." He reached toward Ginny. "This is her niece and her niece's boyfriend. He's new to town, but he and Ginny have had some issues that have kept them from joining the pack."

"Such as?" Rico asked.

Ginny stepped forward. "I've lived the last ten years under a curse that made me impossible to remember. Over the years, I tried to join the pack several times, but it never worked out. Once the group thought there was a strange wolf in their midst..." She shrugged. "It didn't go well."

Rico grimaced. "I can imagine." He looked at Easy. "What about you?"

"Couldn't shift reliably. I can now, though."

Rico seemed to ponder that. "You all plan on joining, then?"

The four of them exchanged looks, but it was Easy who answered. "We'd love to."

Rico finally relaxed. "Good. We'd love to have you." He looked at Easy. "We don't have any other dire wolves in the pack. The ladies will get a kick out of that for sure."

Ginny crossed her arms. "Oh?"

Easy snorted, flattered by her sudden green-eyed glare. He put his hand on the small of her back as he answered Rico. "I'm taken."

"Even better," Rico said. "I don't need to deal with all those hormones. The den is on Sycamore and Luna. Come by any night, but Fridays are when we add new members."

Lucas puffed up his chest a little. "I'll vouch for them."

"Perfect." Rico gave them a little nod. "See you then. I'm off to run."

He shifted back to his wolf form and trotted past them, breaking into a run a few moments later.

When he was out of earshot, Ginny let out a little squeal. "We're going to be part of the pack. I can't wait."

Easy laughed. "They're going to have you on every committee on the books if you're not careful."

She shrugged. "That's okay. I need to make friends."

"And I need a nap," Gwen said. She laughed. "Maybe a shower first, though. Today has worn me out. In a good way. But I'm ready to crash."

Ginny beamed with love. "It's been quite a day, hasn't it? C'mon, I'll drop you guys off at the Manor."

They headed back to the Jeep, piled in, and got on the road home. After they said goodbye to Gwen and Lucas, with plans already made for Friday evening at the den, Easy let out a long sigh.

Ginny looked at him. "You okay?"

"I'm great. Beat. But good. I feel like your aunt, though. Ready for a nap. But I have to get a couple pages in, or I'm going to regret it tomorrow."

"Why don't you work on your book, and I'll take care of dinner? Then you don't have to worry about that."

He took her hand and brought it to his lips, kissing her knuckles. "That would be great. But don't you have work to do, too?"

"Yes, but my deadlines aren't nearly as pressing as yours."

"Hey, in a day or two, when we're back in our routine, let's go out to eat. Just you and me. Like a real couple."

"I'd love that." She grinned. "You know what else we should do?"

"What's that?"

"Take that trip out to see Seymour. I'm sure he feels terrible about what happened."

Easy made a face. "Yeah, I don't know about that…"

"I'm not saying get in the water with him. Just take him some pies and explain what happened and let bygones be bygones. That kind of thing."

"You know I'm in. Especially if it'll make you happy."

"It will." She smirked, maybe because she was getting her way.

Easy didn't care. She was happy, and that was all that mattered. That and her loving him the way he loved her. And he was going to spend the rest of his life searching for new ways to make her smile.

But the first thing he was going to do for her? He already had a pretty good idea about what that was. And if his idea paid off, it was worth whatever cost necessary to make it happen.

CHAPTER THIRTY-THREE

Ginny hadn't counted on it taking three days for them to get out to see Seymour. She knew Easy was busy, knew he was desperately trying to get back on track with his writing, but she also knew he hadn't exactly been home all day for those three days.

Hard to hide your comings and goings from your next-door neighbor.

She couldn't help but wonder what he was up to. Especially when she'd offered to get groceries for him and he'd declined. Same result when she'd asked him if he had any errands to run.

So where was he going, and what was he doing? He'd left three times. Once each day. Each time empty-handed on the way out and the way in.

Not that she was keeping tabs on him. But again, hard not to notice when he lived right next door. And, okay, maybe she was keeping a few tabs. But they'd professed their love for each other, and now he was being a little…sneaky.

Maybe *sneaky* wasn't the right word, exactly, but for the love of Pete, what was he up to?

Ginny sighed and made herself walk away from the window. Tonight, around seven, they were going out to the lake so that Easy could meet Seymour and they could work things out. After that, they were going to grab a pizza at Fritzi's.

Naturally, they'd be going to the bakery on the way to the lake so they could pick up Seymour's pies. She'd called ahead to reserve them, seeing as how they'd be going by so late in the day.

But there were a lot of hours in between now and seven. Hours she needed to spend working and not worrying about what Easy was up to. He was allowed to have his own life and do things without her.

She just itched to know what those things were.

Reluctantly, she sat at her desk, put her headphones on, and got busy. Emails had gotten a little stacked up, and answering them was going to take at least an hour, maybe more. Then there were ongoing projects, new projects, tweaks to old projects...yeah, she had no time to be spying on her boyfriend.

Boyfriend. Heh. She grinned as she opened her inbox.

By six, she was tired of sitting in her office chair and ready to quit, which was perfect since she needed to change for their jaunt to the lake. They were not swimming. That much had already been established.

Ginny wasn't sure Easy would ever get into the same water with Seymour again, but that was fine. She didn't need them to be best buddies, just for them to forgive each other and move on in a friendly manner.

Easy might cast a skeptical eye upon the monster, but he was Ginny's friend, and she wasn't about to give him up. Especially now that her social calendar was going to get a lot busier. She didn't want Seymour to think she was coming less frequently because she no longer liked him. Lake monster or not, Seymour had feelings, and she didn't want him to be hurt.

Living a solitary life was something she understood all too well. Being lonely sucked. She didn't want to contribute to that.

Thankfully, Aunt Gwen could go visit him on her own now, too. In fact, since her memory issues had been cured by the book, she was getting her driver's license back. Her independence had been restored.

Which also meant she no longer needed to live on the assisted-living side of Emerald Manor. Ginny had a feeling her aunt would be moving as close to Lucas as possible.

Or maybe even *in* with him.

Ginny smiled, thinking about how happy he made Aunt Gwen. Finding love at any age was amazing, but for Gwen and Lucas it seemed extra sweet.

She flipped the light on in her bedroom and traded her leggings and T-shirt for cuffed jeans and a fancier knotted-at-the-hips T-shirt. She added some cute jewelry and a pair of sandals, then went to work on her hair and makeup.

She was done with time to spare, so she worked another ten minutes before Easy knocked on her door.

He was smiling when she opened it. "Hi, beautiful."

"Hi there." He looked as handsome as ever in jeans and a T-shirt snug enough to show off his delicious body. "Ready?"

"Yep. You?"

"Yep." She grabbed her purse off the couch, then locked the door behind her as she left.

He took her hand on the way down the porch steps, leaning in to kiss her cheek. "You smell nice, too."

"Thanks. Not sure why."

"Because you're made of sugar and spice?"

She laughed. "I think that's a different little girl."

He opened the door to the Mustang for her, and she got in. "That's right. You're made of chocolate and sex appeal. I keep getting that mixed up."

She snickered, but loved his attention.

He slid behind the wheel and started the car. "Bakery first, right?"

"Right."

At the bakery, Ginny introduced herself to Nasha, who smiled and handed over the pie-laden shopping bags with a curious look.

"You know," Nasha said. "My books show that I've been selling six blackberry pies at a go almost once a week for nearly the last decade. Has that been you?"

Ginny nodded. "That's me, all right."

"Funny," Nasha said. "You'd think I'd remember someone who got that many pies from me week after week."

Ginny just grinned. "I have a feeling you will from now on."

"I hope so." Nasha waved. "Enjoy them."

"We will." Ginny winked at Easy as he held the door for her. "And so will Seymour."

The sky was turning slightly pink and purple as twilight approached. It was a beautiful time of night to visit the lake.

Easy parked in the lot by the old pier, and they walked hand in hand down to the end, each holding a shopping bag. The water was so still it glimmered like glass, and overhead, as the sun set, the clouds had begun to clear, letting the first stars shine through.

She stared up at the pastel sky. "I love this time of night."

"It's really nice." He looked over his shoulder at the shoreline. "Those are just fireflies, right?"

She laughed and nodded. "Lightning bugs don't live anywhere but in the enchanted forest."

"Good."

She took one of the pie boxes out and opened it, waving her hand over the top to send the aroma over the water. "Seymour. I have pie."

"You sure he'll come?"

"For pie? He pretty much can't resist it." She waved more of the scent over the water. "Sey-mour," she called out.

A few seconds later, the water rippled a ways off.

"There." She pointed. "He's coming."

The ripples drove toward them, stopping a few feet from the end of the pier as Seymour surfaced. He chirped at Ginny. Then he saw Easy and bared his teeth.

"Hey," Ginny said. "Listen to me. Easy is a friend. I know he scared you, but he thought that I and my aunt were in danger. He didn't know you and I are friends."

Seymour tipped his head, staring hard at Easy.

Ginny nudged Easy. "Say you're sorry."

Easy smiled and held his hands out. "Sorry about the misunderstanding. I hope I didn't scare you too bad. That was quite a shock you gave us, though."

Seymour made a little trilling sound, then stuck his head into the water and blew bubbles.

Ginny laughed. "I'm pretty sure he's apologizing."

When he came back up, Ginny held out her hand. "Can we all be friends, Seymour? Because I like you very much, and I like Easy very much, and I don't want you to be cross at each other."

Seymour leaned in and touched his head to her hand. She gave him a scratch. His skin was slick and smooth and a little damp.

"Good," she said. "We're all friends."

Seymour leaned in tentatively toward Easy.

Ginny nudged him again. "Scratch his head."

"What if I shock him?"

"Shouldn't that be fixed?"

"It should be. But who knows?"

Ginny smiled at Seymour. "Easy is afraid he might accidentally shock you. The way you sometimes do to me when you're really happy. Don't freak out if that happens, okay? He doesn't mean it. He just can't control it."

Seymour nodded.

Easy reached his hand out slowly, finally making contact with the creature's giant skull. "Wow," he breathed as he scratched. "I am petting a lake monster. This is pretty cool."

He laughed. "Seymour, you're pretty cool."

Seymour barked in agreement, then eyed the pie still in Ginny's hand.

"Yeah, I know," she said. "You want pie. Coming up."

She gave Easy a quick lesson in pie flipping, and between them, they sent the pies sailing into the air one after another.

Seymour caught them all without any trouble, even Easy's first effort that went a little long. When the pies were gone, Seymour slapped at the water a few times to say his goodbyes, then he disappeared into the water, black from reflecting the night sky.

Ginny started to reach for the empty shopping bags, but Easy caught her hands. "I have a couple presents for you. This seems like a good place and time to give them to you."

"Presents? For me? I didn't get you anything." He didn't look like he was carrying anything, so she couldn't imagine what they might be.

"You have given me more than you'll ever

know." He reached into the front pocket of his jeans and took something out, but it was hidden in his closed fist. "I know the sacrifices we made to have our curses removed were necessary, but the truth is you never would have had to give up anything if not for me. I complicated this whole situation."

"Easy—"

"No, it's true. And while I'm not in the least bit sorry for how our lives have intertwined, I am sorry for my part in the pain that giving up your father's bracelet caused you."

She shrugged. "It's okay. My father would have understood."

"I'm sure he would have, because I have no doubt that, to have a daughter like you, he was an incredible man. But I couldn't let it be."

He held his hand out and opened it. She sucked in a breath.

There on his palm lay something that looked very much like the bracelet she'd last seen disappearing into the book of curses.

CHAPTER THIRTY-FOUR

Every nerve in Easy's body was on alert. He watched Ginny's face, searching for any sign that would tell him what she was thinking or feeling. This had to go well. Because if it didn't, the second gift was pointless.

She shook her head. "How did you...you had an exact replica made of my father's ID bracelet. That was so thoughtful. I love it."

"It's not a replica. It's *his* bracelet."

Her mouth came open. She looked at him, then the bracelet, then back at him. "How is that possible? I saw it disappear into the book."

He lifted his palm closer to her. "I just figured in a town like this, nothing was impossible."

She took the bracelet, turning it over in her hands. "This really is my father's bracelet. I recognize that scratch on the edge." She looked at him again. "You have to tell me how you did this."

"You all kept talking about Amelia Marchand and how she's the witch in charge of the town's magic. So I went to see her."

Ginny's eyes went wide again. "You did not."

"I did." He took the bracelet from Ginny and hooked it around her wrist. "Quite a house she's got there."

"You can say that again. So, what, you just asked for the bracelet back, and she gave it to you?"

"Something like that."

Ginny's brows lifted in clear skepticism. "Yeah, not buying that. What kind of deal did you make with her?"

"Just a little trade." A big trade, actually, but he didn't want to ruin the gift by explaining what it had taken to get it.

"Easy." She shook her head as she wrapped her hand over the bracelet on her wrist and put it to her heart. "This is the single most amazing thing anyone's done for me. Outside of my aunt putting her own life on hold to raise me. Saying thank you doesn't really cover what I'm feeling. You know that, right? I am blown away by this."

He smiled. Mission accomplished. "Good. I want you to be happy, and getting that back seemed like the thing most likely to do that."

"That's an understatement."

"Here," he said. "Let me see how it looks on your wrist." He bent his head to see better, and she leaned in, putting her cheek against his.

"Thank you," she whispered. "With all my heart. Thank you."

"You're welcome, Ginny." He looked up at her. His beautiful wolf.

Her eyes were narrowed with expectation. "What did you do to get it back? I want to know."

He took a breath. There would be no living with her until he told her. "I had to make Amelia a promise that I wouldn't leave Shadowvale for a while. Not sure how that benefits her or the town, but I don't think she wanted to just give up the bracelet without getting something significant in return."

Ginny took that in for a moment. "A while? What's a while? How long are we talking?"

He shrugged, reluctant to tell her. "Some...years."

"*Years*?" Ginny blinked. "How many?"

He let a second or two slip by, but there was no easy way to put this. "Ten."

She stared at him like he'd just sprouted antlers. "Easy. Ten years? What about your movie premiere?"

"It'll go on just fine without me."

She put her hand to her mouth, causing the bracelet to slide down her wrist and glint in the moonlight. "Oh, Easy. You did that for me."

He nodded, putting his hands on her waist. "Hey, it's not a big deal. No traveling for a while means more time to write. And I can do all the research I need online. Besides...as long as I have you, life will be great." He grinned hopefully. "I do have you, right?"

She threw her arms around him. "Absolutely. Always. Yes."

He kissed her. "Good, because without you, the next gift would be kind of meaningless."

She leaned back. "The next gift?"

"Yep. That was presents. With an S." He dug into his other pocket, pulled out a small black velvet box, and popped it open.

She took a step back, gasping. "That looks like a diamond ring."

"It better, or I'm asking for my money back." He laughed, nerves making the sound tremble. "I was going to do this at the premiere, but now I figured, why wait?"

She was silent, eyes round and liquid with unshed tears, breath held.

He went down on one knee. "Virginia French, would you do me the great honor of making the rest of my life unforgettable by becoming my wife?"

She nodded, then found her voice. "Yes. I would."

He stood and slipped the ring on her finger. "Then I really have no reason to leave, do I?"

She stared at the rock on her hand, turning it so that it threw sparks into the evening air. Then she looked at him. "Not unless you're with me, you don't."

Then her voice caught. She cleared her throat, swallowing as a single tear slipped down her cheek. "I never thought there'd be a moment like this in my life. That I'd not only find the perfect man, but that he'd remember me and fall in love with me. I never imagined my life would be anything different than what it was. This is a little hard to believe."

"Well, believe it." Easy wiped the tear away, then kissed her again, pulling her close and inhaling her sweet perfume. "I love you, sweetheart."

"I love you, too." Her stomach rumbled as if agreeing.

He laughed. "Maybe we should go get that pizza." He looked at his watch. "Yeah, we should definitely head to Fritzi's. Your aunt and Lucas are waiting."

Ginny looked at him. "They are?" She held up her hand and the ring. "Do they know about this?"

"Yep. I asked your aunt for her permission."

"She must have loved that." Ginny's smile was enormous. "You're such a good man."

He gathered up the empty shopping bags, then put his arm around her as they walked back to the car. "And you're an incredible woman."

She glanced at the ring again. "Hey, did you give this to me now because we're joining the pack in two days? I mean, did you just basically mark me as your territory?"

He laughed. "I have no response to that." He looked down at the big, gleaming diamond. "But now that you mention it, you do look pretty marked."

She frowned at him, but her eyes sparked with amusement. "You're such a wolf. And I love that about you."

"Good, because that's never going to change. So long as I have anything to say about it."

She let out a little chuckle. "I think all of that is in our past." She held up her hand again. "I can't get over this ring. You didn't have to get something so...so enormous."

"Yes," he said. "I did. I wanted your ring to be as unforgettable as you are."

Want to be up to date on all books and release dates by Kristen Painter? Sign-up for my newsletter on my website, www.kristenpainter.com. No spam, just news (sales, freebies, releases, you know, all that jazz.)

If you loved the book and want to help the series grow, tell a friend about the book and take time to leave a review!

OTHER BOOKS BY KRISTEN PAINTER

PARANORMAL ROMANCE
Shadowvale series
The Trouble with Witches
The Vampire's Cursed Kiss
The Forgettable Miss French

Nocturne Falls series
The Vampire's Mail Order Bride
The Werewolf Meets His Match
The Gargoyle Gets His Girl
The Professor Woos the Witch
The Witch's Halloween Hero – short story
The Werewolf's Christmas Wish – short story
The Vampire's Fake Fiancée
The Vampire's Valentine Surprise – short story
The Shifter Romances the Writer
The Vampire's True Love Trials – short story
The Dragon Finds Forever
The Vampire's Accidental Wife
The Reaper Rescues the Genie

For more Nocturne Falls
Try the Nocturne Falls Universe Books
New stories, new authors, same Nocturne Falls world!
kristenpainter.com/nocturne-falls-universe/

Sin City Collectors series
Queen of Hearts
Dead Man's Hand
Double or Nothing

STAND-ALONE PARANORMAL ROMANCE
Dark Kiss of the Reaper
Heart of Fire
Recipe for Magic
Miss Bramble and the Leviathan

COZY PARANORMAL MYSTERY
Jayne Frost series
Miss Frost Solves a Cold Case: A Nocturne Falls Mystery
Miss Frost Ices the Imp: A Nocturne Falls Mystery
Miss Frost Saves the Sandman: A Nocturne Falls Mystery
Miss Frost Cracks a Caper: A Nocturne Falls Mystery
When Birdie Babysat Spider: A Jayne Frost Short
Miss Frost Braves the Blizzard – A Nocturne Falls Mystery
Miss Frost Chills the Cheater – A Nocturne Falls Mystery

Happily Everlasting series
Witchful Thinking

URBAN FANTASY
The House of Comarré series:
Forbidden Blood
Blood Rights
Flesh and Blood
Bad Blood
Out For Blood
Last Blood

Crescent City series:
House of the Rising Sun
City of Eternal Night
Garden of Dreams and Desires

Nothing is completed without an amazing team.

Many thanks to:

Cover design: Design & derivative cover art by
Janet Holmes using images under license from
Shutterstock.com

Interior formatting: Author E.M.S

Editor: Joyce Lamb

Copyedits/proofs: Marlene Engel/Lisa Bateman

ABOUT THE AUTHOR

USA Today Best Selling Author Kristen Painter is a little obsessed with cats, books, chocolate, and shoes. It's a healthy mix. She loves to entertain her readers with interesting twists and unforgettable characters. In addition to Shadowvale, she currently writes the best-selling paranormal romance series, Nocturne Falls, and the cozy mystery spin off series, Jayne Frost. The former college English teacher can often be found all over social media where she loves to interact with readers.

www.kristenpainter.com

58868586R00190

Made in the USA
Middletown, DE
09 August 2019